TRUE SPIES

SHANA GALEN

sourcebooks
casablanca

For Tina, the most remarkable mom I know.

One

ELINOR PACED THE VESTIBULE OF HER LONDON TOWN house, her slippered steps echoing in the strained silence. She couldn't see Bramson, but she knew the butler waited nearby. She pictured him shifting from one foot to the other and wringing his white-gloved hands. Elinor glanced at the tall case clock again and let out a disgusted sigh.

She could not believe he was doing this to her. *Again.* His promises proved meaningless, as usual. She began to tug off her elbow-length gloves. "Bramson," she called.

"Yes, my lady." He stepped out from the adjacent parlor, a blank look on his face. But she saw beneath the facade. She saw the sad shake of his head. The all-too-familiar pity. When had she become someone to pity? No more. Elinor couldn't bear it another day.

She smoothed her gloves back in place. "Have Spencer bring the coach around."

Bramson's brow furrowed. It was the only wrinkle in his otherwise seamless appearance. She studied her butler—his clipped white hair, his black coat and breeches, the unrelieved white of his shirt and neck cloth. Her gaze drifted to the black-and-white checked marble of the vestibule and then to the mirror on the wall opposite. She wore white gloves and a black gown with jet beading. Her skin was pale, and her dark brown hair looked almost raven in the dim lighting.

She was surrounded by the staid, the sober, and the severe, and she had had enough of it. Enough! She was not dead. Not *yet*. But she looked it. No wonder Winn forgot her. And to the devil with him, anyway. The curse, though muttered internally, gave her a zing of elation. *To the devil with him!*

"The coach, my lady?" Bramson asked. "Has his lordship arrived?"

The man knew very well that his lordship had *not* arrived. Every person in the household, save her, had known his lordship was not going to arrive. She was the only fool to believe him. "I shall attend the Ramsgate ball without Lord Keating, Bramson."

Bramson's dark eyebrows arched. "I see. Very good, my lady." His tone indicated he thought this turn of events anything but.

Elinor glanced in the mirror again. "And, Bramson? Send Bridget to my room. I wish to change my gown."

"Eh…" Bramson recovered himself. "Of course, my lady."

She started up the stairs, her legs feeling ten pounds lighter. She was going to attend the ball and dance the night away. Would Mr. Trollope attend? If he did, would she have the courage to waltz with the gentleman? Allow him to put his arm around her and press her tightly to him?

"Mother?"

Elinor jumped, grasping the banister to keep her balance. It was Caroline. The girl might only be twelve in terms of age, but she was an old soul. She had the eyes of a wizened woman. "Yes, dear?" Elinor reached the landing and turned toward her bedchamber.

"Are you about to change?"

Elinor sighed. Even her daughter knew Lord Keating would forget her mother.

"Oh, good. Georgiana and I wrote the first act of a play, and we wanted to act it out for you."

Bridget stepped into the corridor, and Elinor nodded at her. "Find something with color for me to wear tonight, Bridget. I must have something blue or—no." Why not? "Something *red*."

"Are you not staying home?" Caroline frowned. For a moment, Elinor wanted to reverse her decision. She loved her daughters, loved playing with them, spending time with them, watching them grow into young ladies. It was not many years ago, she lamented that she spent *all* her time with her children. It seemed her only entertainment was the juvenile stories of princesses they composed. She'd craved conversation with her peers, and an activity that did not require her to sit on the floor or dress a doll. But the girls had needed her, and it had felt good to be needed.

Now, even that was not true. Elinor did not feel needed at all. Her daughters had governesses and music teachers to oversee their studies, they had their own friends and amusements, and more than once she had offered some advice or tried to participate and felt as though she was an unnecessary appendage.

Caroline and Georgiana *rolled their eyes* at her when they thought she wasn't looking.

Perhaps it was time to seek her own interests and the excitement she'd always craved. She'd read so many accounts of all the bravery during the Peninsular War against Napoleon. She thought of all the daring acts of courage by soldiers and generals. She could not fight a battle, but she could do something less explicit. She could work on the fringes.

She could do something she'd only dared read about and prove she was more than a mother and Society hostess. She could act as a spy.

Excited now, Elinor started for her room. "I told you, Caro, I'm attending a ball tonight."

Caroline looked about. "What about Father?"

"I'm going without him."

Caroline blinked. "What about our play?"

"I'll see it tomorrow, darling." Elinor put a hand on her younger daughter's arm. "You girls should go to bed."

Caroline frowned, looking so much like her father, it cut right through Elinor. "But, Mother, we're not babies. 'Tis not even late."

Elinor opened her mouth to protest, then closed it and shrugged. Why not allow the girls their fun? She was tired of always being the one to enforce bedtime. Tired of each and every one of the thousands of rules children and wives were required to obey. Tonight she would forget about those rules and enjoy herself. Tonight was a new beginning. One without Winn.

"You're right, of course," Elinor conceded. "Stay up as late as you wish." She gave Caro a quick kiss on the forehead and proceeded to her room. Caroline followed.

"Mother? Mother. Are you feeling well?"

Elinor laughed. "I feel perfectly well."

Bridget held out a burgundy gown, and Elinor shook her head. "No." It was too drab. "Let me choose." She didn't miss the look that passed between Caroline and Bridget. Good. Let them look. Let all of London look. She was done living as a hermit because her husband cared more for... anything and everything than he cared for his wife and family. Plenty of married women went out without their husbands. Plenty of men would rather visit their mistresses than escort their wives to the opera or a fête. Elinor almost wished Winn had a mistress. It would have made him more interesting, more human.

Once she would have waited with bated breath for him to return home. Once she would have dressed carefully, anticipating his arrival. But years of whiling away endless hours, nodding to sleep in the vestibule, wearing her best gowns for the sole benefit of the servants, had made her bitter. Winn was never going to change. She did not want to be bitter about the truth. She wanted to escape it—do something exciting and absorbing so she would not have to remember what her real life entailed.

She stepped into her dressing room and scanned the neatly folded gowns. Gray, brown, lavender, black, more gray. Good God! When had she begun dressing like an old woman? There! Her gaze caught on a rectangle of scarlet. She reached for it and tugged it loose, upending the beige gown on top of it and not caring a whit.

"Mother, what is *that*?" Caroline's voice was full of shock and censure. Elinor shook the gown out. It was cut a bit lower than she would have liked but was still far from scandalous.

"This is what I am wearing to the ball," she told her daughter. She carried the gown, its gauzy sleeves and silk skirts trailing like ribbons in her wake, into her chamber. "Here we are." She presented Bridget with her back, and her maid began the task of removing the black beaded gown.

Caroline stood mutely and watched while Bridget helped Elinor don the scarlet gown carefully, so as not to muss her hair. As the maid fastened the last tape, Elinor caught the shake of Caroline's head in the mirror. "Mother, you cannot wear that."

Elinor almost laughed. "Why not?" She turned to Bridget. "Do I have any rouge?"

"Mother!"

"Caroline!" Elinor echoed her daughter's outraged tone. "I am a mother, not a corpse. I do not want to look like one."

From somewhere in the depths of Elinor's dressing table, Bridget unearthed a pot of rouge. Elinor sat to apply it. Caroline's wide green eyes seemed to grow even wider. "Mother," she whispered. "I can see the top of your bosom."

Elinor glanced down at the swells of her breasts. "Good," she said. She studied the effect of the rouge, then tugged a few tendrils of hair loose about her face and stood. "There."

Caroline shook her head. "What will Father think?"

Elinor shrugged. "I don't care." And she meant it.

❦

Somewhere in London, Autumn 1815

The spy called Baron swayed on the steep roof, finding his footing as a piece of the wood structure gave way. He watched it tumble to the ground, watched it turn end over end over end until, finally, it gave a quiet thwack and splintered into ten thousand pieces. He might have paused to consider the thud his head would make if it made a similar journey. But, as a rule, he avoided the most likely scenarios and tried to be optimistic. A moment later, the sound of voices drowned out his optimism.

He glanced over his shoulder as three men climbed through the rotting door to the roof. A bald man pointed at him, and another raised a pistol. Baron teetered on the ledge and slid forward. "Not very sporting of you to shoot a man in the back," he called over his shoulder.

"Then turn around!" one of the men called back.

Not bloody likely.

A pistol shot exploded behind him—a French flintlock holster pistol from the sound of it—and he cursed and ducked. Straddling the vee of the roof, he winced in pain. He was getting too old for this. He scooted forward, while behind him the men started after him, taking wobbly steps onto the steep roof. He welcomed their approach. He preferred a real fight to dodging pistol balls.

"This is the end, Baron!" called the bald man, who Baron now saw had a nasty gash on his cheek.

It wasn't the end. Baron could see the end a few feet away. The roof ended, and the steep drop yawned before him.

"Give us the key, and we'll kill you quickly," the man with three broken teeth and long, stringy hair called.

"Tempting offer," Baron answered, "but I'll take my chances." He scooted forward again and frowned at the distance between the roof and the street below. Looking back over his shoulder, Baron thought he preferred the drop.

"You're dead one way or another," the bald man told him. "Give us the key."

Baron stood, carefully, so as to keep his balance. "You want the key?" He slid toward the roof's edge. "Come and take it." And with a final step, he tumbled off.

"What the devil?" one of the thugs called.

"I didn't think he'd do it."

"Now we'll have to scrape the key out of all his blood and guts."

"Wait a moment. Did you hear him land?"

Baron clenched his jaw and dug his fingers into the gargoyle jutting from the roof's edge. The perfect companion, it grinned madly at him. "Lucky us," he muttered. "One of them isn't a complete fool." He hooked an elbow over the gargoyle's neck and tried to ignore the way his feet dangled freely in the cool night air.

"Go look," one of the men—Baron thought it was the one with broken teeth—said. Baron held his breath, listening to the *step-slide-step-slide* as the man scooted closer. He lowered himself under the gargoyle's head, using only his damp hands to hold on.

Gritting his teeth, he tried not to move, tried to keep his sweat-slick hands locked tightly.

Step-slide-step-slide-step…

A shadow fell over Baron, and in one quick motion, he swung his feet, knocked the gap-toothed man on the side of the head, and sent him tumbling to the street below. The man's scream rent the air, and then with a *smack*, all was silent. Using the momentum from the kick, Baron pushed himself back onto the roof and climbed to his feet just in time to deflect a right jab from the man who'd shot at him with the pistol. Both men lost their balance and fell hard on the roof. Baron slid down on his back, twisting in time to catch the peak. He'd begun to lever himself up, when the thug with the pistol kicked out at him. He hit the side of Baron's head and set his ears ringing. He would have a nasty headache later, but right now he felt only fury. The man kicked again, and this time Baron caught his foot and yanked. The thug lost his grip and slid down the steep roof, clawing for purchase. He caught a pipe near the edge and sent up a thin laugh.

And then, with a creak, the pipe bent, and he slid down and down and down.

Baron rose slowly and let out a breath. The bald man was watching him. The thug took a step forward, then whirled and turned, heading back the way he'd come. Baron let out a sigh and wished he could let the man go. Instead, he started after him, making his way nimbly across the sharp roof. The rotted door slammed shut just as Baron jumped onto the level section. He raced across it, threw the door open, and charged down the stairs after the man.

The building was old, vacant, and black as a crow's feather. Baron heard the slap-slap of the man's rapid footfalls echo through the emptiness. He was gaining on him.

And then the footsteps ceased, and Baron went around the last winding staircase and out the door. At the last moment, he veered to the left and avoided the pistol ball that smacked into the door behind him. "Bloody hell!"

In the shadows stood the bald thug with a man dressed in a sweeping ebony greatcoat. A pistol glinted in his hand. The man looked down to prime it again, but Baron wasn't going to stand still and wait to be shot. With a grunt of frustration, he took off running, the two pursuers all but stepping on his heels. In the distance, the clock of St. Sepulchre tolled. Even though Newgate prison now had its own bell to mark the time of imminent executions, the sound reminded Baron of a death knell. He raced through an alley and dove through a gate as the tenth bell clanged.

"Devil take it," he swore, running toward a high wall and climbing over. One of the men grabbed his ankle, and Baron's kick landed somewhere soft. Soft... Elinor! He jumped down, paused to find his bearings, then arrowed for Mayfair. He was late, and he was damned if he hadn't promised Elinor he would escort her to Lord and Lady Ramsgate's ball. She was going to kill him, he thought as he took a sharp corner, raced across a street, narrowly avoiding a collision with a carriage, then stumbling to the other side. He chanced a look over his shoulder and swore. The thugs were still following him and showed no signs of flagging.

Baron ran, keeping his head down lest he be recognized once he neared Mayfair. He almost would have preferred for Elinor to attempt to kill him. Outright violence would have been preferable to the disappointed look she would bestow upon him in its stead. He hated to disappoint. Ironically, he never disappointed when working. But at home… his record was far from exemplary.

More streets and more alleys, and his breathing grew labored. The carriages multiplied like rabbits, street lamps grew more numerous with each passing street, and Baron knew he was in Mayfair. He ducked into a dark shop doorway and looked to the right. The Ramsgate town house was that way.

He looked left. Home was that way. Should he go home or attempt to make it to the ball? Surely Elinor had not gone to the Ramsgate ball without him. She was too reserved, too meek and nervous to attend a ball unescorted. But he couldn't lead the two thugs to his home.

He ducked back into the shadows when he heard the men approaching. They made more noise than hounds in a fox hunt. At the last possible moment, when Baron was certain they would rush past him, he stuck out an arm and knocked one of the men down. The other raced by, and by the time he'd turned back, Baron had knocked the bald man's head against the window of the shop, shattering the thick glass and rendering the thug bloody and unconscious.

Unfortunately, that left the man in black. The man with the pistol pointed at Baron's head. "Give me the key, Baron."

"You know I can't," he said, keeping his gaze on the pistol. Had the man in black had time to prime it? Was this a bluff?

"You can't run forever."

"Neither can you." Baron was going to take a chance. Standing here, an easy target, was not a position he enjoyed. Carriages streamed past them on the busy street up ahead. The man would not risk the sound of gunfire with so many close by. Baron narrowed his eyes. Would he?

"Don't make me shoot you."

"Have it your way," Baron said and darted toward the busy street. He zigzagged in the event the man in black had primed his pistol, but when Baron didn't feel the hot slap of a ball in his back, he assumed he'd guessed correctly. He looked over his shoulder, saw the man ramming a ball down the pistol's barrel, and cursed. He wouldn't escape so easily next time. The man in black looked up with a grin and ran after him. Baron turned his attention back to the street, almost colliding with a passing coach. He dove around it and continued running, glancing up in time to narrowly avoid a coach-and-four coming from the opposite direction.

Hold. He slowed. Those were *his* Yorkshire Trotters. That was *his* coach! Was Elinor inside? The irony of being all but run down by his own coach did not escape him.

Baron reached the far side of the street and had no time to consider. He turned on his heel and started for the Ramsgate town house. The man in black followed, his ebony greatcoat whipping behind him like a raven's wing. As Baron neared the ball, he ducked down an alley to avoid the lights and the throng of arriving carriages. He heaved himself over a garden wall and tumbled unceremoniously into the Ramsgates' garden. The earl and his countess had strewn Chinese lanterns throughout, lighting the beautifully manicured lawns. Baron hissed and sank back into the more comfortable shadows. He hissed again when he heard the man in black clambering over the wall. He couldn't stay where he was, and that meant he had one option open to him.

One very, very bad option. Dusting the leaves from his lapels, Baron started toward the glittering chandeliers and crescendoing music.

Two

ELINOR STEPPED INTO THE BRIGHT LIGHTS OF LORD AND Lady Ramsgate's ballroom, and her senses were assaulted. A violin's song soared, while a cello tethered the lofty notes to the orchestra's raised dais. The din of voices buzzed like busy wasps, and women in elaborate plumage and sumptuous silks, satins, and velvets circled handsome men in coats and cravats. The clink of china, the mix of perfumes, the heat from too many bodies—Elinor's smile wobbled as the majordomo announced her. Just her. Alone. No Winn at her side.

It felt wrong, all wrong, but she was not going to turn back now. She'd spent enough nights at home, waiting for Winn. Not tonight.

A few guests glanced her way, but the world did not come to an end. No one even seemed particularly scandalized. Taking a deep breath, she straightened her shoulders and moved forward. She had to keep her back straight to stop the bodice of the gown from dipping. As she'd walked through the vestibule at home, she'd remembered why she never wore this gown. The bodice always slipped, and what had been a modest neckline in her bedroom was now dipping scandalously low. She'd tugged it up in the privacy of the carriage, but there was no opportunity now.

"Hello!" Lady Ramsgate glided toward her, wearing a beautiful silk gown of deep green that complimented her dark blond hair and hazel eyes. Lady Ramsgate, one of Elinor's dearest friends, smiled her toothy smile, and Elinor could hardly resist smiling back. "Don't you look stunning?"

Elinor frowned. "It's too daring, isn't it?"

"What? No! It's perfect." Her friend linked an arm with her and began to walk the circumference of the room. "Where is that neglectful husband of yours?"

"Shouldn't you be greeting your guests?"

"In a moment." The countess waved a hand. "In a moment. Tell me, did you dare to come alone? And dressed like this? Oh, I *like* it. I do."

Elinor felt the burn of censorious gazes raking over her flesh—more specifically, her too-bare bosom. "I should take my leave." It seemed she was far braver and ready for excitement when she was at home than when the opportunity actually arose. Oh, she was fooling no one! She'd never be a spy. She could not even attend a ball on her own.

"Oh, no you don't!" Lady Ramsgate said, catching her elbow. "You are going to stay and dance with all the rakes of the *ton*. I want Baron Keating to hear how popular his wife was while he spent another tedious evening poring over ledgers."

"I don't think that's a good idea."

"Poring over ledgers never is." Mary lifted a flute of champagne from a passing footman's tray. "Have a glass or four of this, darling, and we'll see if you don't decide to stay." She handed the flute to Elinor, who dutifully took a sip.

"Now, whom should you dance with first? Ah, I know! You'll want to dance with Mr. Trollope. Or are you calling him *Rafe* now?"

Elinor could all but feel her cheeks turn bright red as her flesh flamed hot. "Shh! Not so loudly."

Mary laughed. "You are blushing like a schoolgirl. It must be love."

"I am going home." Elinor turned. Laughing, Mary yanked her back.

"Very well. I will cease tormenting you. In any case, the infamous Mr. Trollope has not yet made an appearance. Do not fret. The night is young." She glanced around the room, making Elinor nervous. Forcing herself to take a deep breath, Elinor pushed her shoulders down, hearing them pop from the tension. She reminded herself she had come because she wanted a diversion. She had come because she wanted to dance. She wanted to laugh. She missed the company of other adults. She missed the company of a man.

She wasn't quite certain she wanted the company of Mr. Trollope, in particular, but it was lovely to have a man pay attention to her, compliment her, desire her. Yes, she knew Trollope's main motivation was to bed her, but lately she had begun considering giving in to his attempts at seduction. Why not? She did not think Winn would care. He did not want her. And Elinor might be a mother, but she was still a woman. She still craved love and pleasure in her life.

"What about Sir Henry?" Mary asked, tapping a gloved finger on her pointed chin. "He is handsome."

Elinor glanced across the room, wanting to be certain of the gentleman before she replied. "Mary, Sir Henry is a child! I cannot dance with him." She downed the rest of her champagne and took another champagne glass from a footman who, as though sensing he was needed, had stationed himself nearby.

Mary scowled. "He is two and twenty, at least. Besides, darling, he might like all an older woman has to offer."

"No. I'd feel as though I were dancing with a nephew. What about..." She scanned the far side of the ballroom, looking for someone innocuous, someone harmless, someone who did not look as angry and dangerous as the man stalking toward her. She gripped Mary's arm. "He's here!"

"Where?" Mary whipped her head back and forth. "I didn't hear Trollope announced."

"Not Ra—I mean, Mr. Trollope," Elinor said, realizing Winn really was coming straight for her. "My husband."

Mary took a step back, an indication she too had seen Baron Keating plowing toward them. "What happened to him?" Mary hissed.

Elinor shook her head. "I don't know. He looks a bit... rumpled." That was an understatement. Winn looked rough and disheveled and more than a little dangerous. His light brown hair, usually so meticulously styled, fell over his forehead in soft waves almost to his collar. His eyebrows were a slash above his blazing green eyes, and he had a smudge of dirt on one cheek. He wore no cravat, and his shirt was open at the throat. Her heart kicked, and quite suddenly she had trouble breathing.

"He looks good enough to eat." Mary pushed Elinor forward. "I hope you're hungry." And with a whirl, she disappeared into the crush of guests. Elinor wanted to do the same, but just as she turned, Winn caught her arm and swung her back around. She hadn't been mistaken. He looked angry.

"My lord. What a surprise to see you in attendance."

His eyes, a clear emerald, raked over her. Once again, she felt her flesh burn, but for a different reason altogether. This was not embarrassment. This was desire.

Futile desire.

"Did you forget the rest of your gown?" he asked.

Her eyes narrowed. "That is what you have to say to me?" The words were out before she knew what she was saying. In fourteen years of marriage, she had never spoken to Winn in an angry tone. She had never questioned him.

She had been a milksop.

"No apology for breaking your promise?" she continued, gaining confidence. "No explanation for your sudden appearance or why you have a leaf in your hair?"

Looking a bit stunned, Winn reached up, felt his hair, and crumpled the leaf in his hand.

"After all of your transgressions tonight, you have the unmitigated *gall* to comment on my gown?"

He stepped closer, looking—oh, dear—angry. She rarely caught a glimpse of this side of him. "Does it even qualify as a gown, madam? I should think it were some sort of undergarment."

"How would you know? It's been ages since you saw any of my undergarments." She shook her head, fury replacing the last dregs of desire. Who did he think he was? "There is nothing inappropriate about my gown," she retorted, ignoring his deepening scowl. "It isn't any more scandalous than most of the ladies of our acquaintance wear. Only you, sir, are not used to seeing me as a woman. In this gown it is impossible for you to ignore the fact that I am female."

He stared at her, his expression one of shock and rage. Elinor did not think it wise to wait for his reply. That last comment might have crossed a line. She stomped away, then slowed her steps. Why should *she* be the one to leave the ball? Why should Winslow Keating triumph yet again? The orchestra ended the quadrille they'd been playing, and Elinor heard the first strains of the waltz. Glancing over her shoulder, she saw Winn was following her. He had murder in his eyes. Desperate now, she grabbed the arm of the first man she encountered. It was Sir Henry.

"I believe I promised you the next dance, did I not, Sir Henry?"

The poor boy blinked his large blue eyes in confusion. "I—ah, of course, madam."

She grabbed his hand and led him toward the space cleared for dancing. When they were in the center, surrounded by other couples whirling around them, Sir Henry swept her up and began to spin her. "I'm terribly sorry. I seem to have forgotten your name."

"Oh?" Elinor glanced over his shoulder for Winn.

Surely he would not dare make a scene by marching to the center of the ballroom to fetch her. "I am Lady Keating, and that's quite all right. You didn't actually ask me to dance." Where was Winn? She could no longer see him, and his sudden disappearance was making her nervous. Was he approaching from the opposite direction? "I simply needed to escape someone."

"Oh, good."

She glanced back at Sir Henry. "Good?"

"Yes, I did not think I would have forgotten if I'd asked a woman as beautiful as you to dance."

And now Elinor was blushing again. Sweet boy. He didn't mean it, of course, but it was a lovely compliment. She smiled, and for a moment, she forgot about Winn and the girls and the thousand household matters she needed to attend to, and just danced.

❧

Winn would have liked five minutes alone with the puppy dancing with his wife. The man—boy—was ogling her as though she were a candied violet offered on the supper table. And what man wouldn't ogle her? He hadn't even recognized her for a full five minutes, and he had been searching for her. He'd never seen her wear red before. He'd never seen her color so high or her hair in such fetching disarray. This was not entirely true. He had seen her looking thus once or twice.

But not lately. Not in a long, long time.

The shot of lust he felt when he saw her all but knocked him over. And before he had the chance to feel guilty for lusting after a woman who was not his wife, he realized it was indeed his wife, and then anger quickly replaced lust. What was she thinking, coming to the Ramsgate ball with her bosom all but on display? Whom was she trying to seduce? Not him, obviously. Clearly, she hadn't known he was coming, and she never wore seductive gowns when he accompanied her. Usually she wore… well, he could not remember what she wore, because he had not accompanied her for some time, but he was certain it was something far more subdued.

He would have gone after her, dismissed the puppy and danced with her himself, but he spotted the man in black entering through the French doors, which were open to the garden. Winn swore. He was going to have to deal with the thug, and he couldn't do it in the middle of the ball. He would have preferred to return to the garden, but the man in black had spotted him and was making his way across the crowded room.

Lady Ramsgate was a close friend of his wife's, and Winn had been in the Ramsgate town house on several previous occasions. He knew the layout and made for the servants' stairs. The top floors of the house should be deserted. The servants were likely to be busy with all the ball entailed and would not occupy the upper floors at present. Winn moved slowly, wanting to ensure the man in black saw where he was headed and followed. When he felt certain he had been spotted, Winn raced to the third floor, exited into a corridor leading to the bedrooms, and glanced about for a spot to hide.

There was nothing. No potted plant, no chair, no Chinese folding screen. He tried the door nearest him and cursed when it was locked. He raced to the next one. Locked, of course. Where the devil was his luck tonight? He was awful at picking locks— hands too big—but he could use brute force. He took three large steps back, inhaled slowly, then ran for the door, leading with his shoulder. He rammed it, bounced back, and shook his head. His shoulder throbbed, reminding him no part of him was as young as it used to be. Winn examined the frame, saw he'd done some damage, and stepped back again. He eyed the servants' door to the stairwell, knowing he was almost out of time.

With a groan of dread, he rammed the door again. This time he separated it enough to kick it in. He was inside the room and stumbling about in the darkness, leaving the door open a sliver. He stepped behind the door and waited for the man in black to find him.

Winn heard him before he saw him. He was moving quietly down the corridor, approaching the open door. Winn held his breath and prepared to strike. The door opened slowly, the creak of the hinges like a scream in the silent darkness. Someone peered into the room. "Is anyone there?"

Too late, Winn realized it was a servant and not the man in black. He tried to pull his punch, but it struck the man on the side of the head and brought him down. The servant muttered an *oof* and went slack.

"Bloody hell." Now where was the man in black? Winn bent, checked the servant, and was relieved he was unconscious. The last thing he needed was a servant reporting that Baron Keating had attacked him on the night of the ball. He stepped out of the room and closed the door behind him, hoping the man would awake before he was found.

If the man in black hadn't followed him upstairs, he must still be downstairs. With the Ramsgates' guests.

With Elinor.

Damn it! He raced back down the stairs, wishing he'd faced the man down in the gardens, instead of bringing an armed attacker into the same ball as his wife and his friends—well, her friends.

Idiot. Crow would never have allowed him to make such a foolish error in judgment. But then Crow was dead, and it was his own foolish error that had been responsible for that too.

Winn had the presence of mind to ease open the servants' door and check that the corridor outside was empty before exiting. He then made his way back toward the ballroom. He passed several people he knew, but the grim expression on his face did not invite conversation. When he reached the ballroom again, he could not stop his gaze from seeking Elinor. She was still waltzing with the puppy, and now that Winn had the man in black to deal with, there wasn't a bloody thing he could do to stop it. There wasn't any bloody way he could even move close to her. And he wanted to be close to her. Desperately. When had she become a beauty? Had she always possessed that figure?

Winn tore his gaze from her daring red gown and surveyed the room. There. The man in black was standing near the orchestra. Winn started for him, and the man moved toward the French doors, slipping outside. It was a trap, and Winn knew it. He also knew he had little choice but to follow. As he paused just inside the French doors, staring at the moonlit paving stones marking the path into the garden, the waltz ended, and he heard the announcement for supper. He stood aside while the couples, who had been enjoying the early autumn evening, strolled inside, and then he slipped into the darkness.

He had a fleeting thought for Elinor—whom she would sit with at supper—but he couldn't afford to lose focus on the mission.

His focus saved him. The large earthenware vase shattered against the wall just to the right of his ear. Before Winn could blink, the man in black collided with him. Winn went down, rolling once so he was on top of the assailant. But the man had the momentum and rolled him back over. The assailant reared back and punched Winn hard across the cheek. Winn squinted, knowing it would leave a mark.

"Give me the key," the man in black demanded. Did he have a slight French accent? Winn's ears were ringing too loudly for a definitive answer.

"You'll have to take it off my dead body."

The man smiled. "If you insist." He pulled the pistol from his greatcoat, but Winn grabbed the barrel before the assailant had time to aim. For several moments, the two men struggled for possession of the pistol, and then Winn knocked it free, and the weapon slid across the paving stones with a clatter. Winn watched the pistol skid to a stop against a large pot like the one the assailant had thrown at him, and then both men dove for it.

The man in black reached it first, but Winn grasped the man's ankle and hauled him back. He punched him, his right hand glancing across the man's cheek. The assailant stumbled, and Winn grasped his coat and hauled him upright. "Whom do you work for?"

The assailant smiled in response and threw a punch. Winn ducked, but it sent both men off balance, and they stumbled down the wide, low steps leading to the garden. At the bottom, they tumbled onto the grass, and Winn got another punch in before the assailant boxed his ears. They rolled, the branches of a shrub slicing at Winn's face.

Suddenly, the man in black stiffened. And Winn looked up.

Voices.

As of one accord, both men ducked back down into the shadows of the hedgerows and ceased moving. Winn still held the collar of the man in black's greatcoat, and the assailant still had his palm wedged under Winn's chin, but neither moved.

"It is a lovely evening," a woman said. Winn's fingers clutched around the material of the greatcoat. It was Elinor.

"I thought so," her companion—a *male* companion—answered. Winn would have bet his life it was the puppy. "Look. There's the North Star. Bright, isn't it?"

Winn was torn between revealing himself and interrupting the tête-à-tête, or remaining hidden. How was he going to explain what he was doing, fighting an assassin in the Ramsgates' garden? He couldn't, not without more lies and deceptions than even he, a master, could make believable.

He was thankful the hedgerows provided shadows,

but he and the man in black would be visible if Elinor and her suitor decided to go for a stroll.

"The moon is full," she was saying. "I so rarely take a moment to look at it."

Winn wanted to roll his eyes. How utterly predictable—lovers' talk of stars and moons. If he was wooing Elinor, he would speak of...

Winn could not think of what he would speak of, but it would be much more original, of that he was certain. All the talk of the full moon had reminded him of something. The pistol was lying on the paving stones just a few feet from where Elinor stood. The moonlight lit up the white stones. If she should happen to look in the direction of the vase...

"Yours?" the man in black murmured.

Winn looked down. "What?"

"Is that woman yours?"

"No."

"You seem rather annoyed that she is conversing with the *younger* gentleman."

Discovery be damned. Winn reared back and slammed the man's head into the ground. Unfortunately, the dirt beneath them did little damage. His assailant shoved his palm up, and Winn's head jerked back. He struggled to remain on top, but the two rolled, Winn ending up on top again and both of them blinking into the foliage.

"What was that?" Elinor was asking.

"Probably some beast or other. Don't fret. I will protect you."

"Bloody hell," Winn muttered. The man in black laughed. Winn slammed his head into the ground again.

"Perhaps we should return to supper," Elinor said.

"I'll escort you into the supper room," the puppy told her.

"Thank you."

Winn wanted to growl, but at least she was going inside. He prepared to finish the assailant off, but then he heard Elinor's voice again. "Oh, dear!"

He gritted his teeth. If she had seen the pistol...

"I wonder how this vase was broken. I shall have to inform Mary."

Yes, go inside and speak to Lady Ramsgate.

The puppy said something in return, but his voice was fading. Silence descended, but for the sound of the frogs croaking and the lonely call of an owl. Winn looked at his assailant, and the man looked back. By unseen cue, they resumed the fight. Winn slammed the man's head into the ground again before the assailant bloodied his nose. They rolled and finally came apart.

"Enough," Winn, who was closer to the house, muttered. He ran for the discarded pistol. When he reached it, he saw the assailant had discerned his intention and was running the opposite way. Winn gave chase, but by the time he reached the garden wall, he knew he'd lost the man. He could go after him. Five years ago he would have stopped at nothing to catch him. Winn hunched over and attempted to catch his breath. He was tired.

And he needed a drink. He wondered if Lord Ramsgate had anything more substantial than champagne.

Ten minutes later, he peered in the mirror hanging on Ramsgate's library wall. He'd come in through the window and had already drunk one snifter of brandy. He frowned at his reflection. He looked… old. Well, he looked like he'd just come from rolling about in the garden, but he could see lines about his eyes and a deep tiredness in their depths. It seemed impossible, but he felt worse than he looked. And he looked battered and bloody.

He couldn't enter the ball like this. Even if Elinor was entertaining half the men of the *ton*, there was no way to repair the damage to his appearance enough to make himself presentable. He had blood on his lip from his bleeding nose, his knuckles were bruised, and his coat sleeve was torn. He looked down at his trousers, noting they were covered with leaves and stains. He had to return home.

As he climbed through Ramsgate's window, his one thought was that eventually Elinor would have to come home too.

And he would be waiting.

Three

ELINOR DEPARTED FROM THE BALL EARLY. IT WAS barely after two in the morning, and by all appearances, the ball would continue until at least four. Lady Ramsgate had instructed her cook to begin preparations for a light breakfast in case the guests were still in residence at six. She had begged Elinor to stay, offering her a guest room if she wished to send her coachman home, but Elinor declined. She wanted her own bed.

And she wanted to know what had happened to Winn. He'd disappeared without so much as a by-your-leave. Someone mentioned seeing him heading toward the garden, but when she'd ventured there after supper, she hadn't spotted him. Was he that angry at her choice of gown? She could only hope. Anger was better than his usual polite disinterest.

"But Elinor," Mary was saying as Elinor collected her wrap, "I have it on good authority Mr. Trollope will attend. He never goes out into Society before midnight."

"Then you shall have to give him my regrets. I will be exhausted on the morrow as it is, and I have two girls to care for." She started for the door, which was opened smoothly by the Ramsgates' butler. Craning her neck, Elinor searched the line of carriages for her own.

"Your girls are nearly grown!" Mary said, following her. "Why, Georgiana will turn fourteen in a matter of weeks, and Caro is..."

"Twelve."

"Yes, twelve. They do not need you hovering over them every moment."

This was true. The girls were growing up. Why did that make her so inordinately sad?

"Besides, Baron Keating is in Town. Let him chaperone them for a morning," Mary continued.

Elinor laughed. "Winn chaperone? He would not know what to do with the girls if I were not there. He is so rarely at home."

"That's it, isn't it?" Mary pointed a finger at her. "That's why you are leaving early."

"A quarter past two is hardly early."

Mary ignored her. "You wish to see that husband of yours."

Elinor pretended to study the passing carriages intently. "Most wives do wish to see their husbands on occasion."

"And I have never been a proponent of infidelity, but in your case I am prepared to make an exception. Winslow Keating is monstrously inattentive and neglectful of you."

"Mary! Shh!"

"I will not. Why you are still in love with him, I will never understand." She turned and walked away.

Later, when Elinor was settled in the darkness of

the coach, her friend's words rang in her ears. Why was she still in love with Winn? Habit? Foolishness? Hopeless romanticism?

He did not love her. That much was patently obvious and had been since the beginning—well, almost the beginning. He did not flaunt mistresses. In fact, she'd never so much as heard a rumor suggesting he had a mistress, and she had never found evidence suggesting another woman. It was true Winn rarely visited her bed, but then he was rarely in Town. He had inherited half-a-dozen properties all over the country and insisted on supervising them personally. Elinor did not understand why. His father had managed the properties well, giving their supervision largely over to local stewards. There was no reason Winn could not have done the same.

There was no reason he could not have taken her and the girls with him on some of these trips. But he did not. He never so much as offered. The girls had long ago ceased asking where he was or when he would be home. She wished she could stop wondering herself.

The town house was dark when she arrived home, but one of the footmen was waiting and provided her a candle with which to light the way to her chamber. Elinor thought about inquiring as to whether his lordship was at home, but she could not bear the embarrassment and pity. She lifted her skirts and carried the candle up a flight of stairs to her bedchamber. She knew what waited for her there, in the darkest corner of her dressing table, under a pile of ribbons and silks. But she would not succumb tonight. She would not even *look* at them. No matter how alone she felt.

She paused outside her bedchamber, set the candle on the delicate decorative hallway table, and pressed her hand to her belly. She remembered the last time she'd seen him. He'd given her the smudged, hastily written note begging for a rendezvous. She knew his hand-writing by now. Knew the passionate strokes of his pen.

The way he'd looked at her that night! His eyes had burned her with the intensity of his need. The way his gloved hand had rested just a little too long on her arm, so she could feel his heat burning through the thin silk fabric. She knew desire when she saw it. Mr. Trollope—Rafe, as he begged her to call him—wanted her, and the very thought of allowing a man who was not Winn to touch her hand, press his body to hers, touch his lips to her mouth both thrilled and appalled her.

It had been so long since anyone had looked at her like she was anything other than a mother. It had been so long since anyone had looked at her with want in his eyes. She missed being touched, being held, being kissed by a man. A meeting with Mr. Trollope was wrong. She knew it, but she could not seem to resist. Elinor took a shaky breath and turned to her bedchamber.

Bridget, her lady's maid, gave her a sleepy greeting and helped her undress and don a night shift. Just as Elinor sat down at her dressing table—her disobedient gaze straying to the bottom-most drawer—and leaned her head back so Bridget could begin to take the pins from her hair, she thought she heard a sound.

Winn? Her heart—ridiculous organ that it was—began to pound. Her gaze met Bridget's in the dressing-table mirror, and Bridget gave her a subtle nod. Elinor's heart clenched painfully in her chest at the same time her belly did a slow roll. Her face flushed, and her hands began to tremble.

Winn was home. He had not gone elsewhere after leaving the ball.

"I'll comb your hair out and tie it with this ribbon, my lady," Bridget said, indicating a pretty blue ribbon. Elinor only nodded. She couldn't seem to speak. If she had found words, she didn't know what she would have said. That the hair ribbon didn't matter? Winn wouldn't want her no matter how attractive she looked?

She glanced at her reflection in the mirror and noted the beginnings of lines at the corners of her mouth and between her brows. They were faint but would deepen. Her hair had a few strands of gray, but for the most part it remained a rich brown. She didn't think she quite looked her thirty-five years, but she definitely could not compete with the debutantes of seventeen and eighteen. She couldn't even compete when she had been seventeen and eighteen. She'd been in her third Season and all but on the shelf before Winn had proposed.

And now she'd borne two children. She had a mother's figure and the face of maturity. If she'd ever had any hope of making Winn love her, it was long past. "There," Bridget said, tying the ribbon into a bow. "Very pretty, if I do say so myself."

"Thank you, Bridget," Elinor said. "That will be all."

Bridget winked. "You don't have to dismiss me twice, my lady." And she hurried out of the room, closing the door behind her.

Elinor looked in the mirror, turning her head to the side to catch a glimpse of the bow. It looked silly, like something Caroline or, more likely, Georgiana would wear. She pulled it out and tossed her hair over her shoulder, then pulled her robe closed over her night shift. Quietly, she tiptoed toward the door adjoining her room to Winn's.

She could hear Winn's valet speaking to him quietly, and then there was silence. Should she speak to him? Wait for him to approach her? In the morning, his anger would have subsided. Was that what she wanted? The return of her cool, indifferent husband?

She put her hand on the door handle and listened again. His room was silent. Had he gone to bed? She took a shaky breath and tapped on the door, then turned the handle and pushed it open.

He was standing across the room, shirtless, hair tousled, and he turned as she opened the door. The first thing she noted was the fatigue in his eyes. He'd always had the most beautiful, clear green eyes. He'd once given her a pair of emerald ear bobs, and she thought if he had been a woman, they would suit him better, for they matched his eyes perfectly.

The second thing she noticed was it had been quite some time since she had seen him without clothing. His chest was bronzed and hard. He had broad shoulders, powerful arms, and a flat stomach. When he'd turned to look at her, the muscles in his abdomen had bunched and rippled in a way that left her all but breathless. And she still hadn't caught her breath, because she noted he had lost a little weight. His trousers were loose at the waist and hanging at his hips, where a line of dark hair trailed temptingly downward.

She had the mad notion to put her tongue on that trail and follow it down with long, wet strokes. She shook her head. Where had *that* idea come from? Elinor forced her gaze back to her husband's face. He had a day's worth of stubble and what appeared to be the beginning of a bruise on one cheek, and for some reason, it made him look rather rough and dangerous. That and the length of his wavy hair. How long had it been since he'd had it trimmed? She had never seen it this long. For a moment, she wished he were some dangerous stranger who would cross the room, take her in his arms, and kiss her until she forgot to breathe.

She must be overly tired to be having so many uncharacteristic thoughts. "My lord."

He nodded at her, his expression unreadable. Was he surprised to see her? Annoyed at her presence? Taken off guard? "My lady."

She stood in his doorway and waited for him to say more. He looked back at her. Were they reduced to this, then? The formality of greeting each other using courtesy titles? She cinched her robe tighter, and his gaze followed the movement.

"You are home late," he said with a pointed glance at the bracket clock on his table. Elinor saw it was now almost three.

"I hope I didn't wake you," she said.

"No. I was still awake when I heard you come in."

He lifted a snifter of something, probably brandy, and drank. "Did you enjoy the ball?"

"I did. You left without taking your leave."

His brow arched. "You seemed enamored of your companion. I did not want to interrupt."

Elinor frowned. Was this jealousy? But why would Winn be jealous? He had never shown much interest in her before. "I would have preferred you for a companion," she said, "but despite all of your promises, you were not here at the appointed time."

His face darkened. "And so you took it upon yourself to dress like a courtesan and seduce a boy young enough to be your son?"

She opened her mouth to protest, opened her mouth to argue that her gown had been perfectly acceptable, that Sir Henry was too old to have been her son, that she was not the least bit interested in the man… any number of things. And then she looked at Winn. His emerald eyes burned, his fists were clenched, and a vein in his neck throbbed. Why not allow him to seethe a bit with jealousy, if that's what this was? She had done her fair share of seething over *his* slights.

"Frankly," she said, turning back toward her room, "I'm surprised you bothered to make an appearance at all." She pulled the adjoining door closed, but when it should have clicked shut, it was forced open. She gasped as Winn grabbed her wrist and hauled her up against him. His skin was warm, and he smelled like the soap he used in his bath. She looked up at his face and glimpsed what appeared to be a scrape along his temple. She had the urge to lift her hand and ask what had happened.

Her gaze strayed to his lips. Even when she was angry, she could not help but want his mouth on hers. She could not stop a silent prayer that he sweep her into his arms, carry her to the bed, and ravish her. Her heart pounded in her ears, and she waited to see what he would do.

And waited.

He released her wrist and stepped back. Disappointment slammed into her, and she almost crumpled from the weight of it.

"We shall speak about this again in the morning."

She lashed out. "There is nothing more to say, unless you wish to drone on about commitments and duty and tenants who don't pay their rent."

"I do not *drone*."

She raised her brows in challenge. "No, your adventures in estate management are fascinating. I'm certain you are equally fascinated by my tales of garden parties and French lessons. By the by," she added, "Georgiana's birthday fast approaches. If you are not too occupied with more important matters, your daughter requests the pleasure of your company at her celebration."

And with that, she closed the door, shutting out the storm clouds crashing about his face.

❧

Winn took a deep breath and forced himself not to open the door and throttle the woman. His wife. She had never spoken to him thus. And she had never attended a ball alone. And she had never looked so completely ravishing as she had tonight.

He moved away from the door, from temptation, and lifted his brandy again. It wasn't merely the gown she'd worn to the ball. She wasn't wearing anything more alluring than a linen night shift and an old wrapper tonight, but something about her was different.

Or was it?

He pulled the drapes back and peered into the garden. The shrubs threw long shadows on the paving stones, and he spotted a forgotten book lying on one of the stone benches. One of his daughters had probably left it there.

Elinor had always been an attractive woman, but her main appeal was her affection for him. He'd known from the first she was madly in love with him. And he'd known her feelings for him would work to his advantage. She would not question his frequent absences; she would not question his secretiveness or his unexplained injuries. Added to that, he knew from the start she would make him an excellent baroness and be a good mother to their children. After all, he had a duty to more than his country. He had a duty to his title.

His mother had approved of her. After his father's death, she had advocated a quick union and the production of an heir. To his mother's disappointment, there had been no heir, and it did not appear one would be forthcoming. He would have had to share a bed with his wife to produce another child. And while the idea was not unappealing, he had been far too busy these past few years to spend much time sleeping in a bed, much less engaging in any other activities therein.

His nephew would undoubtedly inherit the title

and accompanying estates, and Winn thought the lad would make a fine baron. If Elinor only knew how little time he spent worrying about his title and his lands. Until recently. Recently, he'd been thinking a hell of a lot. Too much. He'd never considered what would happen if—when—he retired from the Barbican group. He hadn't really believed he ever would retire until…

What would he do when his time at the Barbican was through? His children were growing up before his eyes. Soon they'd be having children of their own. And his wife—well, Winn was relatively certain, at this point in their lives, she hardly cared whether he lived or died. If he was not careful, he would end up alone, like Crow. He'd die a solitary old man, with no one to mourn him.

His mother would have said he was too much like his father—absent and inattentive. He shuddered at the possibility that Elinor might follow in his mother's footsteps and marry her groom were Winn to suffer an untimely death.

A slight movement caught his attention, and he blinked, uncertain for a moment as to whether he was imagining things. Ghosts? But no, there was a man sitting on his garden bench, reading the forgotten novel. As Winn stared, the man looked up and gave him a jaunty wave.

Winn cursed.

It was Blue.

Winn threw on a shirt, not bothering to fasten it at the throat, and made his way silently through the house and out into the garden. When he reached it,

Blue signaled to him to move back into the shadows and out of sight. Once away from the house, Winn said, "What the devil are you doing here? I've told Melbourne time and again, I don't like to be contacted at home."

"Sorry, old boy," Blue said, fingering his frilly cravat. "It was unavoidable."

Like Winn, Blue was an agent for the Barbican group. These men were the best the Foreign Office had to offer, remarkable in their talents for everything from combat to code breaking to ferreting out rival spies. Winn did not know the other members of the Barbican. Out of necessity, the members of the group kept their identities secret. Occasionally, operatives worked together. He and Crow had been paired time and again. Winn had actually liked working with a partner, but he couldn't help but think, time and again, that it might have been better if he had worked alone.

Better for Crow as it turned out.

"Melbourne needs to see you," Blue said.

Winn did not know Blue's real name. He was a bit on the short side, at least in Winn's opinion, but not in the least thin or scrawny, though he seemed to want to portray the air of the effete aristocrat. His movements were calculated and smooth. He had a nondescript face, nondescript hair, and startling blue eyes. Every time Winn saw those eyes, he wondered if they could be real. Winn had never seen Blue when not on assignment, so he was a bit surprised at the other agent's yellow waistcoat replete with spangles. His wool coat appeared to be a shade of green that matched his breeches. His pumps—he must have come from a ball—were decorated with some sort of jewel.

Winn frowned. "What are you wearing on your feet?"

Blue, seeming unfazed by the sudden change of topic, turned the shoes this way and that. Yes, those were definitely rubies on his shoes. "Do you like them? I'm afraid they won't fit your monstrous hooves."

"Thank God."

"As much as I enjoy standing about in cold, dark gardens discussing fashion, I am here on business."

"Melbourne wants to see me."

"Yes, first thing in the morning."

Winn sighed. It appeared he was unlikely to catch up on lost sleep tonight. "Very well. Anything else?"

"Yes." Blue held out a hand. "Give me the key."

Winn stepped back. "I don't think so." Normally, he was not so possessive of items he'd been instructed by the Barbican group to obtain, but he'd fought long and hard to hold onto this one. And obviously someone out there wanted it quite badly. He was not going to simply hand it over, not even to someone he trusted as much as Blue.

"Melbourne wants it put away for safekeeping."

"Then I'll give it to him myself in the morning." And with it, he would take the leave he'd been promised. If nothing else, his exchanges with his wife tonight had convinced him he really did need to take a leave of absence from the Barbican group. When Elinor had mentioned Georgiana's birthday, Winn had been momentarily taken aback. It was her birthday again? Hadn't it been her birthday last month? And what was she now? Thirteen? Fourteen? By God, he still saw her as a three-year-old racing about the house with her little sister toddling after her.

And his wife… well, he needed to take her in hand before half the rakes of the *ton* moved in to feed. For once, his personal life would take precedence over the Barbican. And there would not be another time as good as this. He had completed all of his missions and had no others pending. With Napoleon's capture, the world and England were once again at peace. The Barbican could spare him for a few months. "I assure you," Winn said to Blue, "the key will be safe until I deliver it."

Blue said nothing, finally shrugging and stepping back. "Have it your way." He took the beaver hat from under his arm and set it carefully on his head. And still, it perched at a jaunty angle.

"Good-bye," Winn said.

Blue smiled. "Not for long."

Winn had long ago ceased wondering what the devil Blue meant by his cryptic comments. He had also learned Blue was always correct. But he wasn't thinking about Blue when he marched into Melbourne's office at the ungodly hour of half-past eight in the morning. He waited with arms crossed while Melbourne signed a document as directed by his secretary. When he finished, Melbourne waved his man away and looked up at Winn. Winn judged Melbourne to be in his early fifties. The rumor was the man had been a highly regarded operative in his day. Now the still hale and hearty man was the leader of the Barbican group.

"You look like hell," Melbourne said, his eyes narrowing.

"You always did know the way to my heart." Winn took a seat opposite Melbourne. "I was told to come first thing. Did you miss me that much?"

"You're a cocky bastard."

Winn raised a brow. "Could you at least save the insults until I've broken my fast? If I have to slap you with my glove, I don't want to miss."

Melbourne poured two cups of tea from the service on his desk and handed one to Winn. Winn nodded acknowledgement and took the warm cup. Melbourne crossed his arms over his chest. "Little as you like it, you've always been a man who obeyed orders, Baron. That's why you've come so far so fast."

Winn wouldn't have called his ascent in the ranks of the Barbican group *fast*. He was eight-and-thirty and already beginning to feel he was too old for this sort of work. His shoulder was still sore from ramming the door in Ramsgate's town house, and his nose was tender from being bloodied.

Ten years ago he would have laughed outright if a man had told him he preferred sitting in a warm chair by the fire and reading *The Times* with his wife and family to the action of a mission. Now he wasn't so certain he'd scoff.

He sipped the tea. Something was missing in his work for the Barbican group. It wasn't that Napoleon had finally been exiled for good. There were always other villains. But he didn't find the work as fulfilling anymore. Or maybe it was that he'd destroyed the one thing that made the work fulfilling. And Winn couldn't help but think he should have been the one lying in a barren, unmarked grave in Cadiz.

"I have a new mission for you," Melbourne was saying now. "I want you to report to the home of Lord and Lady Smythe at—"

"Wait a minute, my lord," Winn interrupted. Melbourne raised his brows. Winn knew one did not interrupt Melbourne, and he never had before. But he could not listen idly to new orders. "I have an extended leave coming. You all but ordered me to take it before the last mission." Winn reached into his pocket and extracted the key. He set it on the desk and pushed it toward Melbourne with one finger. "Mission accomplished."

Melbourne lifted the key. "Very good. But your leave has been revoked."

Winn shook his head. Had he heard correctly?

"As I was saying, at the request of Lord Smythe—"

"I don't give a bloody farthing about Lord Smythe," Winn said. "I have leave coming."

Melbourne rose to his feet. "And I have men dying. Tell me, Baron, have you heard of a man named Foncé?"

Winn shook his head.

"You will. This key belongs to him." Melbourne twirled the key before pocketing it. "He won't be happy to learn you managed to steal it from him."

"I have many enemies."

"Not like this one you don't. Your leave pales in comparison to the damage Foncé and the Maîtriser group have done to this organization in the last few weeks alone. Agents are dead, Baron. I want every available agent assisting this investigation."

"It warms my heart to learn how utterly indispensable I am to the Barbican group," Winn said, finishing the tea. "But I will take my chances." If he did not take his leave now, Elinor was never going to forgive him. He could not disappoint her yet again or risk disappointing Georgiana too by missing her birthday party.

He would *not* become his father.

"Will you risk the life of your family as well?"

Winn narrowed his eyes. "What are you saying?"

"Your wife and your daughters are in danger as long as this man is free."

Baron clenched his fists. "Then why hasn't anyone caught him? What about Blue or the legendary Wolf? I'm not the only agent you have. What about Saint? He always gets his man."

Melbourne smiled thinly. "As it happens, Agent Wolf requested your assistance. I agreed. It is done."

"No, it is not," Winn said. "You know I work alone."

Melbourne pressed his palms to his desk, his look stony. "I don't recall offering you a choice."

Winn waved a hand. "No need to apologize."

Melbourne's look might have melted steel, but Winn didn't look away. He wasn't working with Wolf. He didn't need another partner. He didn't know Wolf, but he wasn't going to be responsible for the man's widow.

"I'm not apologizing," Melbourne said, "and you are to be partnered with Wolf." He held up a hand before Winn could argue. "This partnership is only temporary. Wolf is not officially a member of the Barbican group any longer, but he is more knowledgeable about Foncé than any of my agents. I need a Barbican man working with him."

"And if I refuse?"

Melbourne's lips thinned. "You'll find yourself in the dungeon filing old cases." The dungeon was the term Barbican agents used for the warehouse under the offices of the group. It was damp, cold, and dark. The number of files was astronomical. Winn knew his eyes would cross within hours of stepping foot inside. Rumor was agents had become lost amid the files and were never seen again.

Winn leaned back in his chair. "Wolf or the dungeon? Difficult choice."

"No, it isn't." Melbourne's expression softened, and Winn curled his hands into fists. He knew that sad-eyed look, and he didn't want it directed at him. The last thing he wanted was Melbourne's pity. "Baron—Winn," Melbourne began, "what happened was a tragedy, but it wasn't your fault. You were cleared of any wrongdoing—"

"Yes, yes, I know. I should be the one with the code name *Saint*. Sometimes even I cannot fathom how virtuous I am. Clearly, I should be granted leave. Failing that—and I know how you hate to part from me—I should be given a new assignment working alone."

Melbourne held his gaze. "Request denied. Meet Agent Wolf at this address. Lord Smythe will introduce you." He handed Winn a card. "Ten this evening, or I'll have your head."

❧

Elinor watched Georgiana glide across the floor with her dance instructor, Mister Winkle. Mister Winkle must have been about sixty; he had been her own dance instructor. He was firm but kind and had a manner that put young ladies at ease. In the corner of their modest ballroom, near the open windows, Caro sat with the girls' governess and painted. It was a bright, sunny day, and a light breeze wafted through the room, rustling the gauzy curtains.

Elinor could think of few places she'd rather be than here, with her two girls, on such a lovely day. Not that they noticed her. They were too busy with their own pursuits. As usual, she was an unnecessary addition. Perhaps if she freed the girls from their studies and took them for a ride in the park later this afternoon...

"My lady." A footman holding a tray stood beside her. Elinor glanced down at the small white note, lifted it, and broke the seal.

My dear Elinor,

If you value my friendship at all, please come immediately. I need you.

Desperately yours,
J

Elinor shook her head. So much for her plans for the afternoon. "Girls," she said when there was a pause in the music, "Lady Hollingshead has sent a note. She needs me for a few hours."

"Oh, might we come?" Caro asked. Elinor did not realize Caroline even knew her mother was in the room. Of course the girl wanted to go. She was close friends with Lady Hollingshead's middle daughter.

"No. Stay and finish your studies. And do not forget to practice the play you have been studying. I was promised a performance tonight."

Georgiana clapped with excitement. "We will be ready, Mama. *The Princess and the Pirate* will play one night only."

"I cannot wait." Elinor turned to leave.

"Mother?" That was Caroline. Elinor paused, knowing she had been foolish to think it would be so easy.

"Yes, dear?"

"Will Father be home for the play?"

Elinor felt her shoulders tighten and her lips thin. "I do hope so, Caro, but you know—"

"—your father is very busy," Caroline finished for her. "That means no."

"I…" But Elinor simply sighed. Let Winn defend himself for once. "I will see you for dinner." She kissed them both on the cheek and then called for the carriage.

It was a lovely day, unseasonably warm for fall. She knew Viscount Hollingshead had a beautifully manicured garden, and Elinor thought she might enjoy an afternoon sitting in a comfortable longue, staring at a clear blue sky dotted with puffy white clouds, and surrounded by a lush green lawn and the last of the summer flowers.

Her illusions evaporated as soon as she stepped foot in Lady Hollingshead's vestibule. The house was in a frenzy of madness, servants running to and fro, crashing into one another, and dropping platters, plate, and silver.

Elinor stepped in front of a harried-looking maid. "Where is your mistress?"

"In the garden, my lady." The girl bobbed a quick curtsy and rushed away.

Elinor narrowly avoided several collisions as she made her way to the garden. The scene outside was as bad as in the house proper, if not worse. As soon as Jane saw Elinor, she rushed to her side. "We are done for. Done for!"

Elinor spotted Mary, Lady Ramsgate, coming toward them. She'd been speaking to a small group of servants, and she rolled her eyes.

"Jane, you must calm yourself. It is only a garden party."

"Only? *Only* a garden party? Do you know who has promised to attend?"

Elinor glanced at Mary, who only shook her head and pressed her lips together. No help there. Elinor looked about at the mad preparations. "The Queen?"

"No." Jane frowned, her blue eyes creasing. "Although that would be very exciting. Someone almost as illustrious as the Queen."

"The prime minister?"

"No. Now I know why you keep referring to this as *only* a garden party. No one of any consequence is attending!"

Elinor sighed. "Jane, I don't think I should guess anymore. Simply tell me."

"The prince regent."

Elinor tried not to grimace. "Oh. Prinny. Well, that should be exciting."

"Yes!" Jane clutched Elinor's arm and looped her other arm through Mary's. "And I want everything to be perfect, but nothing is ready. Nothing! And the party is tomorrow evening."

Elinor glanced about. There was a great deal of

activity, but little had actually been accomplished. Mary finally spoke. "Jane, all you need is a bit of organization."

"I am no good at organizing, you know that. Elinor, could you please, *please* help me?"

"Of course." What were friends for if not to assist in times of need? No matter that Elinor's head was still reeling from Winn's strange behavior last night. No matter that he'd been gone before breakfast, and the girls had not even had a chance to see him. No matter that she would have to be the one—as usual—to witness the girls' disappointment when he did not attend their play. No matter.

The one thing she could do was organize a party.

"Very well. Stand back." Elinor stepped forward.

"Here we go," Mary said, clapping her hands together excitedly.

Elinor raised her hands. "Stop. All of you, stop." She did not raise her voice, only spoke in an authoritative tone. Slowly, the bevy of servants ceased their mad flitting about and looked at her. "Now, gather around and listen carefully. This is what you are going to do."

She laid out a simple list of what needed to be accomplished in order of priority, and then she went about assigning groups of servants to each task, with the highest-ranking servant in charge and the others as assistants. She told them to report back to her in one hour, then calmly walked about offering encouragement, suggestions, and resolving disputes. After an hour, the group in charge of the lanterns had finished, and the others were making splendid progress. The household looked busy and industrious. Even the viscount stepped outside for a moment and peered about at his diligent staff with something akin to wonder.

Lady Hollingshead beamed and insisted on showing him *her* preparations. Elinor let her have the credit and then sent the group of servants who had finished to the kitchen for refreshments for the rest of the staff. Finally, she strode to where Mary sat under a large white canopy. "We should have another update in three-quarters of an hour. I think we are well on our way." She took a seat on the chaise longue and finally had a moment to enjoy the day.

"I don't know how you do it," Mary said, looking about and shaking her head. "Jane was desperate when I arrived, and I simply couldn't think where to begin. Now it seems all is underway." She gestured to Jane and Lord Hollingshead. "Are you going to allow her to pretend this is all her doing?"

Elinor laughed. "Of course."

"And when all falls apart after you return home?"

"I shall come by in the morning to make certain all the last-minute preparations go smoothly. We don't want to disappoint the prince."

Mary smiled. "No, heavens no!" She looked down at her hands. "Will you be attending alone?"

Now Elinor took a deep breath. She would have been much more comfortable discussing party details. "Most probably."

"Then I take it your reunion was not all you had hoped and more."

"It was…" Elinor tried to find the appropriate word. "Interesting."

"Interesting?" Mary leaned closer. "Did you sleep at all last night?"

Elinor laughed, then rose and took Mary's arm. "Let's walk for a moment. We can't talk in private with all this hustle and bustle." They strode into the garden and away from the main house.

When they were some distance from the servants, Mary said, "What happened? Did he have any explanation for his disappearance last night?"

Elinor studied the hedges near her and made a note to tell the Hollingsheads' gardener to trim them. "Of course not."

Mary sighed, and Elinor shook her head. "He chastised me for attending without him and looking like a harlot."

"That is promising. Is he finally jealous?"

"I thought the same thing, and do you know, I do not care anymore."

Mary clapped, surprising Elinor. "Bravo! Why you continued to hold out hope he would fall in love with you is beyond me. He is an idiot not to see how fortunate he is."

Elinor smiled sadly. It was a lovely sentiment, but she did not believe it. She had never truly felt worthy of Winn. He was so charming, so amusing, so handsome. He could have married far better than the likes of her.

"I wish it were so easy to forget him. I look at Winn and my thoughts..." She could feel her face heating. "I want to do things to him I know would shock him. They shock *me*." She scuffed her half boot on the gravel walk.

"Really?" Mary's voice rose with interest. "I don't think they would shock me. Maybe you should try one or two. And then give me all of the details!"

Elinor laughed, then wanted to cry. "He doesn't want me, Mary. And I—you are right. I realized it last night. I deserve more. I want more." She wanted more than a life of planning balls and waiting interminably for Winn to return home. She might not be pretty or witty or fascinating, but she had been a loyal wife and a good mother. She did not deserve his cold disinterest. "Even if Winn were to fall madly in love with me today, it's too late. He's killed the last feelings of love I harbored for him."

"Which leaves the field open for Mr. Trollope. You know how I feel about liaisons."

"Yes, but Mr. Trollope is exciting and passionate and…" Elinor clasped her hands together. "*Dangerous*. And he wants *me*."

"He's a rake, Elinor. It is one thing to dance with him at a ball, quite another to pursue anything more."

"He's not a rake—well, not as much of one as he portrays." She glanced about to make certain no one was listening then lowered her voice. "I shouldn't even tell you this, but Rafe—Mr. Trollope—told me he only acts the rake in public. It's all a facade."

"For what?"

"He's actually a spy."

"A spy? You've read too many accounts of the war."

"But that is exactly how I know he is telling me the truth. Everything he says is in line with what I have read." Elinor looked about again to make certain they were alone. "I told you, I shouldn't even be confiding this to you. He's a spy for the Foreign Office, an elite group called the Babylon group."

"The Babylon group? Did you read about that in *The Times*?"

"No. But the papers did mention an elite group, only not by name. Mr. Trollope is part of this group, and he was one of the men responsible for the capture of Bonaparte. He also passed on key information that led to Wellington's success at Waterloo."

"I had no idea." Mary took out her fan and began wafting it in front of her face. "Why has he not been knighted for his service?"

"I asked him the same thing. He *has* been knighted, but he must keep the honor a secret, because he's still working, and his enemies are always trying to kill him. Someday we will be calling him Sir Rafe."

Mary fanned faster. "Oh, my! That sounds very dangerous."

"Doesn't it? Far more dangerous and exciting than spending all of one's time peering at dusty ledgers and visiting estates."

"Certainly more dangerous and exciting than going to White's or Tattersall's every day." Obviously she was thinking of Lord Ramsgate.

"I want excitement. Passion. And I think I could assist Mr. Trollope in his work. He wants me to meet him at Hyde Park tomorrow morning."

Mary pressed her lips together. "I don't know, Elinor. You are a married woman."

"It is only a meeting, and it will take place in the park. What could happen?"

"What do you *want* to happen?"

Four

THE TWO WOMEN MOVED AWAY, AND WINN LET OUT a slow breath. It had taken all of his considerable willpower not to plunge through the thick shrubbery, grab his wife by her long, graceful neck, and throttle her. Who the hell was this *Trollope*? No member of the Barbican group—Elinor must have substituted Babylon for Barbican—would ever reveal his membership. Winn had never even told Elinor—his own wife—he was an agent for the Barbican. He had never told anyone.

But he wasn't the kind of man who preyed on other men's wives. He wasn't the kind of man who used his position to try and tempt women into bed. Besides, if Elinor knew what the true work of a spy involved—long hours of surveillance in cold, drafty buildings; days hunched over maps and coded messages, strategizing and decoding; meeting after meeting with superiors, debriefing and dissecting one's every move—she wouldn't be so enthralled. The exciting times were few and far between.

And yet, somehow this Trollope had intrigued her.

Winn had not known Elinor longed for danger and passion. She always seemed to enjoy being home with their daughters.

Obviously, he did not know her as well as he thought. When he'd come looking for her in the garden, he had certainly not expected to overhear her contemplating an affair with a man named Rafe. He hadn't been trying to eavesdrop. He'd left his meeting with Melbourne, and with nothing to occupy him until the evening, he decided to join his family at home. It was a pleasant day. Perhaps he might make amends for his recent absences by taking Elinor and the girls riding in the park.

When he'd arrived home, he'd found his daughters busy with their tutors and lessons and his wife gone to her friend Lady Hollingshead. Very well. He would surprise her at her friend's house.

But he'd been the one surprised. Once he'd arrived, he hadn't been able to find her. One of the household staff—the whole place was busily preparing for some to-do or other—had told him Lady Keating and Lady Ramsgate were walking in the garden. He'd gone after them, heard their voices, and was about to reveal himself when his wife had said, *I look at Winn, and my thoughts...*

He'd gone absolutely still. He wanted to know exactly what those thoughts entailed. Elinor had told Lady Ramsgate they would shock him. Winn was not a man easily shocked. True, he and Elinor had never shared much passion, but then his work had always been his passion. Not so anymore. And the devil take him if Elinor's words did not trigger the first stirrings of unexpected desire.

Until she began speaking of another man.

What the bloody hell was he supposed to do now? He wasn't about to allow his wife to go to bed with another man. He didn't know who this Trollope fellow was, but he was going to find out.

❧

Elinor looked up, startled, as the dining room door opened. She and the girls had just sat down to dinner, and they were not expecting any visitors. Georgie and Caro were talking over one another in their excitement about the play they would perform tonight, and Elinor was listening to their happy voices, if not the details of those voices' content.

"Papa!" Georgie, who was sitting closest to the door, squealed. "You're home!" She rose and threw herself into her father's arms. He swept her up and kissed her on both cheeks, then set her down and darted a quick glance at Elinor. If he noticed his younger daughter didn't receive him quite so enthusiastically, he made no sign.

"My lord," Elinor said, sipping her wine as Winn took his seat. "We did not expect you."

"I'm sure you didn't," he said. He was carefully laying his napkin on his lap, so she did not catch his expression, but his tone was unfamiliar. Somewhat strained. He looked at Caroline. "I hear there is a play to be performed tonight. Something about a princess and a pirate."

She nodded at him. All of Caroline's bravado, so familiar to Elinor in Winn's absence, seemed to have leached out of the girl. Winn had that way about him.

When he was present, when he turned those green eyes on someone, he made her forget he'd ever been away and would probably go away again very shortly. Perhaps that was why she had forgiven him so many absences for so long. But it seemed he never turned those green eyes on her anymore and didn't care if she even noticed his absences. And after fourteen years, even someone as pitiful as she acquired some immunity.

And still she couldn't help examining her blue gown and wishing she had chosen something else to wear to dinner. This color did nothing for her, and she already felt drab and dull in Winn's presence.

"I am the princess," Georgie was saying, "and Caroline is the pirate."

"Really?" Winn lifted his fork. "I would have thought you the pirate and your sister the princess. After all, Caro is so gentle and demure."

Both Caro and Georgie laughed. "I think I will make the better pirate," Caro said, finally finding her tongue. "But you shall have to ask Mother for her opinion."

"Why is that?" Winn said, his gaze meeting Elinor's across the table. She gripped her hands in her lap to keep the flash of heat from rising. Oh, where was her immunity now? Was his look intentional? She had to remember it meant nothing. He didn't want her. She wished she had this same effortless flare of attraction for Mr. Trollope. *He* obviously wanted her.

"B-because you never see our plays," Caro said, glancing at her mother a little uncertainly.

Elinor stepped in, hating to see her daughter flounder, especially when Winn should know very well what she meant. "Caroline means to say, we know you are a busy man and undoubtedly have plans this evening."

"No." He bit into a potato.

"No?" Elinor said with a frown.

"I have no plans. I am entirely at your disposal this evening."

"Really?" Georgie said, her face all but glowing. "You will watch the play?"

"I wouldn't miss it. In fact, I am at your disposal tomorrow as well. I will be home *all day*."

He ate another potato, chewing it and watching her. Elinor stared at him. She had no recent memory of Winn ever having a free day to spend entirely with the three of them. He always had work or an appointment. Always. Why was he suddenly free? "You have no engagements?" she asked.

The girls' heads swiveled back to assess their father. "Nothing pressing. So…" He leaned forward. "What shall we do? Perhaps a picnic in the park?"

Elinor's heart jumped into her throat. Did he know? Was this some elaborate way of making her confess to meeting another man tomorrow?

No. It was impossible. There was no conceivable way he could know about Mr. Trollope or her plans for the morning. "The girls have their lessons in the morning," she said before Georgie or Caro could accept Winn's invitation. "You know how I value education."

"Surely it couldn't hurt to miss one day."

The girls squealed, but Elinor raised a hand. "Yes, it could." She had very rarely ever contradicted him in the past, and never in front of the girls or the servants. His brows rose. She did not care. "We have a routine in this house, and I find it best if that routine is followed. I know you have no idea what that routine might be, as you are never here, but perhaps if you were home more often, you might learn it." Elinor clinked her fork on her plate for emphasis, realizing belatedly it might have been better to have had this discussion in private. The girls were shifting uncomfortably in their chairs.

Well, too bad. She was done with pretending everything was wonderful between Winn and herself. She did not care if she angered him.

The girls were staring down at their food, but Winn seemed completely unaffected by her diatribe. "I shall take that under advisement. I leave the determination of the time of day up to you, my lady."

"Thank you," she said because it would have been bad manners not to, and she always liked to model good manners—especially for Caro. But she didn't particularly relish the invitation. Winn was beginning to make her nervous, beginning to make her question, and she found she would rather return to the familiar. She'd been hurt too many times when she thought he had changed, when she thought he might fall in love with her.

She would not be hurt again.

After dinner they adjourned into the drawing room, where the girls disappeared behind a partition to don their costumes. Elinor sat in uncomfortable silence, while Winn looked completely at ease. She didn't know why she should feel so discomfited in her own drawing room. After all, she was the one who occupied it daily. He was the visitor.

"The girls look well," Winn said, glancing at her. "Healthy and happy."

"They are cheered by the novelty of having a father for a night," she said. Where had that come from? She had never been intentionally hurtful before. But perhaps she shouldn't have worried. He seemed unaffected.

"I know. I need to spend more time with them."

She gaped at him. He had never said such a thing before. "They are growing up so quickly," he added. "And I was thinking perhaps it might be time we buy Georgiana a horse. She's old enough to care for the animal."

Elinor's jaw dropped. "You can't do that."

He raised a brow. Did he know how handsome he was when he did that? She inhaled sharply and ignored the way her pulse raced. If he would just cease staring at her with those green eyes and leaning toward her with that muscled body, she could concentrate on being angry with him.

"I'm certain it will be easy enough to buy a good mare from Tattersall's. I'll go this week."

"No! I mean, you cannot simply step back into our lives and buy the children gifts and think that will make up for all the time spent away. You cannot buy their love."

He nodded. "You are right."

To her shock and surprise, he leaned over and took her hand. His was large and warm, covering hers completely. "I fully intend to earn it back." He pulled her arm gently until her face was close to his. His breath tickled her ear, and she shivered. "Using any and all means necessary."

❧

At precisely one minute before ten, Winn stood on the doorstep of the Smythes' elegant town house on Charles Street and knocked. A stone-faced butler opened the door. "Good evening, Lord Keating," he intoned.

Winn frowned. How did the butler know his name?

"I am sorry to say, Lord Smythe is indisposed. You will have to call again at another time."

"I don't think so," Winn said, pushing his way in. He had made the effort to meet with this Smythe, and he wasn't going home now. Melbourne might use the cancelled meeting as an excuse to assign him to the dungeon.

The butler did not sputter or protest as Winn had expected. Instead, he snapped his fingers, and several rather large footmen appeared behind him. Winn had intended to have a quick look about for Smythe, but at the sight of the men, he paused. He was a large man and good at hand-to-hand combat, but he was not certain he was *that* good.

And why didn't he have burly footmen and a butler who knew how to summon them with a snap of his fingers? Not that he had ever needed either, but that wasn't the point.

"I trust you will return later. I will give Lord Smythe your card." The butler held out a small silver tray, his white-gloved hand steady. Winn reached in his pocket, hoping he had thought to bring a card with him, when a man started down the stairs. Winn recognized him immediately. He didn't know the man, but he knew the look and the sober dress.

A doctor.

Perhaps the butler wasn't simply trying to put him off. Perhaps Smythe really was indisposed.

"She's resting now," the doctor said, glancing curiously at the footmen crowding the vestibule. "I shall return in the morning to check on Lady Smythe. Lord Smythe has orders to send for me if there is any change."

"Very good, sir." The butler opened the door for the doctor, then held it for Winn. Winn hesitated. He should go, but he would only have to come back again at what might be a more inopportune moment. If Smythe would just give him Wolf's contact information, he would not have to trouble the man again.

The butler cleared his throat. "My lord?"

"It's quite all right, Wallace," a voice said from the top of the stairs.

Winn looked up and saw a man he assumed was Lord Smythe coming down the stairs. He was of medium height with light brown hair and light-colored eyes. He looked tired and disheveled without a coat, and a cravat dangling down his white linen shirt. He'd obviously run his hand through his hair numerous times, because it was in mad disarray. "Join me in the library, Lord Keating. I apologize for making you wait."

"If this is an inconvenient time…" Winn hedged.

"Lady Smythe is asleep—or giving a very convincing impression of a sleeping person. This is as good a time as any."

"Very well." Winn followed Smythe into his library, and the butler brought two snifters and a decanter of brandy to the desk, poured both men a measure, and stepped back.

"Anything else, my lord?"

"You hungry, Keating?"

Winn paused to consider. He had not eaten much at dinner. He'd been too focused on Elinor, too busy trying to detect any sign of guilt from her. "I wouldn't want you to go to any trouble."

Smythe waved his hand as though a meal might magically appear if he but snapped his fingers. "Food, Wallace."

"Any particular variety, my lord?"

"Yes, the copious variety."

"Yes, my lord. You are ever the connoisseur."

The butler closed the library door, and Smythe gave a weary smile. "He has too much gall, but he knows my secrets, so I don't dare put him out."

"If you ever do, I'll hire him in a moment."

"Would you?" And just like that Lord Smythe… changed. His eyes became hard and piercing as he sat back in his chair and sipped his brandy. The weariness seemed to fall off him, making him look fresh and formidable. "Tell me something, Baron," he said quietly. "Do you have a family?"

Winn frowned. Had he addressed him by title, or did Smythe know his code name? He should have asked Melbourne for more details as to what Smythe knew. "Pardon?"

"You heard me."

"I—" Winn hesitated. He did not like to reveal personal details about his life, but if Melbourne trusted this man, Winn supposed he could offer general information. "Yes. I have a wife and two daughters." He was thinking about that Trollope fellow again. He might mention the name to Wolf. Perhaps the other operative had heard of him. "But the reason I'm here, other than to discuss—"

"How old are your daughters?"

"My daughters?" Now Winn narrowed his eyes.

"My apologies. I didn't mean to overstep. You came to discuss the Maîtriser group. Melbourne sent you, I suppose."

Winn did not show his surprise. "He said you asked for me, my lord."

"Hardly. I don't want to involve the Barbican group any more than necessary. But Melbourne isn't quite prepared to allow Saint and me to walk away that easily."

Winn blinked. "Saint and you?" He did not quite want to believe what Smythe seemed to be implying.

Smythe smiled. "He didn't tell you?' Smythe chuckled and shook his head. "Melbourne does enjoy his amusements. I am Agent Wolf. My wife is Agent Saint."

"You—? What?" His *wife* was Agent Saint? Saint was a man. How could a woman be Saint? Winn could well imagine Smythe was Wolf. He had the look of an agent about him. But would Melbourne have allowed a husband and wife both to operate as agents?

"I've surprised you." He lifted his snifter to drink again, then seemed to notice it was empty. "Melbourne should have told you, but undoubtedly he thought your finding out this way more intriguing."

"Melbourne said you were retired."

"Yes, though Melbourne hasn't officially retired us. He wants us back." And now the weariness returned. "He might have his way after all."

"Is something amiss?" Winn asked. He did not want

to pry, but Smythe—Wolf—seemed defeated. "The doctor was here to see Lady Smythe. Is she unwell?"

"I don't know, Keating. Only time will tell."

Winn wasn't certain what comment to make in response to so cryptic a remark. This was why he usually preferred working alone. He wasn't any use in these sorts of discussions. He and Crow had seemed to understand each other, but then Crow had been his mentor and like a brother to him. "I could come back tomorrow, discuss the Maîtriser group then."

But Smythe wasn't even listening. He was staring out the window, turning his snifter to and fro in his hands. "What does your wife think about the work you do?"

Winn hesitated. Agents for the Barbican were taught never to discuss personal matters with other agents, but then Winn hadn't known agents could marry each other. And it seemed if ever there was a man to ask about balancing marriage and covert operations, it was Smythe. "She doesn't know," Winn said. "She thinks I am away managing my estates."

"Do you have many?" Smythe asked, still looking out the window.

"No."

Smythe raised a brow. "She must think you either a very dedicated overseer or a wretched liar."

"I would have said she trusted me enough not to ask questions. I would have said she believed what I did was for the good of all of us."

"Would have?" Smythe asked. "What has changed?"

"Have you heard of an agent named Rafe Trollope?"

Smythe shook his head.

"Good. I may need you to help me kill him."

Five

FOR PERHAPS THE FIRST TIME IN RECENT MEMORY, Adrian Galloway, Lord Smythe, was glad his snifter was empty of brandy. Otherwise, he would have choked on it just now when Keating spoke. Instead, he slowly set the snifter on his desk, folded his hands, and leaned forward. The man had a hunted look about him. Initially, Adrian had thought Baron was hungry and fatigued after a long day of work. Then he'd considered the other agent's behavior stemmed from the fact that Baron didn't really want to work with anyone on the Maîtriser case.

But now Adrian saw it was something else entirely. Such deductions were a simple matter, when one was paying attention. Sophia would have sensed something amiss and solved the man's problem by now. But Sophia wasn't here, and Adrian wasn't going to wake her at the mere suggestion of murder. Now if they actually killed this Trollope, that was another thing entirely. She wouldn't like to miss out on something like that.

"So you want me to help you kill a man," Adrian said. Plan A was always to go along with another agent's suggestion. He'd move to Plan B, counter suggestion, when he had a better feel for the issue at hand. "Do you want to tell me why we're killing this man?"

"Not particularly."

Plan B was looking better and better. "Do so anyway."

"He's trying to bed my wife." Baron stood and began to pace the library. He was a tall man with a broad chest and brown hair that had need of shears. The man was obviously a good operative. If he hadn't been, he would be dead by now, because such an imposing man would make an easy target. Adrian studied him further, noting Baron had large hands that could probably crush a man's head between them, and long legs that could outrun most pursuers. Baron was known for his unconventional tactics. Adrian wasn't sure what that meant, but judging by the discussion they were having, he thought he might soon find out. To capture Foncé, Adrian was going to need someone who could think unconventionally. Sophia had that talent, but they were both too familiar with the case now. And perhaps too close. They needed someone with fresh eyes and innovative ideas. That was why Adrian had asked for Baron.

But he hadn't expected the events earlier that evening, and he hadn't expected Baron to arrive with murder on his mind. Someone was trying to seduce Lady Keating? Adrian shook his head. He couldn't think of a single sane man of his acquaintance who would be foolish enough to even *think* of bedding the wife of a man like Keating, much less act upon such a suicidal course.

"I see," Adrian said noncommittally. He was treading carefully between Plans A and B now. "And you know this because?"

"You're married, Smythe." Keating paced away from him, then rounded on his heel. "Do all women want excitement and danger?"

Adrian thought of Sophia, lying still and quiet beneath the white and lavender counterpane in her bedchamber. When he'd left her, her dark hair trailed over the pillow like a spill of chocolate, and her graceful eyebrows stood out on her pale skin like angry slashes. No, all women did not crave excitement and danger. Some women craved a family, the birth of a child.

"I would be careful about putting all women into any one category," Adrian said now. "It has caused me some difficulty in the past."

Baron waved an arm encased in a plain but well-made coat. Sophia was always telling him to have more coats and shirts made, but he didn't want to look like a dandy with all the laces and frills. Perhaps he should ask Baron for the name of his tailor.

"Yes, well, your wife is probably an exception," Baron was saying. "In the past, mine has always seemed content to be home with our daughters."

Adrian well knew looks could be deceiving.

"She seemed to enjoy all the Society functions and charitable organizations. But now... now I wonder." Baron dropped down again in the chair opposite Adrian and lifted the brandy that had been sitting untouched.

"What do you wonder?"

Baron stared into his brandy, and Adrian could

almost hear him deciding how much to reveal. "If I even know her at all."

Ah, now this was moving into familiar ground. Perhaps he wouldn't have to resort to Plan B after all. Perhaps there was a Plan C: convince the man to talk to his wife.

"Listen, Keating," Adrian said, leaning back. "I know the kind of life you lead, because I've led it too. All the traveling doesn't make for a very close marriage. Hell, Sophia and I didn't even know we were both operatives until a couple of months ago. But I'll tell you what I've learned and save you the trouble of murdering this man or having to speculate"—ad nauseam, but he didn't say that part aloud—"about what she might be thinking."

Baron raised his brows, looking skeptical.

"All you have to do is talk to her." There. Adrian folded his arms across his chest. He felt rather proud of himself, actually. Sophia wasn't the only one who could be sympathetic or solve others' personal problems.

"Talk to her?" Baron said, sounding less than enthusiastic about Adrian's advice. "And tell her what? I overheard her chatting about bedding another man?"

"I don't know that I'd take that tack…"

"Oh, perhaps I should reveal I'm a member of the Barbican group. Even if I hadn't pledged to keep that a secret, I can imagine her reaction when she realizes I've been lying to her for years."

"Yes, well—"

"Or how about this idea? I go find this *Rafe* and beat the hell out of him, because the more I think about it, the more I think this might actually be some kind of rival operation's method of getting to me."

Adrian shook his head. "Wait. You've lost me."

"Ever heard of the Babylon group?"

"I don't think so."

Baron stood again. "I haven't either. I kept thinking she'd got it wrong, and it was the Barbican group, but I can't think why one of our own would do this. Neither you nor I know of a Rafe Trollope in the group."

"True, but I don't know many other operatives. I'm at sea here, Keating. Are you saying the man trying to seduce your wife is another spy?"

"That's exactly what I'm saying. He works for a group called the Babylon group."

Adrian nodded. "Babylon, Barbican. It's close. But you think this Babylon group might be trying to gain access to you by seducing your wife?"

"The thought crossed my mind."

A shiver ran down Adrian's spine. "Well, why the hell didn't you say this in the beginning? Now we're dealing with a serious issue. We need to find this Trollope."

"And kill him."

Adrian held up his hands. "Slow down. We'll start with torturing him first. We can do that here. If we decide to kill him, we'll probably have to move elsewhere. Sophia will have my head if we spill blood on this rug. We just had it replaced."

"They're meeting in Hyde Park in the morning," Baron said. "I propose we conduct surveillance and dissect our target."

"Agreed. We can make a plan from there."

"I'll take my leave."

"Wait." Adrian stood. "We have another issue." He couldn't let Baron walk away that easily. If he helped the man with this Mr. Trollope, Baron was going to help with Foncé.

"Foncé?" Baron asked.

"Exactly. Saint and I chased the man halfway across Europe, but we lost him. Blue suggested we return to London, thereby luring Foncé here. We have no way of knowing if that will work or not. Perhaps we've read Foncé all wrong. But if I know Blue—"

"No one knows Blue."

That was true enough. "All right, let me rephrase. If Blue's assumption is correct—"

"And when has one of Blue's assumptions ever been incorrect?"

"—Exactly. We have a man who has succeeded in murdering half a dozen of our agents, using rather grotesque methods, and he is presently on his way to England."

"I see your point," Baron acknowledged. "We must be ready for him. We should start with a list of his known acquaintances and previous contacts. The way to best him is to find him before he finds you."

"We surprise him when he's not ready for us. Somewhere he feels safe. The residence of a mistress or another member of his group."

"Right." Baron considered. "Who's going to do all this research? It's tedious, and most agents don't have the time or the knowledge of the Maîtriser group."

"Leave that to me," Adrian said, grimacing inward. "I know the perfect person."

ᐰ

Winn had always been an early riser. Elinor, for all her efficiency in other arenas, was not. He usually breakfasted, read *The Times*, and enjoyed a morning ride before his wife and daughters were even awake.

But today was different. Today he had just accepted his tea from the butler when the dining-room door opened and Elinor entered. She could not hide a look of surprise. "You are here," she said, all but stumbling into the room. She wore a rose-colored day dress cut low enough to expose the swells of her breasts under the gauzy fichu. Her hair, which she always wore simply, had been curled and coiffed and hung in charming coils over her shoulder.

She looked like the girl he had married. No, she looked even prettier than the girl he had married.

"I live here," he answered her. He watched as she considered the obvious retort about his frequent absences and then decided not to make it. Clearly, she was hoping for peace this morning.

Futile, futile hope.

She sat at the other end of the table, accepted her cup of tea from the butler, and seemed to sip it warily. He studied his copy of *The Times* silently and allowed her to consider. If she had not cancelled it, she had a rendezvous this morning with her lover. Winn's presence was clearly a complication. He glanced over the top of his paper and could not help studying her.

Had she always been so pretty? Her skin was milk white, and her cheeks so perfectly pink they looked painted on. She had a small, pert nose both of their daughters had inherited, and dark brown eyes that were amazingly expressive. But her best feature was and had always been her mouth. She had red lips the perfect size and shape for kissing. Her small white teeth were perfectly straight. And there was a tiny freckle just at the curve of the left side of her mouth. He could not even see it from this distance, but he knew it was there. He'd kissed that freckle on many occasions.

Unfortunately, at present, he could not remember the last time he had kissed her. And he could not remember ever having missed kissing her before now.

"Is something amiss?" she asked.

Winn blinked. "No. Why?"

"You are staring at me."

"You are a beautiful woman," he answered, watching as color flooded her cheeks. "I cannot help myself."

The look she gave him was one of confusion and wariness. She did not believe he was being sincere and, further, she did not know how to accept the compliment. The fact pleased him, because it meant others like this Trollope had not yet corrupted her. She had not decided to throw him over yet. Of course, the fact that she was open to corruption was his fault entirely. Why did he not compliment her more? Why did he not kiss her more often? Take her to bed?

Because he was never here. Except... he was here now. "Bramson, leave us for a few moments, please."

Elinor gave Winn a puzzled look.

"Yes, my lord," the butler answered, closing the door behind him.

"Now I know something is wrong."

Winn stood, crossed the room, and sat in the chair beside her.

She scooted to the far side of her chair, increasing

the distance between them. "You have never dismissed Bramson."

"Nothing is the matter." He reached over and took her free hand. She tried to pull it away, but he would not release it. She had not yet donned her gloves, and her hands were warm and soft. "I wanted to speak to you privately."

"Why?"

He must be one of the worst husbands in England to receive this response. Elinor did not even want to hold his hand, much less believe he wanted to speak to her. "Do I need a reason to speak privately to my wife?"

"Winn." She loosed her hand. He let it go rather than engage in a tug-of-war. "Please stop being so mysterious. What is it you want?"

"You," he said without thinking.

She blinked. "I don't understand."

"Another of my failings," he murmured. She really did not know her appeal. He stood and pulled her chair back.

"What are you——?"

Before she could protest further, he pulled her out of the chair and into his arms. He remembered the feel of her. Her body was soft and feminine and ripe with curves. He did not remember it having been so rigid.

"Winn!"

He put a finger on her lips. "Don't speak. It's been far too long since I've done this." He lowered his mouth to hers and kissed her tenderly, gently. It was the kiss he would have given a new lover, a tentative, testing kiss, because he could not remember how she liked to be kissed. Or perhaps he'd never paid enough attention to know.

Her lips remained as rigid as her body, but she exhaled a small puff of warm, surprised air. Her breath was sweet with the sugar and cream from her tea, and he dipped his head again to taste her more thoroughly. His lips met hers with more persuasion this time, and he tightened his hands on her arms, pulling her closer. She did not go willingly, but he sensed desire in her, in the way her breath hitched and her lips yielded slightly.

"Stop," she whispered. It was perhaps the most unconvincing order he had ever heard. Her voice, husky and low, betrayed her need. No man in his right mind would stop after hearing the unspoken craving.

He was obviously not in his right mind. "Why?" He kissed her cheek, the tip of her nose, the flutter of her eyelashes.

"Someone might come in." She stepped back, and he noted the rapid rise and fall of her breasts. Oh, Winn could think of so many places he wanted to kiss, so many wicked things he wanted to do. Why had he spent so much time away? Why had he not remembered what a desirable woman he had married?

"Shall I lock the door?" he asked. He glanced at the table. "I could clear it in a matter of moments." He leaned close and whispered in her ear, "You would look glorious spread naked on that gleaming wood. Perhaps I could take some of the clotted cream and lick it off—"

"Winn!" She jumped back, her face bright red. Had he aroused her or embarrassed her? He moved toward her, and she moved another step back. "You have forgotten yourself."

"No. I've finally remembered." He took another step toward her, and she darted away from him. He was not going to chase her, but he didn't have any qualms about cornering her. "If you object to the dining room, why don't we go upstairs?"

"The maids—"

"—are easily dismissed." He moved closer, and she took another step back. One more, and her back would be up against the window.

"I do not know what has come over you," she said, smoothing her perfectly neat hair into place, "but I am afraid I have an appointment this morning. I cannot accommodate you."

Winn's fingers flexed. He would have liked to throttle her. He knew all about her appointment. How dare she put him off in favor of another man? And Smythe suggested he *talk* to her. Elinor would be lucky if he didn't lock her in her room for the rest of the year. "I see." He could have allowed her to go then. He was meeting Smythe in Hyde Park anyway, but Winn didn't want to make it quite so easy. "I'll have my valet fetch my coat and hat then," he said.

Her eyes widened. "What? Why?"

"I thought I'd go with you."

"No!"

He raised a brow, and she took a step back, bumping into the window. Now he had her trapped. "You object to my company that fervently?"

"I don't object to your company."

He stepped closer, planting his hands on the

windowpane so he framed her head and those fat, glossy curls. He wanted to take one and wrap it around his finger. "I am glad to hear it. Where are we off to?"

"I…"

He could see her thinking, devising a lie. And what surprised him was that if he had not known she was lying, he would not have known it was a falsehood. He did not know her tells.

"I have some shopping to do, underthings."

He smiled.

"For the girls."

His smile dropped. Even though he knew she was lying, the thought of buying underthings for his daughters unnerved him. He did not want to know what the girls wore under their skirts. As far as he was concerned, they did not exist under their skirts. And he did not want to know otherwise.

"So I'm certain you would rather stay at home."

He could not argue. He had her physically cornered, but she had more than outmaneuvered him mentally. "I will wait patiently for your return."

She gave him a puzzled look, for which he did not blame her. She ducked under his arm and started for the door, but he could not allow her to go that easily. He did not know what would happen in the park today, but Winn was not going to allow Elinor to meet her lover without thoughts of her husband on her mind. With lightning speed, he reached out, grasped her arm, and spun her back to face him.

"What—?"

He silenced her with a kiss. No gentle, tantalizing kiss this time. He wanted heat. He wanted to sear the memory of his lips on hers, his body pressed to hers, his arms holding her tightly—sear all into her mind. He wanted her to feel the lasting traces of the heat of their kiss all the way to Hyde Park and back. His mouth slanted over hers, his lips parting hers so he could taste her. She cried out in surprise, but he took without mercy, and soon she was clinging to him just to keep upright. He pushed her back against the window, cushioning her with his arms as he wrapped them around her waist.

Outside, the wind battered the windowpane. The day had dawned dark and blustery. He could feel the cold seep through the wool of his coat, but he was far from chilled. Elinor was so warm—her mouth, her skin, the small sigh she made now when his tongue met hers. She was still stiff and unyielding. She did not want him to kiss her, but, like it or not, she *did* want him. She *did* desire him.

He allowed one hand to roam over the indention of her waist and down the swell of her hips. He caressed the curve of her bottom and pressed her to him. She gasped, and he caught the sound with his mouth. He remembered her lips. That much he had not forgotten. They were so soft and inviting, and he found himself succumbing to the pleasure of kissing her.

Now, who was seducing whom?

He broke the kiss and trailed his lips along her cheek until he reached her earlobe. He nuzzled the silky curl she'd tucked behind her ear and breathed, "Don't make any plans for this evening. I want your"—he kissed the tender flesh of her ear—"undivided attention."

"Winn—"

"And you might want to find somewhere for the

girls to play this evening. They might wonder when they hear you crying out in pleasure."

She inhaled sharply as his tongue teased her skin, and then he brushed his hands up her sides and traced his thumbs over her nipples. Her body was trembling, and he knew he was going to have trouble allowing her to walk away. He wanted her. Badly. He kissed her again, and this time her mouth met his eagerly. Winn might have smiled at his victory if it wasn't also a defeat. His own desire had built far more than he liked, and now he must stand back and watch while she went to meet another man. Slowly, while she still sought him, he pulled back.

Her face was flushed and her eyes as dark as the midnight sky. Her fichu did little to constrain the straining of her breasts as she struggled to catch her breath. Winn clenched his hands to keep from ripping that flimsy material away and feasting on her soft skin.

"You should go," he said, his voice edged with steel. "While I am still amenable to your departure."

"Yes." She nodded and looked this way and that as though confused as to where she was going.

Winn gestured to the door. "That way, madam."

"Of course." She stumbled past him, hurrying toward the door. Her hair was not quite so perfectly coiffed anymore. And damn him if he didn't find her more alluring with it slightly mussed. She reached the handle and opened the door, but before she could step outside, he said, "Ellie."

She stopped, her posture as rigid as that of a man who has just been shot.

"I'll be waiting for you."

Six

ELLIE. HE HAD CALLED HER *ELLIE*. ELINOR COULD NOT say the last time he had used the sobriquet with her. Years, she thought. Years and years.

She sat in the Keating town coach and sped toward Hyde Park. There were few other conveyances about this morning. It was early and chilly, and she imagined the members of the *ton* much preferred their warm beds to the biting wind. This morning she could also see the appeal of a warm bed, a warm, naked man sharing it with her.

She shook her head. Damn Winn! Why did he have to kiss her this morning? Why did he have to whisper in her ear and make her blood thrum in her veins today? All of these years she had wanted him, waited for him, hoped he would notice her, desire her, seduce her. And now, today, when she had finally given up, he sought her out. Did he know or suspect? She did not see how he could, unless he'd found the letters she'd kept in her dresser…

But he was not home enough to have even spent any time in her bedchamber, much less searched her dresser. And if he had been in her bedchamber, Bridget would have told her. The household servants were loyal to her. They'd realized long ago Winn was not the one who ensured their salaries were paid. So how did he know? But if he knew about Mr. Trollope, wouldn't he have been angry? He would not have kissed her. Which meant this must be an incredible coincidence, and she was allowing her imagination to run wild because she felt guilty for betraying Winn.

Not that she'd betrayed him. Yet. She was only going to meet Trollope. That was all. She hadn't even allowed him to kiss her. She'd accepted his love letters, that was true enough, but she hadn't responded in kind. She'd been cautious, despite the fact that Rafe Trollope was wild and exciting. She was not certain this was what she wanted. She was not wild and exciting, though at the moment, with her heart pounding and her lips still warm from Winn's kisses, she felt rather reckless. She took a deep breath and tried to shut out the image of Winn pulling her into his arms. She tried to forget the feel of him pressed against her. He was so tall and so strong. She could barely wrap her arms around the breadth of his shoulders. And yet, for such a large man, he was never clumsy, never inelegant. Indeed, today he had moved with all of the sleekness of a lion as he caught her about the waist and pulled her against him.

Against his chest. His hard chest. His hard, muscled chest.

She licked her lips and closed her eyes. This was not helping matters. She should be thinking of Trollope, with his sun-touched golden hair and his emerald-green eyes. Drat! That was Winn who had the green eyes. Trollope had... she could not remember the color of Trollope's eyes.

She glanced out the window and noted Hyde Park was just ahead. Elinor sat up straighter. She would take note of Mr. Trollope's eyes this morning. She would memorize their color, and she would kiss him too. That would help her to forget Winn's persuasive mouth. By the time she returned home, her thoughts would be centered on Mr. Trollope and the exciting new adventure she was about to embark upon.

She frowned, a moment of panic infusing her. There was one detail about her relationship with Trollope she had not mentioned to Mary. She'd told him of her interest in his work, and he'd offered to allow her to help him with his next mission. She was excited at the prospect of seeing mention of her work—not her name, of course—in *The Times* at some point in the future. How thrilling it would be to know she had done something more important than plan a ball or scrub a child's face clean. And perhaps when she and Trollope were working together on their dangerous mission, they would fall in love. Trollope told her he was half in love with her already, and she knew his motives were anything but pure. Still, at least there was one man whose interest she had captured.

The carriage slowed and stopped, and Elinor peered out of the window. The park was deserted at this hour. She did not even see Trollope. But he had told her he would keep out of sight until she was away from her driver. They did not want any witnesses to their meeting. Mr. Trollope worried about foreign agents and spies, and even though Elinor had assured him her driver was not a foreign spy, Mr. Trollope did not wish to take chances.

A groom opened her door and handed her down.

"I prefer to walk alone this morning, Jacob."

The groom's eyes widened. "B-but my lady," he finally managed. "I'll be sacked for certain."

"The park is empty. No one will ever know, and I shall be perfectly fine. I will stay within sight of the carriage."

"My lady, please."

"Another word, and *I* shall sack you."

Jacob closed his mouth abruptly, and she set off. She tried to walk for a while before looking over her shoulder to see if Jacob was watching her. Like a good servant, he was. She waved at him and meandered toward some trees. Feeling like an idiot, she pretended to spot something fascinating and ducked into the small copse. The ground beneath her feet was spongy and soft, and now that she was out of the sun, she felt the chill. She shivered and peered around the woodsy enclosure. "Mr. Trollope?" she hissed. "Ah… Rafe?" She had not used his Christian name before, but what was the use in holding on to societal conventions at this point? She was breaking them simply by being here. "Rafe!"

Elinor sighed. It seemed she was destined to wait for men who deigned never to make an appearance. She turned, prepared to return to Jacob, who was probably apoplectic at her disappearance, and then gasped. Mr. Trollope was standing behind her, smiling.

He made a deep bow, sweeping his hat in an arc before him. "My lady."

Elinor put a hand to her racing heart. It pounded, and not only from surprise. Trollope's good looks always took her breath away. "I thought you were not coming," she breathed.

He glanced behind him as though ensuring he were not followed. "I was unavoidably delayed."

Elinor swallowed. Had he come straight from a mission? He looked a bit breathless. He stepped closer and took her hand in his gloved one. "I am so pleased you came today, Elinor. May I call you *Elinor*?"

She nodded. "Of course."

He squeezed her hand, and she wished she could remove her gloves and touch his skin. She looked up at him, then back down to meet his eyes. She had forgotten he was not nearly as tall as Winn, or as broad-shouldered. He was actually rather slight and quite slim. Beside Winn, she always felt petite and delicate. Trollope made her feel like she should hunch over a bit and have Bridget lengthen and tighten her stays.

And she really must cease thinking of Winn! Here was Mr. Trollope with his golden-blond hair, his lion-like brown eyes, and his charming smile. He was the catch of the *ton*. Every young lady was swooning over him, and he wanted her. Elinor.

He tugged her hand and pulled her closer. She hesitated slightly, uncertain what he meant to do. She had never kissed a man other than Winn, and she was not certain if she was prepared to do so now. But, fortunately, Mr. Trollope merely bent and brushed his lips over her gloved knuckles. "You look ravishing today."

Elinor wanted to be pleased by the compliment, but she had the sense this was something he said to every woman. She had taken extra care with her appearance, but did she look *ravishing*?

"I could not sleep for thinking about you," Trollope said, looking up at her from under his long lashes.

Elinor frowned. His lashes were longer and thicker than hers. That seemed immensely unfair. She studied his face. "You look well rested."

"I assure you I am not. I could not wait to hold you in my arms." He tugged her hand again and pulled her smoothly into his embrace. "May I kiss you?" He moved to press his lips to hers, and she tilted her head back. But niggling thoughts invaded what should have been a romantic moment. Why had he asked to kiss her? Why not simply do so? She wanted to be swept away, not queried.

"Kiss me, Elinor."

She frowned. Why did *he* not kiss *her*? Why did he not press his lips to hers and steal her breath away? Elinor took a deep breath and closed her eyes. This was, after all, what she'd come for. Mostly. But just as their mouths met, she heard a sound like a muffled curse. She opened her eyes, and a startled robin flew at her, narrowly missing her face with its wing. "What was that?"

Trollope was eyeing the trees. Elinor looked up as well but saw nothing other than branches and brightly colored leaves. The reds, yellows, and oranges of autumn were in abundance in this wooded section of the park. "I don't see anything, but we cannot be too careful."

Elinor nodded. "Of course. Perhaps you should explain the mission now. My groom will pursue me if I am out of sight much longer."

Trollope's brow creased in annoyance. "I thought I told you to come alone."

"How am I to come alone? It was difficult enough to leave the house without Lord Keating attending me."

Mr. Trollope mumbled something about choosing a better venue in the future; then he smiled. "One kiss, then I will tell you all of the particulars of the mission." This time when he reached for her, Elinor moved deliberately out of range.

"We're too exposed here," she said.

His brows came together. "Fine. As I told you, I work for an elite organization."

"For the Babylon group."

"Shh!" Trollope grabbed her arm and pulled her deeper into the copse. "You mustn't speak the name out loud. There are spies everywhere."

Elinor blinked. "Oh, I'm sorry!" It was a stupid mistake. He had told her before not to say the name of the group aloud.

"You are forgiven, but be more cautious in the future, or I shall have to find another agent to work for me."

"Of course." Elinor's heart was pounding again. Finally she was going to be a secret agent and participate in missions. She was almost giddy at the thought of the adventure. Trollope needed her, and she wanted to be needed. "What would you have me do?"

"I need you to give another agent a message."

Elinor nodded. She could do that easily, and how exciting to meet another agent! "What is the message?"

He glanced over his shoulder again. "I cannot write it down."

"Of course not."

"You will have to remember it."

Elinor nodded again. "I have an excellent memory."

"Very good. The message is *oranges and lemons, say the bells at St. Clement's.*"

Elinor blinked. "A rhyming song?" She had sung that with Caro and Georgiana when they were barely walking. "That is not a message."

"It is in code," Trollope said, his tone impatient.

"Oh." Code. Of course. She had not thought of that. "To whom shall I give the message?"

"Will you attend Lady Hollingshead's garden party?"

"You know I will. We are good friends."

"He will be in attendance."

"How will I know him?" They were whispering now, their heads close together, and she had to admit this was so much more fun than supervising Georgiana's French lesson.

"You will know him when you see him."

"How—?"

"Lady Keating?"

Elinor jumped at the sound of her name. "It is my groom, Jacob."

Trollope's face paled. "You should go before he spots me here. We would not want him to inform your husband of our rendezvous."

"No." She did not want that either, but she did think a veteran spy like Trollope would be less worried about a man as benign as Winn. "But how will I know the agent?" she asked as Mr. Trollope made for the trees on the other side of the copse.

"I have faith in you, my Elinor. We will meet again

soon to discuss the next mission, and next time it will be somewhere very, very private." He kissed her hand and was gone.

"Lady Keating?"

She turned. "I'm here, Jacob. Coming!"

✦

"It's about time the bloody groom stepped in," Winn said, watching his wife walk back to the carriage with Jacob. "What the devil is he doing if he's not protecting my wife from vermin like that?" He gestured to the trees where Elinor's lover had taken shelter.

Smythe looked bored, which was quite an accomplishment, as they were balanced precariously high in a tree. "I assume she ordered him to wait. Poor man. He cannot win—sacked for dereliction of duty or sacked for disobedience."

"I'll have a word with him."

"You had better speak to all of your servants then. In my experience, wives usually have control over matters pertaining to the household. Especially when the master of the house is frequently away."

Winn scowled. What else was going on in his house he did not know about?

"There is good news," Smythe said.

"What is that?" Winn wanted to know. His wife had almost kissed another man—would have if Jacob hadn't distracted the couple. He would have jumped down and killed this Trollope that moment if Smythe hadn't held him back.

"Trollope is not a spy."

"Oh, that." It was small comfort to know the man seducing his wife was a liar.

"He has probably used the story in the past to woo women. Clearly your wife is giving him more difficulty than he anticipated. He actually has to concoct a mission for her."

Winn smiled. That was true. Leave it to Elinor to make things difficult. "But now she'll be approaching random men and speaking to them of oranges and lemons."

"Let me take care of that. In the meantime"— Smythe gestured to the trees where Trollope was making his way back through—"I believe we have a rake who needs to be taught a lesson."

"You are correct, Smythe. And I want him all to myself."

Winn pulled his hat low over his brow and jumped down, surprising Trollope enough so the man let out a high-pitched squeal. Wolf, similarly disguised, landed beside him a moment later. "I suppose no one ever taught you to share, Baron," he muttered.

"Who the devil are you?" Trollope asked, stepping back. Smythe flanked him, cutting off his escape.

"I am afraid I cannot reveal that information to a potential rival agent," Winn said.

Trollope glanced wildly behind him, noted Smythe, and Winn saw all the blood drain from his face. "Potential—?"

"You are an agent for the Babylon group, is that correct?" Smythe asked. Winn scowled. He wanted the privilege of making the man look a fool.

"I-I don't know what you are talking about,"

Trollope sputtered, looking from man to man with wide eyes.

"Likely story," Winn said. "Unfortunately for you, we have a double agent in our employ, and she has identified you."

"She?"

"That is correct."

Trollope shook his head. "No, Elinor cannot be an agent."

"Why? Because you made up that mission in order to seduce her?"

"But I did not know she was a-an agent. I'm not a spy. I've never been a spy."

"Of course not," Winn said sarcastically. "We don't expect you to admit your involvement in Bonaparte's escape scheme so easily."

Trollope waved his hands frantically. Behind him, Smythe was having a difficult time not laughing.

"But I don't know anything about an escape scheme. I don't know Bonaparte. I'm not a spy."

"And I'm certain the phrase *oranges and lemons, say the bells at St. Clement's* means nothing to you as well."

"It's a song, a children's rhyme. Nothing more." He was all but screeching with fear now.

"It's the password for the spies involved in Bonaparte's escape plan," Winn told him. "And do you know what it means that you have given it?"

Trollope shook his head. He looked perilously close to tears. Winn's enthusiasm for beating him bloody was waning.

"It means we have to kill you." Winn pulled out his pistol.

"No!" Trollope screamed.

"A pistol ball to the brain is a quick, painless death."

Smythe cleared his throat. "But perhaps you'd rather die by having your throat slit?" Smythe tapped Trollope on the shoulder with the blade of a long knife he produced from his pocket. Winn had no idea where it had come from, but he had to give Wolf credit.

"No, please!" Trollope was all but crying now. "Don't kill me."

"It's too late for that," Winn said. "You know too much."

"I know nothing! Nothing!"

Winn cocked the hammer of the pistol. He hadn't even primed it with gunpowder. Trollope screamed, and then he looked down. Winn's gaze followed. Liquid dripped onto the brown and yellow leaves under Trollope's feet, and a wet spot grew and grew in the crotch of his breeches.

Winn shook his head, and Smythe was laughing out loud now.

"Please." Trollope fell to his knees. "Do not kill me." He clasped his hands, begging.

Smythe shook his head, raised his hat, and mouthed, *let him go*.

"I will allow you to go under one condition," Winn said.

"Anything!"

"You must admit to the entirety of the *ton* that you are a fraud and a womanizer."

"I'll do it."

"And you must never speak to Lady Keating again. If you do, she has orders to terminate you immediately."

"I shall not even acknowledge her."

"Good," Winn said.

"Let's go." Smythe gestured to Winn.

"One last thing." Winn drew his fist back and slammed it into Rafe Trollope's pretty face. Trollope fell backward and uttered a sob. Winn left him lying among the wet leaves and walked out of the copse with Smythe.

"Feel better?" Wolf asked.

"Marginally."

"Good. Might we begin work on the Maîtriser case then?"

"Tonight," Winn said. "This afternoon we have a garden party to attend."

Seven

SOPHIA, LADY SMYTHE, WAS TIRED OF LYING ABOUT IN bed. It was true Adrian had forbidden her so much as to sit up. It was true the doctor had cautioned her that rest was necessary. It was true that she had fainted.

Mortifying, that. She had never fainted before in her life. When she had come to and Adrian had told her what had happened, she had almost punched him for lying. But then she'd become light-headed again and had to settle for a potent scowl.

But she felt much better now. Cook had fed her hearty broths and warm, buttered bread. She'd had her fill of tea and cakes. Wallace, her butler, had made certain the household was quiet and she had no visitors. And now she was in want of diversion.

She wanted to do something useful, especially as she knew Adrian was out doing something entertaining. He had not told her his plans, but he was not at home, and she was willing to bet he was involved in some dangerous plot or another, getting himself chased or shot at, and she was missing all of the fun.

And so when he entered their room at half-past

nine in the morning, creeping quietly so as not to wake her, she gave him an annoyed look.

He gave it right back to her. "Why are you out of bed?" he asked, going to her directly. She was standing at the window, looking down at the street.

"I'm not tired," she said. "It's morning."

"The doctor said you should rest," he pointed out.

She glared at him, challenging him just to try and order her back to bed. "Yes, but I think we both know it won't make any difference. If I'm going to lose the baby, I'll lose the baby whether I rest or not."

"You are not going to lose this baby."

She began to pace, and she saw him flex his fingers. He would have liked nothing more than forcibly putting her back to bed. "I'm not going to lie in bed and fret for the next several weeks. Not only will it drive me mad, it won't do any good. I told you before, if I am with child, I'm going to approach the pregnancy without fear. What happens will happen. I cannot sit about idly imagining the worst."

"Sophia." He stepped in front of her and enfolded her in his embrace. The feel of his warm, strong arms around her made something in her soften, and then she surprised herself by falling against his chest and burying her head in his shoulder. She needed his strength now, more than ever.

"I want what you want," he whispered into her hair. "And perhaps I have an idea that will satisfy both of us and the doctor."

She leaned back and raised her brow. "Oh, really? Is this some sort of plan?"

"No, merely a suggestion." And he told her about his meeting with Baron in Hyde Park.

At the end of his summary, she shook her head. "So you spent the morning skulking about the park, listening to this lovers' tryst? And I thought you were off having an adventure."

"I don't skulk."

"My mistake. I don't understand why Keating didn't simply confront his wife or the two of them together."

Adrian sighed. "Because we needed to determine whom we were dealing with. This Rafe Trollope might have been one of ours or a rival spy."

"And now that he's dealt with, you and Baron will find Foncé and the Maîtriser group?"

"We will formulate a plan."

She refrained from rolling her eyes. Adrian and his plans. "Of course. And in the meantime," she said, moving away from him and leaning over to straighten the brush and comb on her dressing table, "you want me to stay home and thumb through piles of dull documents on the Maîtriser group while you have all the excitement."

"No."

"No?" She looked up, holding a silver brush in one hand.

"Keating and I will discuss Foncé this evening. Afterward, I thought I might assist you with research."

She smiled. "It could be quite the romantic evening."

He pulled her back into his arms and kissed her lightly. "A stack of files, a glass of wine, a brace of candles, and the two of us filling pages of parchment with notes on strategy. I think it will be our most romantic evening yet."

❧

When Elinor returned from Hyde Park, the first sound she heard when she stepped into the vestibule was laughter and music. The girls were laughing, which was a surprise, as she expected them to be deep into their studies by this hour.

She gave Bramson a bewildered look, and he shook his head and sighed. "Lord Keating, Miss Keating, and Miss Caroline are in the music room, my lady."

"And where is Miss Pilar?"

"I believe Lord Keating dismissed the governess for the morning."

Elinor raised her brows. The household and the girls' education were hers to oversee. How dare Winn interfere? She did not interfere in his sphere. "Thank you, Bramson."

He bowed, and Elinor marched into the music room, a sharp retort on her tongue. But when she opened the door, the words died. Winn was seated at the pianoforte, his back to her and the girls flanking the stool where he sat. He was playing Haydn's "Un cor si tenero," and the girls were calling out the names of arias. "Is it 'Prüfung des Küssens'?" Caro asked.

"No. Try again."

"I know!" Georgiana said. "It's 'Mentre ti lascio, o figlia.'"

Elinor was impressed. Georgiana's music teacher had been earning his salary. "No. Try again," Winn said.

Elinor stared at him. She had forgotten he could play the pianoforte. Not only that, she had forgotten how utterly charming he could be. It seemed today was her day to be reminded. She might have slipped silently into the room and observed longer, but she did not want to be reminded of Winn's charms. She had all but put Winn and his charms behind her and embraced a new romance with Mr. Trollope. And now, on the day she was to start her new adventure, Winn had the audacity to remind her why she'd fallen in love with him in the first place.

"It's 'Un cor si tenero,'" she said.

Three heads turned toward her, and she smiled. "I would have thought you'd recognize it, Georgiana."

"I do, Mama. Now that you name it."

"Have you returned from your shopping so soon?" Winn asked. Elinor could have sworn there was a mocking tone in his voice, as though he knew she had not really been shopping.

"Yes. I need to prepare for the Hollingshead garden party."

"Very good. I am looking forward to it." Winn returned his attention to the piano and began playing another aria.

"Are you planning to attend?" she asked. The last thing she needed was Winn making it difficult for her to deliver Trollope's message to the secret agent.

"I am invited, I assume."

"I know!" Caro interjected. "It's 'Heil und Segen'!"

"No." Winn shook his head. "But you are close. It's Bach."

"Why should you wish to attend the garden party?" Elinor asked, coming around the instrument so she could see everyone's faces. "I did not think you cared for such amusements, and you made an appearance at the Ramsgates' ball so recently."

"Is it 'Was die Welt'?" Georgiana asked.

"No," Winn said.

"'Wer Gott bekennt'?" Caro asked.

"It's 'Domine Deus, Rex coelestis,'" Elinor said, frustrated with the slow progress of their conversation.

"Mama!" Georgiana whined. "This is our game!"

"I'm sorry, but I am trying to speak with your father. And you are supposed to be studying mathematics with Miss Pilar this morning."

Caro groaned. "I detest mathematics."

Winn rose. "Your mother is right. I have distracted you from the Pythagorean theorem for far too long. Run along and find Miss Pilar."

"Oh!" Caro stomped her foot petulantly. "But I don't want to learn about mathematics. I want to stay with you."

Winn leaned over and kissed Caroline on the cheek, surprising the girl and Elinor both. "I am afraid if your mother insists upon attending this garden party, I must dress. I will see both of you later, at which point I should have a surprise."

"Really?" Georgiana clapped her hands together. "I cannot wait." She took Caro's hand. "Come now, or he may change his mind."

Elinor watched the girls scamper away and turned her gaze back to Winn. He sat and smiled, but she was not charmed. Well, not much. And she was especially not charmed when he began to play the pianoforte again.

"I am not insisting you attend the garden party at all," she told him. "You are free to do as you choose."

He nodded and continued playing. "That goes

without saying. I choose to attend the garden party with you. Someone must stand at your side and fend off your suitors."

She blinked at him, uncertain how she should respond. She'd never had any suitors, save him.

"Do you not need to dress for the afternoon's entertainment?" he asked, his fingers racing over the keys. She had difficulty looking away from those fingers. They were thin and long and elegant, and she could imagine them touching every inch of her naked body. She blinked and tried to focus on his face. But that was no good either. She could not seem to stop staring at his mouth, and his mouth conjured even more sinful thoughts than his fingers. It was the music. That had to be how he was bewitching her.

"Do stop playing!" she ordered.

He raised a brow and lifted his hands from the keys. "Certainly, madam."

"You have some surprise for the girls? I thought we agreed that all such *surprises*—ponies and such—should be approved by me."

He rose and took a step around the pianoforte so he was within arm's reach. Elinor stepped back. She had felt far more authoritative when he was seated and she standing. Now she was reminded how tall he was, and how easily he could wrap her in his arms.

"I am not one of your children, Ellie," he said. "I don't obey your orders." He stepped closer, and she stepped back.

"Don't call me that."

"Call you what?" He moved closer.

"Ellie. It is not my name." Her back bumped the

pianoforte, and she tried to scoot around the edge, but he pinned her with his body and planted his hands on either side of her waist.

"It is my name for you."

"I would appreciate it if you would call me by my given name."

"I don't give a bloody farthing what you would or would not appreciate."

Her eyes widened. Where had her aloof husband gone? This man's eyes were burning with intensity and… was that desire? She dared not hope, not only because she did not relish having those hopes dashed yet again, but because what she saw in his eyes made her nervous.

"I will go to Tatt's tomorrow to choose a pony for Georgiana."

Elinor put her foot down, literally. "No. She has had little to no experience riding, and—"

"I thought of that."

"—she is too… you thought of that?"

"Yes. She has not spent much time outside Town."

Elinor bit her lip. It was the only way she could avoid saying: *And whose fault is that?* She could not count the number of times Winn had promised to take them on a tour of the Lake District or to sample the waters at Bath and then later reneged. Biting her lip had the added bonus of slowing her breathing. This made it more difficult to breathe in Winn's scent, something she had always thought dark and tantalizing. She had not been this close to him this often for months, and her defenses against him were considerably weaker than she had anticipated.

"I thought both of the girls might benefit from some time with my mother."

Elinor gaped at him. She shook her head. Now she knew this was not the man she had married. That man was not on speaking terms with his mother. She'd had to beg him to invite the woman to their wedding.

To be fair, it was not actually the dowager baroness he objected to, but her much younger husband—one of her former grooms. The union had been something of a scandal, but no doubt the woman felt she had done her duty by the deceased viscount and was entitled to enjoy her remaining years however she saw fit. At least that was Elinor's view—not that she expressed it. By all accounts, the late Baron Keating had been rather a bore—much like Winn. Rather, much like the Winn Elinor was used to. She did not know this new Winn at all.

Elinor had very rarely visited Keating's country home, but she did know of its renown for breeding and raising horses. Winn had grown up around thoroughbreds, but he'd never shared the family passion for breeding. Still, she was certain were he to evaluate the horseflesh at Tattersall's, he would choose the perfect horse for Georgiana.

"Georgiana and Caroline could benefit from riding lessons. Where better for the girls to learn than Montworth House?"

"I don't understand." Elinor's head was spinning. "You are suggesting we go on holiday to visit your mother?"

"No. I am suggesting we send the girls. You and I will stay here. Alone."

Elinor was not at all certain she wanted to stay alone with Winn. Her nervousness was increasing. She had not felt like this around him since he had courted her—if it could have been termed courting. "Do not be ridiculous. I shall accompany the girls to your mother's. After all, I haven't seen the dowager in years."

"No, you won't." Winn shook his head. "We have a garden party to attend, and I intend to send the girls this afternoon."

"But they haven't packed!" Panic seized Elinor, and not because she worried Caro and Georgiana would not have the right gowns. She had never been away from her daughters for more than a night. Now Winn was sending them away for an indeterminate amount of time.

Winn gave her a look as though he knew exactly what she was thinking. "The nanny—what's her name?—will assist them," he said calmly.

"But I haven't spoken with them about how to behave."

Winn raised a brow. "They are twelve and nigh fourteen. If they do not know how to comport themselves by now, they never will. In any case, my mother is perfectly capable of dealing with any sort of recalcitrance Georgiana or Caroline exhibit. I assure you, my brothers and I were far more difficult to manage."

Elinor blinked. Winn had been difficult to manage as a child? She had never heard him say so before. She had always thought he had been birthed perfect. "But…" She struggled to think of another excuse. He'd said he sent a note to his mother, and she'd been asking for years to see the girls, so there was no objection there. The dowager lived in Richmond, which was a short distance from London and ensured the girls would not be traveling after dark.

"But?" Winn asked, with that annoying eyebrow still cocked.

"I suppose I have no further objections." None that she would voice, at any rate.

"Good." He did not move away so she could pass. Instead, he remained rooted in place, locking her behind the pianoforte. She was not used to this behavior. Why did he all of a sudden seek her company? What did he want from her? Was it merely to torture her? She'd spent so many hours, days, weeks, wishing he would notice her, and she had finally managed to tamp her longings for him down to a manageable level. She did not think she could stand it if he made her love him again. She could not bear the loneliness and longing she'd feel when he inevitably forgot her.

"I must dress for the party and tell the girls the good news."

"Of course," Winn agreed. But he did not move. He was looking at her, his clear green eyes focused wholly on her. Elinor felt her heart begin to pound. Was there something wrong with her appearance? Did she have leaves in her hair? Dirt on her face?

"You shall have to move aside, if I am to go, my lord." She could hear her voice shaking.

"I find myself quite content right here, my lady."

Elinor swallowed. "I don't understand."

"Don't you?" He notched her chin up so she was forced to look at him. The desire she saw in his face caused heat to slash through her. What game was he playing? She shook her head.

"No," she whispered. "Do not do this."

He frowned. "Do not do what? Kiss you? You are my wife. I have the right to kiss you." He leaned down, and she put a hand between them.

"Winn, please do not do this to me. You know—" Her voice broke, and she swallowed and attempted to steady it. "You know how I have always felt about you. I know your feelings are not the same, and I have come to terms with that." She stared down at the green piping on the spencer she'd worn to meet Trollope at Hyde Park. She did not want to look in Winn's eyes at the moment. It was humiliating that she should have to mention this again, but she did not know what else to do. She would no longer allow him to manipulate her affections to suit his purposes.

"You have come to terms?" he asked. "What does that mean?"

How was she to answer that question? By saying she no longer cried herself to sleep every night? No, she still had some pride. "It means I have learned to be content without you. I do not want you imposing yourself on my life again.

"Now"—she pushed past him. Rather, he allowed her to push him aside—"if you will excuse me, I wish to say good-bye to my daughters and ready myself for my friend's party." And she walked out of the music room without turning back. She finally breathed when she reached the nursery. Elinor stood on the other side of her daughters' door and listened to their giggles and innocent chatter. Her back burned from what she imagined had been the intensity of Winn's stare. She'd walked away from him, though. She'd done it. She had never thought she would be strong enough to walk away from him, much less push past him. But she had done it, which meant she could do it again.

She closed her eyes and remembered the first time she had seen him. He'd been so handsome, so cocky, so obviously bored with Society. After two Seasons, Society was her life. The balls, like the one where she'd first seen Winn, the on-dits, the rides in Hyde Park. Her mother and father had been minor gentry, and she knew it strained their finances to give her even one Season, much less three. That had been her last chance to snag a husband.

She hadn't been staring at Baron Winslow Keating with any hope he'd ask her to dance. She wasn't beautiful or engaging, rich or titled. A man like Winn would have no cause to notice her.

But he had.

He'd caught her staring, flashed a smile, and started across the ballroom.

The girls giggled again, and Elinor pressed a hand to her heart. It pounded as it had the night she met Winn. There were many times she wanted to regret her marriage, but how could she when it had produced her life? For Georgiana and Caro *were* her life. But perhaps a week or so away might be good for her as well as for them. They would be safe and well cared for. And she had a mission for the Babylon group. She did not want to involve her family in that business.

Elinor took a deep breath and opened the nursery door.

Eight

WINN STOOD BESIDE THE PIANOFORTE FOR SEVERAL long moments. He was speechless. Truly speechless. He did not think he would ever be able to remove the echo of Ellie's words from his mind.

I have learned to be content without you.

Winn supposed he deserved that one. He had not been around much, and what exactly had he expected Elinor to do in his absence? Pine? He had not pined for her. A small voice inside him piped up with the suggestion that perhaps that had been because he'd always known how much she loved him and had known she was home pining for him. He'd felt certain of it. But somehow, somewhere, she'd learned to be content without him. She didn't want him anymore. She didn't love him anymore.

And he deserved that as well. He'd never been in love with her, and he'd never lied to her and pretended he was. If she wanted to hold on to false hope, that was her affair. Except she was no longer holding on to false hope. And he was no longer *not* in love with her. He wasn't exactly in love with her either, but his feelings were not what they had been. Something about her had changed. Something had forced him to see her differently.

All of which meant absolutely nothing, because she'd told him, *I do not want you imposing yourself on my life again.*

Who the hell says something like that to another person? He'd never imposed himself on her life. Had he? Well, he had this morning, but what the hell was he supposed to do? Allow her to run off and meet another man? If that was what she wanted, she was going to have to learn to accept a lot more than him imposing himself on her.

The truth was he had missed her—or at least the idea of her. He missed his daughters. He wanted his wife and his family. Yes, he was late to this realization, but he'd had the realization all the same. He was weary of the Barbican group, tired of being an operative.

Unfortunately, his wife had tired of waiting for him, and his girls had grown up while he'd been away. Now he would have to win Elinor back—a feat he was certain he could accomplish. She had been easy to win initially. All he'd had to do was to smile and ask her to dance, and she was his. He could charm her again.

Except he also had to find the head of the Maîtriser group, which was the most dangerous group the Barbican had ever encountered. Foncé had killed half a dozen elite, all-but-indestructible Barbican agents, and the sadistic madman had left his mark, carving the letter *M* into their bodies. This was not an assignment Winn could afford to take lightly.

But if he didn't win Elinor back now, he might

lose her. Perhaps he should have sent her away with Caroline and Georgiana. He didn't care about their riding skills. He wanted the girls out of harm's way. It was his own selfishness that kept Elinor near him. He feared if he sent her away now, she might never return.

And after this morning, he was curious as to how her "mission" would go. Smythe had promised to take care of it, but what did that mean exactly? Winn started for the stairs. There was only one way to find out, and that meant attending the garden party.

Winn had never liked Lady Hollingshead. He had no particular fondness for any of his wife's friends, though after hearing Lady Ramsgate's injunctions against marital infidelity, he felt more warmly toward her. He supposed he could not fault Elinor if her friends were empty-headed gossips. Almost every woman in the *ton* fit that description. It was not as though Elinor had many choices. And still, if he'd had his druthers, he'd have rather endured the torture of having his toenail pulled out—again—than suffer a garden party.

Several hours later, after a silent drive, they arrived at the garden party. Lady Hollingshead greeted them with her usual effusion, then flitted off to take care of some crisis or other, dragging Elinor with her. Winn watched his wife calmly take control of the situation, and marveled that he had managed to choose his mate so well.

She had not been one of the beauties that Season his father had died. The late baron had been thrown from a horse—a Thoroughbred with too much bottom—and died instantly from a broken neck. Winn had mourned his father, though he'd barely known the man. He could recall only about half a dozen brief conversations with his father in all his twenty-something years. He'd sworn he would do everything in his power not to emulate the man. And, of course, he'd turned out exactly like him.

From the start, Winn's focus had never been on family. When he met Elinor, he'd scarcely paid her any attention. He had every excuse for his behavior. He'd been shocked by his father's sudden death, his mother's involvement with her former groom shortly thereafter, and the imperative from his family that he marry and produce an heir posthaste. But the truth was Winn had just embarked upon his career with the Secret Service and had begun to feel he might have a future in serving his country thusly. He'd been enjoying the work and feeling, for once in his life, as though he was making some sort of contribution, and then his world had come crashing down.

He'd chosen a wife because he'd been told to. He hadn't been looking for beauty. He'd been looking for a woman who would not refuse him; who was not so silly he could not stand to be in her presence, thereby making the task more difficult; and who had a family with decent connections.

Elinor had been the perfect choice. He'd married her, consummated the union, and gone on with his career in espionage. He did not see why the fact that he was Baron Keating should curtail his involvement with the Foreign Office. It was true his family had been disappointed he had not produced an heir, but several of his brothers had male offspring, and Winn had no qualms about leaving the title to one of their progeny. Having grown up surrounded by brothers, Winn found he liked his daughters. He liked the sweetness of little girls, the way they held each other's hands, the way their hair curled beside their rosy cheeks, the way they skipped and sang just because. Oh, there were the typical female dramatics, as well, but that was why libraries had been invented, was it not? He could go inside, close the door, and shut out the crying jags.

But something had happened since he'd returned from his recent business on the Continent, and he was at a loss as to how he might explain it. His perfectly forgettable wife had become... unforgettable. It was not only that she managed his household seamlessly. God knew how. She could not predict whether he'd be home or away, but if he did appear, his place at the table was always set, and his valet was always on duty. The larders were stocked, the servants paid, the children educated, and the family status maintained.

That in itself would not have impressed Winn as a younger man, but with age and experience came a new realization that not every household was managed so well. And when he began to look at his wife with new respect, he noted something else. At some point in their marriage, she'd grown beautiful. The unremarkable girl of twenty-one whom he'd married had become a ravishing woman in her thirties. Winn did not think women were supposed to do such things. He especially did not believe mothers of two children were supposed to grow in attractiveness. Shouldn't she look haggard and worn? Why was her hair so glossy, her skin creamy, and her figure full and sensuous? When he'd been away from her shortly after their marriage, he'd rarely thought of her. But in the last few days, he could not seem *not* to think of her.

"If you could stop staring at your wife for a moment, you might see me attempting to garner your attention."

Winn turned around at the familiar voice and blinked at Blue. At least he thought it was Blue. Blue always managed to blend in with his surroundings, to appear completely unmemorable. But this man with Blue's signature bright blue eyes looked as though he wanted every eye in the room on him. He was what Lady Hollingshead would call *dashing*.

"What are you wearing?" Winn gestured to Blue's caped greatcoat, which he had not removed; his Hessian boots, shined to reflect like a mirror; and the fussy cravat and high stock at his neck. Blue's hair was a dark brown and waved luxuriously down to his shoulders. He looked like some sort of Italian lothario.

Blue gestured toward a corner near a set of bushes, and Winn followed him. The spot was secluded and afforded the men a view of the party but sheltered them from sight. "Wolf said you needed a secret agent."

Winn frowned. "Not an actual agent."

Blue looked at Winn as though he were an idiot. "Precisely. I am in character. That much should be obvious."

Winn narrowed his eyes, trying to see Blue how others might. "I suppose if I were looking for the caricature of a secret agent, I would look at you."

Blue bowed with a flourish. "Am I correct in assuming the woman you were ogling is your wife, the one with the coded message to give me?"

"I was not ogling her."

Blue said nothing.

Winn shifted. "I was thinking, and my gaze traveled all about the crowd."

"She's an attractive woman, Baron. You do not need to justify yourself to me."

And yet Winn could not help but wonder how much Blue knew. Had Smythe told him Elinor was involved with another man? He felt suddenly inadequate, and the feeling was entirely new to him.

"If you will excuse me," Blue said, tossing his cape over his shoulder, "I must look secretive and mysterious."

"You win all the good assignments," Winn muttered.

Blue smiled. "I do, don't I?"

And with a dramatic glance over his shoulder, he walked off, only to slip, completely unsurreptitiously, behind a column. Winn watched the ladies watch Blue and wondered, fleetingly, if Blue was married. What kind of woman would Blue choose? The agent looked out from behind the column, then ducked back behind it. More importantly, what woman would have Blue?

And then he had his answer, because Elinor had obviously spotted the decoy and was making her way toward him. She, however, was actually doing so quite unobtrusively. If Winn had not known her intention, he would not have guessed her destination.

The woman had hidden talents.

And he would be damned if any other man was going to catch a glimpse of them.

≈

That was him! Elinor sucked in a breath, then let it out slowly. She excused herself from Lady Hollingshead's side with some paltry excuse and made her way to the refreshment table. She could see him better from that vantage point.

Yes, that must be him. Mr. Trollope had said she would be able to spot the contact, and if that man wasn't a spy, then she didn't know what one was. He looked exactly as she imagined a spy would look.

Oh, but he was handsome, even more handsome than Rafe Trollope! She could all but imagine him listening to her message, then sweeping her into his arms and kissing her senseless.

Not that she would allow such behavior, of course. Winn would certainly object. She looked about but did not spot her husband. If he had bothered even to remain in attendance, that was. He'd probably slipped away to take a nap or play at cards with some of the other dull gentlemen. The thought actually reassured her. Perhaps he had not changed as much as she feared. Perhaps her heart was not really in jeopardy, and she had nothing to fear from that quarter.

She stopped to chat with several ladies of her acquaintance as she made her way toward the column where the spy had hidden himself. Had he spotted her? Was he waiting impatiently for her message so he could dash to the rescue of King George or Queen Charlotte? Elinor moved with a bit more haste until she was finally standing in front of the column. She cleared her throat, hoping that would catch his attention. "Sir, are you perhaps waiting for a message?" She did not dare look at him.

He answered without revealing himself. "I am. And I find myself in some haste. Life or death, you understand?"

"Yes." She turned to look at him, but he put a hand on her shoulder. "It is better if you do not see me clearly."

His hand was warm and strong on her shoulder, and

she took a shaky breath. "I understand. The message is *oranges and lemons, say the bells at St. Clement's.*"

The man was silent, and then he squeezed her shoulder. "Thank you. I cannot tell you the service you have done for your country."

"No, she hasn't," a familiar voice said. "All she's done is recite a children's song."

Elinor gasped and turned to see Winn glaring at her.

"Take your hand off my wife, Blue."

The secret agent lifted his hand from her shoulder. "My lord," Elinor began tersely, "this matter does not involve you."

"Perhaps I might…" the secret agent began.

"Oh, I think it does," Winn said, narrowing his eyes at her. "Any time you deliver messages for your lover, it involves me."

Elinor's heart lurched into her throat. So she'd been right! He *had* known. That explained everything. But Mr. Trollope was never going to trust her with a mission again. She had to find some way to salvage this. "Winn, I promise I will speak to you about the matter momentarily. It's not what you think."

"No, it's not what *you* think," Winn said. "Your Rafe Trollope is not a spy. He lied to you."

She blinked at him. "But how do you know Mr. Trollope is a spy?"

"He's not a spy."

She folded her arms across her chest. "And you know this because?"

"Because I am."

She stared at him, uncomprehending. Was Winn so jealous he would fabricate lies?

"And with that revelation," the secret agent standing between them said, "I will take my leave." He bowed and took her gloved hand, brushing his lips across her knuckles. "It was a pleasure to meet you, my lady." He glanced at Winn. "Baron, working with you is never dull." And the man sauntered through the crowds mingling in the garden and disappeared into the house.

"Do you know that man?" She clenched her fists as a new idea occurred to her. "Did you ask him to pretend to be a spy in order to fool me?"

"No."

She raised a brow.

"Not exactly."

"Explain, please."

"I think it would be better if we discussed this at home." He gestured at the guests milling about, several of whom were watching them curiously.

"Oh, why is that, Lord Spy? Do you need to protect your secret identity?"

He put his arm around her waist and pulled her close. "Would you lower your voice?" he said through a forced smile. Elinor doubted this display of false affection was fooling anyone. "I'll explain everything in the carriage."

"I am not going to leave. Lady Hollingshead needs me here. Not to mention, I haven't seen Lady Ramsgate yet." Her argument was ridiculous, but she didn't care. Winn had obviously spied on her and manipulated her so she would look the fool. The last thing she wanted was to return home with him.

"Elinor, you are either going to come with me willingly or—" He broke off abruptly, his attention riveted on the Hollingsheads' party. She followed his gaze and saw the so-called secret agent was back and walking quickly toward them.

"What's this?" she asked. "Did you forget to pay him?"

"No." He took her arm, his grip firm and almost painful. "Listen to me, Ellie, I don't know what this is, but whatever happens, I need you to do as I say."

"Am I supposed to believe this is all real?"

"Elinor, I don't care what you believe. Just do as I say, understand?" Something in his tone made her look at him more closely. He was deadly serious. She had never before seen such an intense, serious expression on his face.

"What is going on?" She tried to back away, but he hauled her beside him just as the man she'd met earlier stepped before them.

"I need to speak with you, Baron." The man's blue eyes flicked to her. "In private."

"I'm not leaving her alone until I know what this is about."

"Very well. On my way out, I spotted an agent from the Maîtriser group coming in."

Elinor frowned. The message meant nothing to her, but Winn's hand on her tensed. "Are you certain?" Winn asked the man he'd called Blue.

Blue gave him a look.

"Did he spot you?"

Blue sighed. "Are there any other inane questions you wish to ask, or do you wish me to take the lead on this?"

Winn's gaze shifted to her, and Elinor gave him a shaky smile. She could tell he was thinking of the best way to make her leave but she was not going anywhere. She was beginning to believe this Blue might really be a secret agent. Either that, or this was all an impossibly elaborate ruse designed to trick her. But why would Winn want to trick her? And why would Winn be involved with a secret agent? She did not believe for a moment his story that he was a spy. Winn? Winn liked to go on and on about ledgers and balances and crops. He was not a spy.

"Let me take her to safety and then—"

"There's no time for that," Blue hissed. "There he is."

Elinor whipped her head to look, but Winn grabbed her chin and held it in place. "Not so obvious," he said through clenched teeth. "We don't want him to know we're talking about him."

"Why?"

"Because then he might decide to kill us."

In the middle of the Hollingsheads' garden party? She did not think so.

Winn took her arm and linked it with his. "Now, we three are going to go for a leisurely stroll to look at the daffodils." He pointed to some bushes on the outskirts of the garden.

"Those are roses," she pointed out.

"I don't care. Just walk."

She did not see how she had much choice. After all, Winn was pulling her along on one side, and the man he called Blue was prodding her on the other. Twilight was settling in, and once they reached the roses, Winn said, "Sorry." He pushed her through them, and she belatedly raised her hands to protect her face from thorns. She was unable to protect her dress, however, and she heard the material rip when her skirts caught.

"Are you mad?" she yelled before he clamped a hand

over her mouth and pulled her into the shadows. The roses grew along a wall marking the perimeter of the Hollingsheads' gardens, and she could feel the cool stone against her back. A moment later, Blue was beside her.

"There weren't any brambles available? I don't think my coat is completely shredded," the spy quipped.

"I'm sure your tailor will appreciate the business." Winn was still holding one hand over her mouth, and with the other he was parting the bushes and peering through the roses. Elinor yanked his hand down. He gave her a sharp look. "Not a word, or I'll gag you."

Her jaw dropped in outrage, but she didn't dare voice her thoughts. He was looking at her fiercely, and she did not want to test whether he would actually follow through on the threat.

"Now, here's what we're going to do," he said to Blue, his voice low and filled with authority. God help her, but he really did sound like a spy.

"Too late," Blue, who was also peering through the roses, remarked. "He's heading this way, and he's bringing a friend."

Both men were silent for a long moment, during which Elinor had the urge to look through those rose bushes herself. What, exactly, did they see?

"I don't think he saw us," Blue said.

"No." Winn shook his head. "No, but I can scarce believe our good fortune."

"Why is that?"

"Because we are not all as lucky as you, Blue."

Elinor heard the low rumble of men's voices approaching and guessed that the man they'd been watching was coming their way. Winn's arm slid

around her waist, and she felt his warm breath tickle
her ear. "Not a word, do you hear me? Not a sound,
or we are all dead."

She swallowed, fear rippling through her. What was
going on? She had thought she wanted excitement and
adventure, but she had not bargained on the danger.
She had not considered she might be risking her life,
that she might never see her daughters again.

She covered her mouth. Was this why Winn had
sent the girls away? To keep them safe from whom-
ever was on the other side of those roses?

"You're fine," Winn whispered, his voice oddly
reassuring, considering he'd just told her she could die
at any moment. "I'm right here." Winn stiffened, and
Elinor heard one of the men on the other side of the
roses speaking.

"What time is he due to arrive?"

"Any moment. He's capricious at best."

"If he does not make an appearance, my employer
will not be pleased." There was more than a hint of a
threat in the man's voice. Elinor crouched back in the
shadows, and Winn squeezed her hand. She had not
even realized he was holding it.

"I never promised to serve him on a platter. I said
you would gain access. You are here."

"And he is not."

"Give him time. He likes to make a grand appearance. And when he does, he'll demand all the attention. You won't be able to squeeze near him."

The other man chuckled long and low. "Leave that
to me."

Elinor's nostrils burned with the smell of cheroot

smoke that lingered and then faded away. A moment later, Winn spoke, his voice low. "The prince?"

"Who better fits that description?" Blue answered.

"Before we jump to conclusions, I'd like to see whether Prinny even received an invitation."

"He did," Elinor said. Both men turned to look at her. She shrugged. "Lady Hollingshead is my friend, and she was very excited about the prince attending. It was all she could speak of the last time I saw her. But you don't mean to say—"

"I'll go directly," Blue interrupted her. Elinor watched in amazement as he scaled the wall and disappeared from sight.

"Where is he going?" she asked.

"To stop the prince from attending."

She blinked. "He knows Prinny?"

Winn considered. "I think it's more of a case of the prince knows him."

"Oh." She brushed a rose petal from her cheek. "Lady Hollingshead will be so disappointed."

"She'll feel worse if the prince regent is assassinated in her garden."

"And just how can you be certain that's what those men were discussing? And what is this Maîtriser group?"

"I can't answer that."

"Because you are a spy."

He inclined his head.

"Bastard." Before she could even think what she was doing, she'd slapped him hard across the face. With her arms in front of her face, she tore her way through the roses, past the guests, past Lady Ramsgate, who called after her, and out into the night.

Nine

WINN STOOD IN THE SHADOWS OF THE ROSES AND FELT the full sting of the slap. It had not hurt him, not literally, but it had hurt his pride. He'd lied to her. She was entitled to her anger and outrage. But he'd always thought if she ever realized his secret, she'd be proud and pleased. She'd understand the reason for the deception.

Clearly, he'd been deceiving himself.

He would have liked to have gone after her, but it was futile. He couldn't offer explanations—none that would satisfy her, at any rate. Why even try? And so he followed Blue over the stone wall, grunting with effort. How the hell did Blue make these feats appear so easy? A few moments later, Winn flagged a hackney and headed for the offices of the Barbican group.

His town house was dark and quiet when he arrived home several hours later. It was early for Elinor to have retired, but he remembered the girls were at his mother's house. Without their company, she had probably taken dinner in her room and stayed there. No doubt she wanted to avoid him. He was not going to allow that.

He went to his room, dismissed his valet, and knocked perfunctorily on the door adjoining their rooms. He did not wait for an answer, merely opened the door and entered. The room was dark, but he could smell the smoke from her recently extinguished candle and see the tension in the outline of her form on the bed. "I know you're not asleep," he said.

"Did you deduce that with your powerful spying skills, or did you ask the servants?" she retorted.

Sarcasm. He had not anticipated that. He approached the bed, and because he did not want to stand over her, sat down beside her. "We should discuss this."

Her back was to him, and she angled her shoulder away. "I do not want to hear anything you have to say. You've lied to me for years. Why should I believe anything you have to say now?"

Why should she? And why should he even make any effort? They could go on as before. In fact, it would be easier for both of them. He would no longer have to lie.

But that wasn't what he wanted. He wanted her, and he'd been married long enough to know he'd have to make amends. "I don't want to lie to you anymore."

She laughed, a short bitter laugh. "Why not?"

Because he desired her now—not just her body, but all that she symbolized—family, home, love, and—very well, he wanted her body too. "I'm trying to make this right," he said finally.

She rolled onto her back, and in the light from the hearth, he could see her dark eyes watching him. Her hair, gloriously long and thick now that it was uncoiled, tumbled like a silk skein over her pillow.

"Are you? And what if I do not want your amends? What if I plan to run away with Mr. Trollope?"

Winn glared at her. "That nincompoop? He's not even a real spy."

She shot up. "I didn't want to marry a spy! I wanted to marry a husband, and it seems I married a man who pretended he would be a husband when he was really a spy. So maybe this time I shall try a man who pretends to be a spy, and he will end up being a husband." She moved to climb out of the bed, but he grabbed her wrist and hauled her back down.

"*I* am your husband. Do not forget that."

"Why not? You forget whenever it suits you."

"I've never forgotten. Not for a moment. I've always been faithful to you." Her hair brushed against his arm, making his skin come alive.

"Am I supposed to believe that? You've never wanted me."

He heard the pain. She had hidden it well, but he knew he'd hurt her. No more. "I want you now." He yanked her against him. "Desperately." And he closed his mouth over hers and took possession. How dare she speak of leaving him? Did she think he would allow her to go? She was his wife, the mother of his children. Yes, he would be the first to admit he'd made mistakes, but he was ready to rectify them. Anger surged in him, but he knew that beneath the anger, the emotion he did not want to admit was fear. He feared he was too late. He was losing her.

But not without a fight. And since she was a woman and his wife, he couldn't fight her with fists or knives. He would have to fight her with passion. Winn pulled her close, pressing her body against his. She burned his skin, even through the fabric of their clothing. She was so unbelievably warm. He remembered that about her. On the few occasions he'd slept in her bed, she'd kept him as warm as any fire.

Holding her close, he could feel the softness of her breasts press against his chest, the silk of her hair dance across his forearm, and he wrapped a hand in the thick ribbon and claimed her. He slanted his mouth over hers, opening her to him. She moaned, and the rigidity in her body melted away. She had never been able to resist him. He'd always loved that about her, the way she always wanted him, the way she responded eagerly to his every touch or caress. He was ashamed to admit he never thought much of her pleasure in the early years of their marriage. Initially, he'd been a young, impatient lover. And then—there was really no excuse. But he was no untried youth now and he knew her body and her needs well enough to anticipate what would please her. He would give her an experience she would not soon forget. He wanted to claim her, brand her as his own.

He stroked her tongue with his own, suckling it, all the while moving his free hand up her back. When he reached the neck of her chemise, he tugged it, loosening the strings so it fell off one shoulder. That shoulder shone pale and round and tempting in the flickering firelight. He dragged his mouth from hers and kissed the smooth skin, trailing his lips to her collarbone, and feeling her shiver at his touch. He pulled her gently down onto the pillow, released her hair, and using his teeth, tugged the bodice of her chemise down, revealing, inch by inch, the fullness of her breasts.

She was half-bared to him now, and he wondered if he'd ever truly looked at her, ever truly appreciated her beauty. Because she *was* beautiful. Her body was round and full, her breasts filling his hands, her nipples hardening against his palms. He touched his mouth to them, surprised by the silky softness. Were all women so soft? It had been years, before his marriage, since he'd been with another woman. He could not even remember. Ellie was all he could think of now. Ellie was all he wanted.

He took one nipple in his mouth, and she moaned loudly. Rolling the hard nub with his tongue, he gently sucked and tugged until she was moving restlessly beneath him. His hands slid down, the urge to feel the heat at her core so strong that though he feared he moved too fast, he could not resist. One hand cupped the curve of her hip, and he felt her hand, which had been clenching his shoulder, glide down to grasp it.

"Stop."

Winn did not think he could have heard her correctly. Surely she did not mean what she said. She was breathing as hard as he, her voice equally hoarse, her skin flushed with arousal. He dragged her chemise up her legs, and she clutched his hand. "No. Stop."

There was no mistaking the order in her voice that time. She meant it. He looked up at her, saw the hardness in her gaze.

"What is it?"

"Do you think this changes anything?" She gestured

to the two of them, their bodies tangled among the rumpled sheets. "Do you think this will make me forgive you for all the lies, all the deceptions?"

He pulled away from her and watched as she yanked her chemise back up to cover her nakedness. "What do you want from me?"

"Nothing. I've asked for nothing. *You* came to *me*."

He stood, raked a hand through his hair. She was telling the truth. She had never asked or demanded anything from him. "Perhaps you should have asked for something."

"And what good would that have done?" She rose, wrapping some sort of shawl lying at the end of her bed around her shoulders. "One thing you never lied about were your feelings. You never said you loved me. You never said you wanted me."

"I want you now." He felt like an idiot saying the words. Why should he have to try and convince her he wanted her? Hadn't he showed her quite clearly a moment before?

"Why? Because you feel threatened by another man?"

"No." But he realized that must be exactly how it appeared to her. He glanced at her face, at her dubious expression. "Listen." He crossed to her, took her shoulders. He looked down at her, having forgotten how much shorter than he she was, how petite and feminine. "I will admit I was not pleased to find out about this Trollope fellow, but I've been thinking about you—about our marriage—for some time."

She folded her arms across her chest. "Go on."

He frowned. What else was he supposed to say? Perhaps if he changed the wording…? "I've wanted you for months," he said.

"So you're in love with me now?"

Winn hesitated. What did marriage have to do with love? No one married for love.

The hesitation cost him. She pulled away from him and shook her head. "Nothing has changed, and this time I will not allow you to come in, sweep me off my feet, and then leave again when the mood suits you."

"I do not leave when struck by a mood. I have orders."

"Ah, yes. Of course. Speaking of which, don't you have a prince to save?"

Winn scowled at her. "I have it under control."

"Oh, good. I suppose it is only me you do not have under control, at the moment."

It was as good an observation as any and irked him. "I do not want to control you."

"Then what *do* you want from me? This?" She gestured to the bed. "Is that what you want?" She dropped her wrap and allowed the chemise to fall off her shoulders. Winn reached forward, catching the material before it could expose her.

"No. Not like that."

"Then what do you want?"

He wasn't certain how to answer. He had not really considered what he wanted. He wanted a wife and a family. But was it the reality he wanted or some fantasy? He looked at Elinor now, struck by the fact that the reality might be more work to obtain than he had considered.

"Since you seem at a loss for words, allow me to assist you," she said. "You said you no longer wanted to lie. Why do we not begin by telling all of our secrets? You know mine. You discovered my flirtation with Mr. Trollope—and ended it quickly enough. Now, it's your turn."

Winn gritted his teeth. This was what men groused about in the hallowed halls of the gentlemen's clubs—White's and Brooks's and their ilk. Women, it seemed, always wanted the impossible. "Elinor…"

She raised her brows. "Yes?"

She was going to make this as difficult as possible, obviously. "I cannot tell you my secrets. My business is highly confidential, and you do not have clearance—"

She shrugged as though this was exactly the answer she expected. "Well, that is that, then." She brushed her hands together as though he were dirt and she were dusting him away.

"What is what?"

"We are at an impasse. You cannot give me what I want, and I cannot give you what you want."

Winn was familiar with impasses. He was a master of dealing with impasses. "I'm certain we can find a way around this. Is there something else I can offer?"

"Besides yourself?" She shook her head. "I do not think so."

Winn drew in a slow breath. Of course she would choose to interpret his statement as though he were keeping himself from her. "It is one aspect of my life I cannot share," he said.

"Oh, I see." She nodded. "Share something else about your life, then."

Winn opened his mouth then snapped it shut again. Bloody hell! How had he fallen into this trap? "I…"

"Go ahead. Share something else."

He sighed. Heavily. He could think of absolutely nothing else to tell her.

"That's what I thought." She crossed to the door adjoining their rooms. "Good night, my lord."

Winn stared at the hazy rectangle of light cast from the lamp in his room. He knew when he was beaten—or, if not beaten, he knew when retreat was the best course of action. Retreat and retrench, Melbourne always said. Winn strode through the door, hearing it shut behind him.

He stared at his large, lonely bed. Retrenchment. Yes, that was what he needed.

❧

Elinor had not slept well. She had not slept at all, truth be told, but why should she bother to tell the truth, even to herself? Winn did not seem to think it necessary. He seemed to think it perfectly acceptable to hide the fact that when he was away from her he had a completely different life. He was a spy, for God's sake. He was protecting the Prince of Wales from assassination plots, and the rest of the country from God knew what else. They'd been married for fourteen years, and she'd never known. She, like a fool, had believed him when he'd said he was going to supervise the Keating estates. But what man spent that much time at his estates? He must have thought her the worst kind of fool. He must have laughed at her gullibility with each new lie he told.

She had known, when she threw down the gauntlet, how he would respond. Of course he could not tell her about his secret life. She knew something of spies from her reading, knew they had such codes of secrecy. But she wanted him to know how it felt to be in an impossible situation. He'd put her in one for years.

When slivers of sunlight peeked through her drawn curtains, she stopped pretending to sleep and rose. A good, hard ride was what she needed. She was not much of a horsewoman, but she enjoyed being outdoors. She would ride in the park nearby and clear her head. And perhaps if she was fortunate, Winn would find somewhere else to glower, and she would not have to see his dour expression at breakfast.

She summoned her maid, dressed, and made her way through the quiet house to the front door, where she waited for the groom Jacob to bring her a mount. Oh how she missed Caroline and Georgiana. She did not realize how often she had used them to assuage her loneliness. She did not realize, until they were away, how often they served as a buffer between Winn and herself. Now she was glad for the freedom to do as she pleased but also uncomfortable that she could not use her daughters to escape Winn.

She was afraid she would have to face him at some point, and knowing Winn—not that she did—that would be sooner rather than later.

Jacob finally appeared, rubbing sleepy eyes and leading a sweet bay mare. Elinor thanked him, but when she refused his offer to accompany her, he stood firm.

"Lord Keating spoke to me personally, my lady. Told me not to let you out of my sight. I'll be sacked if you go alone."

Elinor rolled her eyes and consented. He was unassuming and would not intrude upon her need for solitude. Mayfair was all but empty this time of the day, and she thought she might just walk the horse through the quiet streets instead of heading for the park. There, she would feel obliged to run the mare, and that might take more strength and stamina than she possessed after last night.

She did not know how she had managed to resist Winn. She could not remember a time when he'd touched her like that, and she wanted, more than anything, to give in to his caresses. She wanted his mouth on her, his hands, his body covering hers. She wanted him more than she ever had, but she knew if she gave in to the desire she would never be able to resist him again.

And when he left again—because he would; she knew that if nothing else—she would fall into an even deeper despair than she'd felt before. She'd drawn upon hidden reserves of fortitude and told him to stop touching her, seducing her. At first she had not even believed herself. She certainly hadn't sounded convincing, but when Winn hadn't immediately acquiesced, she began to mean it. Was he so arrogant that he assumed she would never refuse him?

Probably. After all, it was not as though she ever had.

She allowed the horse to trot a little, lost in her thoughts and the novelty of the deserted streets. Here and there a maid bustled with a basket full of produce, but for the most part, this part of the city was not yet awake. She turned back toward home. Elinor could remember, as a new mother, rocking Georgiana back to sleep in the early morning hours when the city was silent. She'd had a nurse, of course, but she'd so enjoyed that quiet time with her daughter, she had defied convention and told the nurse to go to sleep. This morning reminded her of all those years ago. She should have felt happy and fulfilled, but all she could think was how she wished Winn would fall in love with her. He'd robbed her of even the simple pleasure of motherhood.

Now it seemed he wanted her, but she still felt something was missing. Perhaps because he still was not in love with her. Would she never realize that some dreams were unattainable?

Would she never be satisfied with her—?

Suddenly her horse reared, and Elinor grappled to keep her seat. She clutched the reins with all her strength and murmured soothing words, but when the mare came back down, she shied to the side, and Elinor saw what had spooked the animal. Two men wearing hats low over their brows and with mufflers obscuring the lower part of their faces were approaching from a dark alley, and one was reaching for the horse's bridle.

Elinor brandished the whip she had remembered but rarely used, and shouted, "Step aside! I do not have any money or jewels."

Jacob raced to her side, whereupon one of the men raised a pistol and shot the groom. Elinor screamed. She'd not been truly frightened until that moment. She had been concerned, but deep down she did not really believe the men would accost her in the streets of Mayfair, just blocks from her home. It was practically unheard of. Poor Jacob. Her assailants ignored her screams, and the taller one succeeded in grasping her horse's bridle and holding her steady.

"Release my horse at once!" Elinor commanded. She raised the whip, striking at the shorter man, who was coming for her. The man caught the end of the whip and yanked it from her hand. The shorter man grabbed her and hauled her off the horse. She kicked and screamed until his hand covered her mouth, silencing her. A moment later, she was dragged down the dark alley and shoved into a carriage. The drapes were drawn, and the interior of the conveyance was black as night. She blinked, momentarily blind. She reached out, her hands touching the soft velvet squabs and heavy brocade draperies. And then her hand touched something warm, something encased in soft material, but something undeniably human.

She drew back with a hiss and looked up. She could just make out the eyes of the man seated above her. His knee was in front of her face, and she jerked back, appalled that she had touched his leg.

"Good morning, Lady Keating. Or should I call you Mrs. Baron?"

Ten

"WHAT DO YOU MEAN, YOU CANNOT FIND HER?" Winn demanded of Bramson several hours after breakfast. He had not seen Elinor all morning and had assumed she was attempting to avoid him. He decided to allow it for the moment, taking breakfast alone while she dined in her room. He read the paper, checked ledgers in his library, but when midday approached and she was still hiding, he had had enough.

He marched to her room, knocked on the door, and was informed by her maid that the baroness had gone out riding early this morning. The cold chill of unease skittered up Winn's back and down his arms. He knew this feeling. He knew it well, and he did not want it associated with his wife. He'd pushed the maid aside, ignoring her gasp of outrage, and searched Elinor's room. Her clothing, valises, and mementos were still here—at least from what he could ascertain from a cursory glance.

But if she had gone riding early this morning, where was she now?

He made his way to the mews and questioned the

grooms there, who looked relieved to see him. They had been worried about her ladyship and the groom who had accompanied her and were uncertain as to what to do about her long absence. Once again, Winn cursed his frequent travels. It was obvious the staff was not used to him being in residence and did not think to go to him with their worries.

Next, he enlisted the footmen to search the house for any sign of her and also to inquire—discreetly—at Lady Ramsgate's and Lady Hollingshead's residences. Shortly thereafter, Bramson had informed him that Lady Keating was not to be found.

Winn paced his library, scowling. "Are you saying she has simply disappeared?"

"No, my lord. I am saying *I* do not know her whereabouts. Would you like me to call for a magistrate or the Bow Street Runners?"

"Good God, no." The last thing he wanted was to involve Bow Street. He was a spy, after all. It was his job to ferret out people and information. But his unease was growing. He did not want to acknowledge what he now feared to be the truth: something had happened to Elinor. Pickpockets? Thugs?

Perhaps it was nothing quite so horrible. Perhaps she had merely fallen from her horse, hit her head, and was lying unconscious in some filthy street. No, that was not dire at all.

Bloody hell! Why had he allowed her to order him out of her bedchamber last night? He should have insisted upon staying close to her. But that was ridiculous, of course. He'd never worried about being close to her before.

And just now he was beginning to realize that perhaps he should have.

"I will find her," he told Bramson now. The butler nodded and rushed to fetch Winn's coat and walking stick. When the man stepped out of the way, Winn drew a key from his waistcoat pocket, inserted it into his desk drawer, and slid it open. Inside was a case holding a pair of Forsyth & Co. dueling pistols. He was about to open it and remove them, when a sharp knock sounded on the door. Bramson opened it without waiting for permission.

"What is it?"

Bramson handed him a white note. The fact that the proper butler had not bothered to take the time to bring the note on a tray told Winn it was important. "This just came for you, my lord."

Winn broke the seal.

"The courier said it was urgent."

Winn glanced down, recognized Melbourne's handwriting, and cursed before he even read the contents.

∽

Elinor sat in a well-appointed drawing room, a cup of tea balanced on her knee, and stared at the man before her. He was tall and broad-shouldered, though not as tall or as muscular as Winn. His eyes were bright blue, which made a stark contrast to his lush black hair. It fell in waves to his shoulders and framed a handsome, Gallic face. He had dark brows and a generous mouth, and he seemed inordinately fond of smiling.

He was smiling at her now, though the expression

did not quite reach his eyes. Those eyes were as cold as glaciers. Looking into them made her shiver.

"And so, madam, I ask again, with as much civility as I am able to muster, what is your role in the Barbican group?" His accent was French, cultured, and smooth as silk. She would have liked to answer him. If she had known what he was talking about, she would have. He was a difficult man to resist.

"I told you. I do not know who or what the Barbican group is."

He lifted one dubious eyebrow. "Are you saying you have lived with one of the most formidable spies in the Barbican group, and you have never heard of it?"

Elinor looked down at her cup of tea. She had not even tasted it, and it no longer warmed her knee. The delicate cup rattled against the saucer now as her nerves jumped. He had asked her this same question several different times, and she had evaded it as best she could. She did not want to compromise Winn, though she did not know if he was truly a member of this Barbican group or not, but she did not know how much longer the man before her would remain cordial if she did not give him an answer.

"I..."

He waved a hand, dismissing her answer before she could give it. "I have it on good authority that you are married to the spy called Baron."

"My husband is Baron Keating. As to whether he is a spy, that seems rather unlikely." She managed to still the rattling cup and look the dark-haired man in his bright blue eyes.

"You are a good liar, madam. I would almost believe

you. Except…" He trailed off, and though she did not want to fall into his trap, she found herself compelled.

"Except?"

"Except I do not believe my source lied." He rose, and Elinor tensed at the way his dark form cast a shadow over her. The cup began to rattle again. Oh, why had she gone on a ride this morning? Why had she not stayed at home in her safe, warm bed?

And why had she ever thought it would be glamorous to be a spy?

"W-why is that?" she asked, looking up and up, into his cold eyes.

"Because before he told me what I wanted to hear, I carved my name into the bare flesh of his chest." He knelt before her, snatching the clinking teacup and saucer out of her grasp. "He begged for death, and I granted it after he told me what I wanted to know—the identities of the spies Baron and Blue."

Elinor swallowed. She could feel her skin burn where a knife might slide over her bare flesh. "And what name did you carve?" she asked, though she could not have said what motivated this question. Only that she wanted to know the name of the man who would take her life.

He smiled, bowed, and kissed her hand. "Monsieur Foncé, madam. At your service."

❧

Winn was cold. The fire burned hot and bright, the logs crackling and popping, and Winn shivered. Melbourne pressed a snifter of brandy into his hand.

Winn looked at it, and a voice from across the room said, "Drink. You look like you need it."

Winn squinted, staring at the man sitting calmly in the armchair across from him. Why shouldn't Agent Wolf be calm? It was not his wife in the grip of a murderer.

"Let's go back over this again," Wolf was saying. "We'll start at the beginning."

Winn wanted to punch him. He resisted, because in Adrian Galloway, Agent Wolf, he saw himself. How many times had he sat across from a man or woman who was frantic with worry and panic? How many times had he been the cool, aloof voice of reason?

Every time. Until this one.

Until it was Elinor.

"I don't want to go over it again," Winn said, interrupting Melbourne and Wolf and their tedious recounting of the few events all of them had recounted innumerable times. The two men looked at Winn, and he knew their looks. Indulgent looks because they were sympathetic. They were trained to humor the victim, console him.

Well, Winn was no victim, and he did not want sympathy. He wanted action.

"I want to do something. We sit here and talk, while somewhere out there"—he gestured wildly with his hand and sloshed brandy over his wrist—"Foncé could be carving my wife into tiny pieces."

"He doesn't carve them up," Wolf said. "He—"

"I don't give a bloody farthing what he does!" Winn yelled and threw the brandy glass against Melbourne's wall. It shattered, and brandy ran like blood down the wood paneling. "I want her back. Now."

"So do we," Melbourne said. He held up a hand to stay Wolf, who had risen and looked ready to strike. "But we do not know where he has taken her. We do not know his whereabouts."

Winn understood this, but he thought running in circles and chasing his tail would be preferable to sitting in this room any longer. This wasn't supposed to happen. He was the operative, not his wife. His family and his position were not supposed to intersect.

"Let's look at it from another angle," Wolf said. Winn clenched his fists, and Wolf took a step back. "Hear me out. We know Foncé has Lady Keating, because the man we had assigned to watch the known operatives from the Maîtriser group saw them take her. But even he did not know, initially, who she was. He followed the riderless horse back to the mews and inquired as to whose residence it was."

"This information is nothing new," Winn said.

But Melbourne put a hand on his shoulder. "Wait. I think I see where he is headed."

"My point," Wolf said, "is that if our own man did not know who Lady Keating was, how did Foncé's men know to take her? Not only did they take her, they made sure the groom could not follow them. This was no random abduction. We know Foncé too well for that. Somehow Foncé was able to discover the spy Baron was on to him, and he was able to link you with Lady Keating."

"Which means he knows your true identity," Melbourne said.

"Yes." Wolf acknowledged this with a quick nod, far too quick for Winn's taste. He'd worked for years to keep his identity secret. And now it was known to the most dangerous man in Europe, a man picking off Barbican operatives seemingly at will. "If we can discern how Foncé was able to link Baron and Lady Keating, we might turn up something new."

Melbourne nodded.

The room was silent but for the hiss and pop of the logs in the fire. Wolf and Melbourne looked at Winn, and he stared at the smoke rising up into the chimney. "Bloody hell," he swore. Winn cut a glance at Melbourne. "Why did you need that key?"

"What key?" Melbourne asked smoothly.

Winn took three steps, grabbed Melbourne by the throat, and pushed him onto the desk. "I am in no mood for spy games," Winn hissed.

Wolf was beside him in an instant, but Melbourne shook his head. Winn knew Wolf was a match for him. If the other spy wanted to tussle, he was not certain who would emerge the victor.

"I suppose at this point, you have a right to know."

Winn didn't answer, and he didn't release Melbourne, either.

"We believe the key is to one of Foncé's safe houses. One of our operatives managed to steal it from the man we think may be Foncé's second-in-command."

"*Believe* and *think*," Winn all but spat. "Are we gypsy fortune-tellers or spies? Is there anything you *do* know?"

"You asked about a key," Wolf said quietly. "Is there something *you* know?"

Winn looked at him and released Melbourne. "The Ramsgate ball. I was chased by a man in black to the ball. We fought over the key, and while we were fighting, he managed to ascertain that Elinor was my wife."

Melbourne was adjusting his cravat, but he paused to stare at Winn. "That information might have proved important before this."

Yes, Winn had already considered that. If he hadn't been so jealous over Elinor's puppy. If he hadn't been shocked by her gown. If he'd been doing his job…

If, if, if…

His life for the past year had consisted of ifs and whys and so much blame he could hardly shoulder it. And now he had made another grievous error, and this one hurt his family. Except… Winn looked at Melbourne. This time the blame was not entirely upon his shoulders.

"Why didn't you tell me the key had something to do with Foncé?"

Melbourne shook his head. "I tell you what you need to know." The older agent stalked toward a decanter of brandy, but Winn stepped in front of him.

"And you think I don't need to know I'm dealing with the minions of a madman out to annihilate the Barbican group?"

"It has not been policy to—"

"My wife may be dead because of your inane policies!"

"Winslow, I know you want someone to blame," Melbourne began.

"Yes!" Winn slammed his fists against the wall. "I want someone to blame. Someone besides me, because I cannot be responsible for another death."

In the silence that followed Winn's outburst, Winn

heard a man clear his throat. Slowly, he turned and saw Blue standing in the doorway. His hair, which had been long and flowing only the afternoon previous, now appeared cropped short. "Is this a bad time?" he said, brows raised.

"What do you have?" Melbourne demanded.

"A body," Blue said.

Winn sank to the floor, head in his hands.

∽

She was going to die. Elinor knew this for a certainty, and yet the thought itself would not stop looping itself through her brain.

It was quickly followed by: *I will never see Caro and Georgiana again.* And then: *I will never see Winn again.*

Though, as for the last one, she was not certain whether she was upset that she would not see him because she was still in love with him or because she now hated him enough to want the opportunity to kill him.

She suspected it was a combination of both. Unable to sit still in the small upper chamber where she'd been taken when Foncé had ordered her out of his sight, Elinor paced under the barred window, her hands clasped over her roiling belly. She felt ill. She felt as though she would go mad with not knowing when she would die and how. She counted her steps, thirty-three across the room and thirty-three back, and wondered if this was how those French nobles condemned to the guillotine had felt. They'd known they were to die, known the horrible way it would happen, but could do nothing but pace and pray for a miracle that would never come.

Oh, how she hated Winn. How could he have done this to her? Had he never thought of anyone but himself? Had he never considered his foolish playing at spying could be dangerous? Or maybe he knew this all along and did not care. Maybe he cared more for the thrill of espionage than he did for her or their children.

And where was he now? Did he even know she was gone? Certainly her absence had been noted by now, but was he a good enough spy to realize who had taken her? And could he rescue her? Would he even try?

Elinor was not certain of any of it. She was no longer certain who her husband was.

But of one thing she was certain. If she wanted to escape, she was going to have to do it on her own. She paced and planned and finally rang the servant's bell.

She'd been so shocked that she'd pulled the rope, so shocked that she was actually going to go through with her daft plans, that she had to sit down for a moment because her legs wobbled too much to support her. She'd half fallen on a stool in front of a mottled dressing mirror, and in the warped glass, she could see her reflection.

Loose pieces of hair clung to her cheeks and forehead in sweaty ringlets, her dark eyes were wide, and her face was as pale as a specter's. No, she thought with a shake of her head. This would not do.

She smoothed her hair back, pinched her cheeks to give them color, and took several deep breaths. She stood, straightened her gown, and was calm and composed when the door opened to admit the servant. It was a hulking giant of a man, and he did not look pleased to have been summoned. Some of Elinor's calmness fled, but she was determined to avoid at least the appearance of anxiety. After all, this Foncé could not see her pounding heart or hear her mind screaming in complete and utter terror.

"What do you want?" the man growled. At least that was what Elinor thought he said. He had a strange accent, and she had to guess at half of his words.

"I wish to be taken to see Mr. Foncé, if you please."

The servant shook his head. "If Foncé wants to see you, he'll ask for you," he said, or something to that effect.

"He will want to hear what I have to say, I assure you," she said, doing her best to sound firm and commanding. She'd had years of experience managing a household and ordering servants about. Despite her nervousness, she could play this role in her sleep. "If you do not take me to him, he is going to be most displeased. After all, if I'm forced to sit here and think and wait, I may change my mind."

The servant frowned, his heavy brows coming together over the prominent ridge of his forehead. "I'll be back."

He exited, and she heard the key turn in the lock. She would not allow herself to consider the possibility that Foncé would not want to see her. She had not lied when she said her resolve would fail if forced to wait.

After what seemed an interminable amount of time and too many trips across the thirty-three steps of the room, she heard footfalls again. Quickly, she smoothed her gown and stood at attention again. The servant opened the door and motioned for her.

Elinor was equally terrified and elated. It was working! Her plan was working! But did she even want it to work? She really had no other choice, unless she was content to sit in this room until Foncé decided he no longer had need of her and carved her to pieces. Besides, she could be brave. Winn did this sort of thing all the time, she supposed. Was he braver than she? Impossible. Elinor had birthed two children. She had faced their temper tantrums and their battles of will. She had nursed them when their fevers were so high she was not certain the girls would live through the night. She had gone without sleep or sustenance and emerged on the other side only a little worse for wear. And what the experience had taught her was that she could do anything if she must.

She could face this Foncé. She must.

She was shown into a library of sorts this time. It unnerved Elinor slightly that the venue had changed. She had planned where she would sit and what she would say, with the drawing room in her mind. But the library would have to do. It was a darker room, and the drapes were drawn, but Foncé had lit several lamps. Their flickering light glinted off the metal of the knives he was polishing.

Elinor took a fortifying breath and forced herself to enter the room when the servant mumbled something she assumed was her introduction.

Foncé did not speak. He looked up at her and polished a long knife with a rectangular blade. Elinor thought it might be called a meat cleaver.

"Thank you for seeing me," she said. He did

not ask her to sit, as she had expected, so she stood awkwardly before him.

"I hope this is important," he said, placing the cleaver down and lifting a smaller, more delicate blade. "I am busy, as you see."

"It is important, and I shall endeavor to be brief. I think I may be of service to you."

Foncé continued polishing, but he raised a brow with interest. Elinor frowned as she watched him. Was it her imagination, or had he removed a dark crimson material from the blade? She clenched her hands into fists and hid them in her skirts. Her nails bit into her palms, and she focused on that sensation rather than the wicked knife being cleaned before her.

"You seem interested in my husband, the man you think may be the spy Baron."

"I know he is Baron."

"And you've taken me in order to lure him out."

"In part. I thought you might make attractive bait." He set the delicate blade down and lifted one with a hooked end. Good God, what was the purpose of that?

"I regret to inform you that if Lord Keating is this Baron, he will see this is a tactic to capture him and not rise to the bait."

Foncé stroked the blade. "That is unfortunate for you."

"But perhaps not for you. Perhaps I could be of some assistance."

Foncé's expression did not change, and Elinor felt panic creeping closer and closer. If he did not like her proposition, she was doomed. "Why would you assist me, *ma cherie*?"

"Because I would hope you would repay kindness with kindness and allow me to go unharmed."

"I see." Foncé lifted another weapon, this one a long blade with a forked end. "And what can you offer me that would entice me to accept this proposal?"

"I will lure Baron out so you may capture him."

"I do not need your assistance. I will have him eventually."

"But why wait, when I can make certain he is yours before morning?"

Foncé stroked the implement he held in his hand, and Elinor could imagine the sharp prongs piercing her flesh. "Go on," he said.

"I'll send a note, and we will make it seem as though I was able to smuggle it out. I will tell him I overheard your plan to take me to Almack's and kill me."

Foncé's eyes narrowed. "Why would I take you to an assembly room?"

"Because it is symbolic. If you were to kill me there, it would show the *ton* no one is safe, and because it shows you have the power to access such exclusive venues. Lord Keating will understand the significance and come for me."

Foncé shook his head. "He is no fool. He will make certain the locale is secure before the prescribed time. When he discovers it is not, he will not come."

"He will come. If I ask him to. If I assure him we can escape." And she could assure him that quite honestly. She knew Almack's as well as her own house. She knew the back exits and the tucked-away rooms. "I can also sneak you in. I know the owner. He will let me in."

"I see." Foncé looked thoughtful. "And why would you do this for me?"

Elinor gestured to the knives. "I do not want to die, for one."

"And you have no qualms about betraying your husband?"

She shrugged. "Ours is no love match. We have a marriage of convenience, like the rest of Society. In truth, I hardly know him. He is rarely, if ever, home."

Foncé set the forked implement down, and Elinor let out a breath she had not known she was holding. "How can I trust you?"

That was the question she had hoped would not arise. But Foncé was an intelligent man. He saw the flaw in her plan. "I give you my word," she began, as she'd rehearsed in her room.

He shook his head. "Not good enough."

Elinor wanted to curse. She had been so close! "I know no way to prove myself. You shall simply have to trust me."

"I do not think so, madam." He lifted a small, delicate scalpel. "But I think I might know a way to ensure your cooperation."

Eleven

"IT WAS NOT THE BODY OF LADY KEATING," BLUE SAID from somewhere far away. Winn could hardly hear the other agent for the rushing sound in his ears. "But the news is not good, nonetheless." He trained his bright blue eyes on Melbourne.

"Go on," the secretary said. Somehow Winn managed to move into a chair. Elinor was alive. Foncé had not killed her. Not yet. Winn did not have to bear the responsibility for the death of his wife and the mother of his children. Not yet.

"It was our man inside the Maîtriser group, I'm afraid."

Wolf's head snapped up. "We have a man inside the Maîtriser group?"

"Melbourne is just full of surprises, isn't he?" Winn muttered.

"Not anymore," Blue said ominously. "A friend of mine with the Bow Street Runners reported a body floating in the Thames and suggested I might have an interest in taking a look."

"And?" Melbourne asked.

"And it was our man."

"How do you know Foncé killed him?" Wolf asked.

"Because he'd carved his name on the man's chest. It is a departure from his usual practice, but I have no doubt it was his work."

Winn put a hand to his eyes and rubbed the bridge of his nose. His head pounded, and his eyes were dry with fatigue. He closed them briefly, feeling them burn under his heavy lids. "I don't suppose this man gave you any information as to Foncé's whereabouts," Winn said, opening his eyes and looking at Melbourne.

"He had not managed to determine that information yet," Melbourne said. "I'm afraid we are no further along than we were before."

"So what now?" Winn demanded. "Do we sit here and wait for Elinor's body to wash up? Do I twiddle my thumbs while that murderer carves her up?" The image of her tender porcelain flesh flashed in his mind. His fingers could still feel the silkiness of her skin. His hands could still test the weight of her breasts. He could not imagine that glorious flesh marred by the crude red slashes of Foncé's tools. Would Caroline and Georgiana ever forgive him for not saving their mother? Could he ever forgive himself? He'd not yet forgiven himself for Crow. He did not think he ever would.

Melbourne was speaking to Wolf. "Saint has found nothing yet?"

"She has uncovered several interesting possibilities, but research is a slow process."

"Yes," Blue murmured. "Especially when the researcher is Saint."

Wolf shot him an annoyed look.

"I have one or two operatives in Town," Melbourne said. "I could send them on surveillance. Perhaps they might turn up something."

Winn felt his hopes sink. Research. Aimless canvassing. These strategies would not save Elinor. Not in time, anyway.

A sharp knock sounded on the door, and Melbourne cursed. "Now what?" He stalked to the door and threw it open, revealing a clerk in black, cowering in the casement. "I said I did not wish to be disturbed!"

"I know, my lord, but this just came. It is addressed to Lord Keating. His butler sent it as soon as it arrived at his house."

Winn jumped to his feet and snatched the vellum from the clerk's trembling hands. He all but ripped it when breaking the plain red-wax seal, but what he saw made it possible for him to breathe again. "It's from her," he said. Skimming the words she'd written and trying to make some sense of them, he closed his eyes and attempted to focus.

"It's a trap," Wolf said.

Winn opened his eyes and glanced at the room of men. They all wore the same expression. Without even having read the missive, they knew what it contained. Winn knew too. It *was* a trap.

And he had no choice but to fall into it.

⚜

The man had said his name was Tolbert, pronounced *toll-bear*, and Elinor thought it suited him. At least the *bear* portion of the name suited him. Her servant had given his name grudgingly and only after they'd been in the closed carriage on the way to the rendezvous for three-quarters of an hour. After she'd written the note, closely supervised by Foncé, she'd paced her room for hours, waiting for Winn's response. She'd had the note sent to her home, with instructions for Bramson to forward it to Lord Keating if he was not at home. But she had not really known if Winn would receive the note or not. She suspected he was wherever spies in London congregated, and no one—not even Foncé—knew where that was.

But somehow the note had found him, and he had penned a curt reply that he would see her at the appointed time and place. As she and Tolbert sat outside Almack's and waited for the clock to reach nine o'clock, she wished she could part the carriage drapes and scan the surrounding area. Was Foncé lurking nearby? Was Winn arriving outside Almack's even now? She lifted her hand to the drapes, parted them slightly, but Tolbert snapped them shut in front of her face with a whoosh. "No peeking."

Elinor sat back, feeling duly scolded. Hadn't she been a baroness when she left her house this morning? Hadn't she been afforded every respect and courtesy and deference possible? And now servants snapped drapes shut in front of her face, and she could do nothing to object, because he was armed to the teeth and would slit her throat without a second thought.

Five long minutes ticked by, and Elinor heard distant church bells clang nine times. The sound seemed strange to her for some reason. Wrong. She glanced at Tolbert, but except for a peek through the curtains, he did not move. Elinor thought about inquiring as to why he was allowed to look through the curtains when she was not, but in the weak light from the carriage lamps, she could see the glint of metal from one of his knives, and she bit her tongue.

Was Winn waiting for her, even now? Was he waiting outside Almack's, wondering if she was coming, wondering if this was all a trick, wondering if she would leave him waiting? The irony of Winn waiting for her was not lost on Elinor, but for once she did not wish their positions reversed. She wanted to be with him. Somehow she knew if she could just reach him, fall into his arms, all would be well. He would find some way to save them. He had to.

Tolbert parted the drapes again and nodded. "Let's go."

Elinor could not think what might have changed since the last time he had looked, but she was glad finally to exit the conveyance. As soon as she stepped out, she halted.

"What is going on?" This was not Almack's. They were in front of a house she did not know.

"Change of plan," Tolbert said.

"What?" How could Foncé change the plan? It was *her* plan!

But now as she looked at what appeared to be a hotel of sorts, Elinor knew she was the one who had been duped. Foncé was no fool, and he had obviously found some means of changing the meeting location without her knowledge. This was his territory, not hers, and she felt completely at a loss.

Her belly tightened with a sickening dread. She had led Winn into a trap.

Perhaps he would not come. Perhaps he would be able to rescue them both. She was all but useless now.

Tolbert kept close to her, a concealed knife pressed to her side and his hand on her upper arm as he led her to the door of the hotel and then through the public rooms and up the stairs. Elinor had a quick glimpse of several women and men conversing in a drawing room, but nothing looked untoward to her. The hotel looked much like any other. She considered crying out for assistance, but her companion seemed to sense her urge and dug the knife in deeper. Tolbert, who had only ever lumbered when she had been waiting on him, moved at a punishing speed. Elinor was disappointed at the quick glimpse she caught of the rooms. She had no sense of it from such a hasty perusal.

As Tolbert pushed her up a second set of stairs, she tried to imagine Winn walking these same worn stair runners only moments before. She closed her eyes briefly and allowed herself to be propelled by Tolbert. She tried, desperately, to feel Winn's presence. At their home in Mayfair, she always knew when he was in residence. There was a subtle change in the feel of the house—a quietness, a tension, a holding of breath that commenced when he walked through the door. And even if the house had not changed, she changed when he was near. Her skin became warm and sensitive, even the softest material seeming to chafe uncomfortably. Rooms that had been chilly only moments before seemed unbearably hot. Her clothing felt tight, her hair heavy, her hearing intensified. It was as though every part of her coalesced and focused on Winn.

But she did not feel him now. Try as she might, she did not sense his presence anywhere. Her heart, which had been pounding quite a staccato, now thumped heavy and painful in her rib cage. She began to fear he had not come. She began to fear he had suspected the trap and would leave her to Foncé's whims. Her chest sagged as her heart seemed to double in weight. If her plan failed so spectacularly, she knew she would not live out the hour. She would have had to be blind not to see how much Foncé anticipated carving her up with the ghoulish implements he lovingly referred to as his tools.

"Here," Tolbert said, stopping before an ordinary door, which was closed, as were the other doors along the corridor. Elinor had not even noticed they had reached the landing for the stairs and started down a corridor. Now she blinked and attempted to take in her surroundings. The walls of the corridor were bare of portraits or other ornamentation. A few stubs of candles burned in a brace a little ways down the hall, but no other light illuminated the shadowed corridor. The carpet beneath her feet was worn but not yet shabby. The door before her was wood and painted white. The paint had yellowed slightly, but except for a small section near the handle that was peeling, was still in good repair.

"Go on," Tolbert ordered her, motioning with the dagger. He put his hands on his hips, revealing a brace of pistols, additional daggers, and other weapons she did not want to consider. Elinor prayed Winn was behind the door, because she did not have the first inkling as to how she was going to evade Tolbert

before Foncé arrived. Clearly, her grand delusions of
saving the day were only that—delusions. And now
she was completely at Foncé's mercy. He would never
keep his word and release her when and if he captured
Winn. And did she want to be released if her husband
was dead because of her foolishness?

She put her hand on the door's handle, turned it,
and was surprised it opened. It swung wide, revealing
a dark room without even a fire in the hearth. She
hesitated and tried to take a step back, but Tolbert's
foot blocked her exit. He jerked his head toward the
room, and she shuffled inside. The door closed with
a bang behind her, and she jumped at the unexpected
sound. The room seemed devoid of windows and was
black and cold as a cave. And yet she sensed she was
not alone. "H-hello?" she whispered. "Winn?"

Something or someone moved in the far corner.
Light flickered, and she blinked as a small candle sputtered to life. It did little to illuminate the man seated in
the corner of the room beside the bed. He was dressed
in black, and no inch of skin was visible. She thought
she might have been able to detect the glint of his eyes,
but she was uncertain.

Something felt wrong, and she inched backward.
She darted her gaze about, searching for some means
of escape, but there was nothing.

"Come closer," the man said. It was not Winn, at
least the voice had not sounded like his. It was accented
and quite deep. Winn had a tenor voice with all the
trappings of the British nobility in his clipped words.

"I…" She did not know what to do, what to say.
What had Foncé planned for her?

"Come closer," the man demanded again.

Elinor looked over her shoulder at the closed door behind her. Tolbert and his arsenal stood on the opposite side. She was not getting out that way. And in a very short amount of time, Foncé and his men would descend on this room and take her and whoever this man was prisoner.

"I am terribly sorry," she sputtered. "I think I have the wrong room."

"Take off your coat," the man said.

Elinor frowned. Had he misunderstood her? "But I—"

"Take off your coat." His tone did not brook any argument, and she felt compelled to fumble with the buttons and shrug off her spencer. She looked about for somewhere to place it, but could not see any furniture save the bed limned by the candle. She moved closer, laid the garment on the bed. Her fingers grazed the coverlet, and she was taken aback to discover it was satin.

"Take your hair down."

Elinor frowned, looked at the door and then at the man. "Sir, I'm afraid you have the wrong woman. I am here to meet—"

"—your husband. I am aware. I won't hurt you."

His words did not reassure her.

"Take your hair down," he ordered again.

Elinor was confused, but she dutifully began removing the pins from her hair. Not wanting to wake Bridget this morning, she'd styled it herself and quite simply. It was easy to uncoil it so her long tresses fell to her back. Instantly, she felt vulnerable and exposed. The elaborate coils and curls of her coiffed hair were familiar to her. She'd been wearing it thus since she was a young girl. It was a shield, a protection as much as any article of clothing. And now that her hair hung down and her coat had been removed, she began to feel helplessly unprotected. "But my husband was supposed to come," she protested before the man could speak again.

"He sent me. Put your hands on the bed."

Elinor did not believe she could have heard either statement correctly. Why would Winn send another man in his stead? She had promised a romantic interlude in the note, all the while penning it, knowing Winn would see past Foncé's words and know she needed his help. But perhaps he had misunderstood? Clearly, this man had taken the missive at its word.

"I am afraid there has been some mistake," she began. She looked at the door. Perhaps if she informed Tolbert the wrong man had been sent to meet her...

"There is no mistake," the man across the bed said. "Put your hands on the bed and bend over."

Elinor stood completely frozen. She was devoid of options. Tolbert was behind her, and soon Foncé would be arriving. He would kill her and this man, and in the most heinous manner imaginable.

In front of her, across the wide expanse of the bed, was a randy man who wanted to bed her. Had Winn really sent him? If so, was he a spy? Could he help her escape Foncé?

"I grow impatient," the man said, the threat in his tone clear.

Her hands trembled as she placed them on the satin coverlet. The material slid through her fingers as her hair slid over her shoulder, blocking her limited view of the room. But she sensed movement. The man was coming toward her.

What was she going to do? She could not stand here and allow herself to be raped. Perhaps when he was behind her, she could scramble over the bed or knee him in his nether regions. She had to do something.

He was behind her now. She could feel his warmth, and then she jumped because he slid his hand along her ribs, over her breasts, and then down her arms.

"If you know who Foncé is," she said quietly, trying to keep her voice steady as his hands roamed her hips, "then you know the danger we are in. He has taken me prisoner, and he knows my husband is a spy."

His hand closed on her ankle and then traveled up her calf, under her skirts. She trembled with fear as his fingers slid higher. This was her last chance. She had to make her escape now.

She kicked back, her heel slamming into something hard and solid. She heard a grunt, and the hand holding her knee let go. Quick as a cat, she scrambled onto the bed. She was halfway across when an unforgiving vise gripped her ankle and hauled her back.

She kicked and thrashed, trying to break free, but he did not release her. She grabbed handfuls of the comforter, but the smooth material slid through her fingers. And then she was jerked to the bed's edge, flipped over, and her hands pinned.

She fought harder, biting and kicking, and wriggling to free herself.

"Stop fighting," the man ordered. "Listen closely if you want to survive."

❦

Winn could feel the sharp rise and fall of her breasts as she struggled against him. Unfortunately, the action was doing nothing to cool his desire. He had not expected to react to merely touching her body. He'd been searching for hidden weapons, because one could never be too careful, and one could not afford to trust anyone—not even one's wife. But what should have been a perfunctory search turned into erotic torture as her rounded bottom pressed against his hardening flesh. Now he held her tightly and fought to regain control.

"Winn?" she asked.

He'd forgotten to disguise his voice, but it served him well, as she ceased struggling, and he could think again. "You sound surprised. Did you think I was going to leave you in Foncé's clutches?"

"I didn't know what to think. This... this building wasn't in my plan. This is all wrong. And Foncé—he's mad, and he knows who you are."

"I realized that when I determined that he'd abducted you."

"You knew?"

"I'm a spy, Ellie. It is my job to know these things."

"But then why didn't you come for me? Why did you allow this?"

He could not see clearly, but he thought he saw her hand gesture toward the room. He pushed up and away from her. The feel of her warm flesh, her bare arms, was muddling his brain. He needed distance. "How else was I supposed to reach you?"

"But we're trapped here. I wanted to meet at

Almack's. I thought I could escape from there. Foncé must have changed my letter."

"There was another note enclosed with additional instructions," Winn told her.

"How dare he!"

"Elinor. Listen." He'd cut her off because her argument was valid and, unfortunately, useless. If he'd really been the expert spy he claimed, he would have known Foncé's location, and all of this would have been unnecessary. Instead, he had been forced to walk into a trap, knowing, even as he stepped into the room indicated in the note accompanying Elinor's missive, he was going to be ambushed. "We don't have much time. Foncé will be here in a few moments."

She jumped up. "Then we have to go. We have to escape before he reaches us."

"And exactly how do you propose we do that?"

She stared at him for a long, long moment. "You don't have a plan?"

Of course he had a plan. He wouldn't be a very good spy if he didn't have a plan. Winn just didn't think Elinor would like his plan very much, as it involved allowing Foncé to capture the both of them. It was risky, but what choice did he have? He could either refuse the meeting, in which case Elinor would still be in Foncé's hands, and the leader of the Maîtriser group would be considerably less happy with her, or he could come to her aid and allow himself to be taken. Assuming he could escape later, the Barbican group would then know Foncé's whereabouts. If he was not able to escape—or not able to escape with

Elinor... Winn did not particularly wish to consider that outcome. In fact, when he'd discussed his plan with Melbourne, Wolf, and Blue, none of the three men had mentioned the possibility of failure either.

It simply was not an option.

"I'm going to take care of you," he said to Elinor now. "Whatever else happens, stay with me. I can take care of you, if you stay with me."

She shook her head. "I don't like the sound of that. I don't want to be taken care of. I want to be rescued."

"And I'd like to oblige you, but there is no way out of this room except through that door, and I doubt your henchman is going to allow us to pass."

Elinor shook her head in a disbelieving gesture. "Can't you hit him over the head or something? Render him unconscious so we can flee?"

"To what purpose?" Winn asked. "I'm certain Foncé has every exit guarded. In fact"—he consulted his pocket watch—"I imagine he is on his way up the stairs right now."

Elinor's head whipped toward the door, and he saw naked fear in her eyes. "Ellie." He stepped closer, put his hands on her arms. "I told you I will take care of you."

Booted steps sounded in the corridor outside, and she shook off Winn's hands. "Do not talk to me. Do not even speak to me!"

Winn refrained from pointing out those were the same thing. "I'm not going to allow anything to happen to you," he said as the door burst open.

But, really, how was he going to keep that promise?

Twelve

SEVERAL HOURS LATER, ELINOR SUPPOSED SHE WAS going to have to rescue herself, as Winn did not seem capable of doing so. What kind of spy allowed himself to be captured? Not a very good one, obviously. She supposed she was going to have to rescue the both of them, for now they had been returned to Foncé's lair and were running out of time.

She glanced at the cellar floor, where Foncé's men had left Winn's crumpled body. Tolbert had carried her husband, who was almost as tall as that big bear of a man himself, as though he were a small child. Except he dropped him in Winn's current resting place without much care. Tolbert had then grabbed her arm, prepared to drag her back to the room she had occupied earlier. Once again, she'd assumed her authoritative look and stance and demanded she stay with her husband. She'd pointed to his unconscious form. "He needs me. Just you try and make me leave his side."

Tolbert had not wanted to deal with her rebellion, and he'd lumbered up the cellar stairs and closed the door, leaving only a weak candle burning. Elinor shivered now. It was cold, dark, and that candle would not last the night. Soon she would be in complete darkness in the cellar of a madman. How long until Foncé made his way down here equipped with his *tools*? He'd seemed to take enormous pleasure tonight in watching his men punch and kick Winn, who did little to defend himself. Elinor had tried to stop them, but Tolbert had held her firmly.

Earlier on the carriage ride back to Foncé's head-quarters, she'd checked Winn's breathing, relieved he was still alive. Now, she bent down and checked it again, pushing him onto his back. The floor was hard, but the position looked more comfortable than the one he'd been left in. "Winn?" she whispered. "Winn?"

No response. Elinor rose and lifted the candle, placing it on the floor so she could see him better. She hunched down and ran a finger over the bruises beginning to appear on his temple. "That is going to give you a terrible megrim," she said to herself. "And your eye is going to be black before the end of the day tomorrow." She combed a strand of his hair away from his face, allowing her fingers to linger on the hard plane of his cheek. When she was not with him, it was easy to forget how handsome he was, especially now that his features were relaxed. He often looked so cold and hard. She rarely saw him in unguarded moments.

She brushed some dust from his forehead and smoothed the lines on his brow. Even in unconscious-ness, he frowned. "I sincerely hope this wasn't your plan," she murmured, loosening his cravat and the buttons of his linen shirt, "because it's not what I would consider a success." Not that her own plan had been any more productive.

Tolbert had tossed her spencer in a heap on the stairs when she'd begun to argue with him, and now she made her way to it and pulled it over her gown. At least it would ward off some of the chill. She did up the fastenings of the spencer and then went back to check on Winn. His breathing seemed easier now, the breathing of a man deep in slumber.

Just like a man to sleep during a crisis.

She looked around the cellar, hoping to spot a possible escape option. But with only the candle for light, she could not see anything not directly in front of her. She supposed she would have to wait until morning to explore the cellar further. It did not appear to have any windows, but Foncé might have instructed his men to board them up. In the morning, telltale slivers of light would peek through, and she would have an idea of the cellar's vulnerabilities.

That was, if she lived until morning.

She rubbed her eyes. Two nights of little sleep were finally catching up with her. No one had hit her, but she had a megrim herself all the same. She looked back down at Winn in his greatcoat. He looked warm enough. Perhaps if she lay beside him for a few minutes and closed her eyes, she would feel better and would be able to think clearly again.

She woke when Winn groaned, her every sense coming instantly alive. She'd fallen asleep, and for far longer than an hour or so. The candle had sputtered out, leaving a pool of wax at the bottom of the holder and on the cellar floor. She sat quickly, wincing at the pain in her back and shoulders. She was not used to sleeping on the floor.

Winn groaned again, and Elinor turned to him, rising to her knees. "Winn? Are you all right?"

"Am I alive?" he muttered.

"Yes."

His eyes squinted open, and she could see one was red and bloodshot. "Was I unconscious?"

She nodded. "Yes. All night." Elinor realized it must be morning. The cellar was no longer pitch black, only gloomy and shrouded.

"Is there any way you could hit me over the head again?"

"Winn!"

He held up a hand. "Not so loud." He braced himself on an elbow, and she tried to help him rise. "Let me do it," he said, his voice surly. "I need to see how bad the damage is." He rose to a sitting position. "It feels like I was dragged behind a horse."

"Foncé's men weren't exactly gentle with you last night."

"No." He gritted his teeth and pushed to his feet. "Where's the fun in that?" He wavered, and she jumped beside him, putting her arm about him to steady him. He scowled. "I said I didn't want help."

"You're going to fall on your face."

"Don't coddle me."

"Fine." She stepped away. "Fall down then, but don't think I'm going to drag you behind me when I escape."

He lifted a brow, a look that appeared comical over his swollen eye. "You have an escape plan?"

She frowned and peered quickly around the cellar. No visible windows or doors, other than the one at the top of the stairs. She imagined it was both locked and guarded. "I'm working on one."

"Oh, good."

She put her hands on her hips. "You might sound a little more enthusiastic. After all, someone has to save us."

"And you think you can do it?"

"I can do a whole lot more than you! All you've managed to do is allow yourself to be captured, beaten within an inch of your life, and rendered unconscious for the last six hours or so."

"Oh, don't you worry about the inches of my life," he said through clenched teeth. "I have a few left." He seemed to study the cellar now. "At least you listened and managed to remain with me."

"Yes, a lot of good that did me. I can't see any way out of this place, and I imagine once Foncé has breakfasted, he's going to want some entertainment. In case you haven't realized it yet, you and I are the entertainment."

"I know exactly what he's capable of."

"Then why did you allow yourself to be captured?"

"Because, madam, there are larger considerations than you or I. Your capture gave the Barbican group the perfect opportunity."

"Wait a moment." She held her hands out in front of her. "Are you telling me that you planned this? That you did not come to rescue me at all?"

"I'm still hoping to rescue you."

"Don't bother." She turned on her heel and marched toward the cellar walls. She was going to find a way out of this place on her own. She was done with spies and husbands and men in general. There were a few streams of light coming from one of the corners, but the area was barricaded by crates and what looked to be the remains of the house's previous kitchen. She spotted a stove lying on its side and a broken table. The table she might move, but not the heavy stove.

Winn was behind her, still talking. "Ellie, we've been looking for Foncé for months. This was our chance to find his headquarters."

She whipped her head around and stared at him. "And so you used me?"

He opened his mouth and seemed to consider. "I wouldn't say that. You are doing a service to your country."

"I don't want to do a service to my country." Not anymore. She was through with spying. "I want to go home."

He reached for her, and she slapped his hand away. "Don't touch me. We've been married fourteen years. Fourteen years of lies and deceit. Fourteen years when I have asked almost nothing of you. I asked one thing from you. One." She held up a finger. "And you won't even give me that. You care more about your precious spy group." She spun back, using her anger to heave the table out of her way. Then she started stacking crates up toward the slivers of light coming through.

"You actually expected me to rescue you?" His voice sounded incredulous.

She shook her head. How was it possible she had married such an idiot? "It would be lovely if once"—she lifted another crate—"just once, you pretended to care about me."

"I *do* care about you."

She slammed another crate down. "No, you don't! Do you know what it was like for me when we first married?" She kept stacking crates, studiously avoided looking in his direction. Her vision blurred from all the dust in the cellar, and she swiped at her eyes. "I was a new bride. Away from my parents for the first time. I was in a new house. My whole life had changed, and all I wanted was to please you—my new husband. That's all I wanted."

"Ellie—"

She felt him move closer, and she skirted away. "But you couldn't even pretend you cared for a few days. As soon as we were married, you were gone—away on one of your missions, I'm sure. I waited for you every day and every night. I would have been elated with a simple note." But she'd received nothing. And when he had come back, he hadn't seemed to remember she was his wife. She'd changed her hair, her gowns, hosted a ball, but nothing drew his attention. "Nothing I did would ever make you love me. You didn't even *notice* me." She swung around now to face him. "What is wrong with me, Winn? I know I'm not beautiful or witty or terribly accomplished, but I am your wife. Can't you even rescue me?"

He stared at her—at least she thought he did. Her eyes were watering too much—horrid dust—to see him clearly.

"Ellie, I'm so sorry." He reached for her again.

"No!" She jerked away. "I do not want your apologies. Not now. It's far too late for that. Just answer my question."

"There was and is absolutely nothing wrong with you. I was a fool."

"No, I am the fool. What did you say a moment ago? *You actually expected me to rescue you?* How you must laugh at my foolishness."

"Never. Ellie—Elinor, I was never going to be able to rescue you. That was a trap. Surely you knew that."

"Of course I know that now," she said, throwing a crate in his direction. "This is not how *I* planned it. But you are a spy. I expect you to be capable of escaping a trap."

He was silent for a long moment, and she glanced over her shoulder to look at him. "Never thought about that, did you? Never thought about *actually* rescuing me."

"Of course I did."

"Liar." She kicked a crate, angry at the way her eyes burned with unshed tears. She would not cry. He'd never loved her. Nothing had changed. Why cry now because she had more evidence for what she already knew to be true?

"Elinor." He put a hand on her shoulder, and she shook it off and went back to stacking the crates.

"This conversation is not over."

"It is for me."

There was a long silence, then he cleared his throat. "What are you doing?"

"I'm escaping."

"Forgive me for stating the obvious, but I see no window or door."

She jabbed a finger at the light streaming through the slats near the top of the cellar walls. "See that light?

It's coming from somewhere. I thought perhaps the windows or a door might be boarded up. I want to climb up and take a look."

"Huh." He put his hands on his hips and looked up at the ceiling.

"Huh? Your response is *huh*?"

"It's not a bad idea."

She rolled her eyes and went back to stacking crates.

"Elinor."

She ignored him and continued working.

"Elinor." He took the crate from her hand, set it down, and took hold of her shoulders. "I…"

She waited for him to continue. Never had she seen him look so completely uncomfortable. Never had she seen him stumble over words.

"You…?" she prompted.

And still he didn't speak.

"Is this going to take long? I have an escape to plan."

He clutched her shoulders. "Will you forget about the bloody escape? I'll take you out of here."

"Forgive me if I have my doubts."

"I was terrified. There. Is that what you wanted to hear?"

"Not particularly." Although she had never heard him say anything actually expressing an emotion before, so this was a novel moment. She might have enjoyed it if she did not have crates to stack and an escape to plan. She wanted him to release her. "Let me go."

"I thought you were gone. I thought you were dead."

She stilled and forgot about her escape plan for a moment. "You were terrified for me?"

"And me. I didn't know how I was going to go on without you."

"I imagine as you always have."

He shook his head and brushed a finger along her cheek. "No. That's no longer possible. I find, wholly unexpectedly, you have become necessary."

She shook her head. She could not be hearing him correctly. "Necessary for what?"

"My happiness. I need you, Ellie, and I was afraid I'd lost you."

Elinor wanted to melt. She wanted to feel warm and happy and exactly as she'd always imagined she would when she dreamed about this moment. She remembered her first dance with Winn, and the feel of his strong arms around her. She remembered the first time he'd called on her, endured a quarter hour of her mother's simpering, and the stuffy drawing room of her family's rented London town house. She remembered the first time he'd kissed her—at the wedding breakfast.

She remembered the first time she'd told him she loved him, and his response, "What does marriage have to do with love?"

She'd been shocked to realize he didn't love her, but then why should she have been? He'd never said as much, never acted like a man in love. But she couldn't help feeling deceived. He'd made her love him with his wit and charm, and though he must have known her feelings, he never did anything to discourage her.

And now, after all of that, he said he needed her. She should think it all the most wonderful turn of events. But there was one small point that bothered her. "And yet, you did not rescue me."

"Bloody hell. What do you want from me? If I spirited you away, how many countless others would die? I cannot let my feelings interfere with my work. Too many people are counting on me."

"*I* was counting on you!"

"Do you think it was easy for me to allow myself to be captured? To watch Foncé walk out of that room with you and not know if I would ever see you again? To pray to God and all that is holy I was not hurt so badly that he carved you up before I had a chance to tell you, just this once, what you mean to me?"

Elinor shook her head. Why was he saying this? Was it another lie? To what purpose? "I don't understand," she finally answered.

"Neither do I." And he pulled her hard against his chest and crushed his mouth to hers. At first Elinor could not move, and she wanted to fight him. She wanted to reject him for all the times he'd turned away from her. But Winn was holding her too close and too tightly, and she had no choice but to succumb. Gradually he relaxed his hold slightly, cradling her head with one hand and cupping her cheek with the other. His kiss gentled, became something sweet and poignant. Unable to resist, and feeling the old rush of excitement at his touch flooding through her, she opened herself to him. The cellar and Foncé and her escape plans faded away for the moment, and there was only Winn. Winn surrounded and enveloped her, and she had no fears, because she knew he would take care of her.

He trailed kisses over her eyes and her cheeks, touching his lips lightly to her temple. "Ellie, Ellie."

I love you, she thought. *Damn it! After everything, I still love you.*

But she did not say it. She would never say it again.

"I know what you are going to say," Winn murmured.

She raised a brow. That was good, because she had no idea.

"We need to think about escape."

She hadn't been about to say that, but it seemed like what she should have been thinking of saying. She nodded.

"While I like your tower, and I am always a proponent of unconventional methods, I do not think it our best strategy in this situation." He bent and lifted a shard of broken wood lying on the ground.

"And what is our best strategy?" she asked, relieved he was finally willing to discuss escape options.

"Let me show you."

❦

Winn believed in a straightforward approach whenever possible. As he had told Elinor, he was not averse to the unconventional. He was known for his unconventional methods, though what one man considered unconventional, another considered direct and efficient. That was the case today. Conventional wisdom said to find a back door exit, but the most efficient path—unfortunately also the most lethal—pointed him toward another approach, an approach Foncé and his men would least expect. And it was a hell of a lot better than spending a quarter hour making a crate tower only to discover there was no way to exit the cellar.

Winn knew of one certain exit—the one at the top of the cellar stairs.

Elinor was looking at him expectantly, her cheeks pink and her hair loose and tangled about her face. There was a smudge of dirt beside one eyebrow, and he itched to wipe it away. She looked more beautiful than he could remember. Scenes of her throughout their lives together flashed before him—the light behind her at the altar of the church where they'd married, her softly rounded belly when she was carrying Georgiana, the way she'd looked down at Caroline and crooned to her softly in the middle of the night when she did not know he watched.

She'd always been beautiful—this woman, this wife, this mother. It was he who had not taken the time to notice or appreciate it. She had been right about that at least. But he'd never known she blamed herself. If he could only go back, he would have done it all differently. He would have loved her as she deserved to be loved.

But he could only go forward, and he might have hurt her too badly ever to win her back. His gut twisted in knots when he even thought it, thought he might be too late to save their marriage.

But he could still save their lives. He took her arm and steered her toward the wooden stairs leading out of the cellar. Slats were missing, and the wood was so warped it listed to one side, but it had survived the weight of that hulk of a man carrying him down here, so Winn felt fairly certain it would support the two of them. "We walk up those stairs, ram the door, and face Foncé's men directly."

She stared at him.

He raised his brows. "Well?"

"I thought you were hoaxing me."

Winn scowled.

"That is your solution?" Elinor asked, glaring at him.

"What is wrong with it? We have the element of surprise in our favor."

"What is wrong with it? For one"—she lifted a finger—"we are outnumbered."

Winn waved his hand. "I am not going to discuss this with you. I'm the operative, and I say we are going up the stairs."

"Secondly," she said, tugging his shoulder before he could start up the steps. "The door is locked. I already tried it."

He frowned at her. "I'm not worried about a locked door." He started up the stairs again, but she pulled him back.

"Very well, you may be strong, but you cannot fight all of them. Foncé has at least five guards here."

Why was he even listening to her? He had the experience, not she. Of course, every point she made was valid, but what concerned him more than dealing with whatever lay on the other side of that door was waiting for Foncé to decide he was ready to deal with Winn. "Not every guard is in front of that door. It's early. Some are sleeping."

"But all of them have weapons. You are unarmed."

"It's never stopped me before. And I have this." He raised the wooden section of board.

She reached for him, another attempt to delay him, but he grabbed her hand, kissed it, and placed it by her side. "I'm going, Elinor. Trust me on this."

He was halfway up the steps when he heard her mutter, "Do I have a choice?"

But she came after him. She followed him up the stairs and stood a few steps below him while he studied the door. She'd told him it was locked, but he tried it anyway. He didn't relish battering the door and making all of that noise unless it was necessary. It must have been latched on the other side, because he could not open it.

"I told you," she muttered.

He ignored her and pushed against the door. One thing was certain. There was not a bar across the door, and that meant he could probably hit it hard enough to break the latch. "I'm going to break it down," he said, his voice hushed. He had to lean close to her so she could hear, and he could smell the floral scent in her hair. "Stay close to me. I don't know what we'll find on the other side. Step down one more. Give me some room."

She did as he bade her, and then he felt her tug on his shoulder again. "Elinor." He all but growled her name, but when he turned to her, she reached up, took his face between her hands, and kissed him.

He was so taken off guard, he didn't even have time to kiss her back before she pulled away. "What was that for?"

She looked sheepish. "It might be my last chance."

"Don't count on it." He grinned. He turned back around, rolled his shoulders, took a breath, and slammed into the door. The wood splintered loudly and parted, but the door didn't whoosh open. On the other side, Winn looked into the wide eyes of one of Foncé's men. The man raised a pistol, and Winn ducked. The wood above him splintered, raining down on him like oak needles. Winn jumped up, cursed, and kicked the door hard. The tactic was loud but effective. The door came off its hinges—the bloody latch still didn't budge—and Winn jumped into a room that looked like it had been designed for use by servants bringing food from the kitchen to the main floors of the house.

As soon as Foncé's man saw Winn come through the door, he ran for the exit, but Winn scrambled after him, cutting his own leg on a slab of sharp wood at the bottom of the broken door. Winn tackled the man just as he reached the door, wincing at the pain in his leg. Fortunately, they were in the back of the house, and it would take Foncé's men a moment to reach them. The fewer men to fight, the better.

"Winn!" Elinor's voice snagged his attention, and the guard rolled and slammed his pistol into Winn's cheek. Winn's vision went slightly gray, and he dropped the jagged board he'd planned to use as a weapon. With his fists his only option, he wrapped one hand around the man's wrist and grabbed his scraggly brown hair with the other and rammed the man's head against the floor.

The useless pistol fell to the floor, but the guard wrestled one hand under Winn's chin and shoved Winn's head up. Winn looked over his shoulder at Elinor, who stood in mute horror in front of the battered cellar door. "I could use some help," he said, jaw tight.

Her brows came together, and then she blinked.

"Oh! Of course. What should I...?" She looked about and then reached for a lamp. Winn could only pray she would hit Foncé's guard and not him. She started for him, and Winn released the man so the momentum of their wrestling bodies propelled them over. He hit a table, but the guard was on top. He couldn't give Elinor a better target. "Now," he yelled. The guard drew a fist back. "Now!"

The lamp shattered over the guard's head, and the man went limp. Winn threw him off, sat, and dusted porcelain debris from his clothing. He glared at Elinor, who was staring with what appeared to be concern at the guard.

"He's fine," Winn said. "You waited long enough to hit him."

"I wasn't certain where to hit him."

"A moment more, and I might be the one unconscious."

"So now what?" she asked.

He rose to his feet. "Now we escape." He reached for the door, his hand pausing on the handle when he heard the sound of approaching voices.

"Oh, no," Elinor moaned.

Winn couldn't have said it better.

Thirteen

SOPHIA LAY IN BED, UNABLE TO SLEEP. IT WASN'T Adrian's soft snores keeping her awake, and it wasn't worries and wondering about what was going on inside her body that kept her awake. Not tonight.

Rather, not this early morning. She peered at the bracket clock on her bedside table. In the dim glow of the hearth fire, she could just make out the hands. Half-past three. So much for the additional rest the doctor had prescribed her. She closed her eyes, snuggled closer to Adrian, who put an arm around her in his sleep, and tried to relax.

But something was not right. She had missed… something. Her eyes opened again. Something about the Maîtriser group. Something about Foncé. But what? *What?*

Adrian had told her Baron had been taken by Foncé. The operative had known he would be captured. Adrian and Blue had tried to track Foncé, but he'd proved too elusive. This was also to be expected. Baron had devised the plan, because being taken captive and imprisoned at Foncé's headquarters was the only way to know where the madman was hiding.

But Sophia didn't believe that. Not entirely. Baron wanted to protect his wife. He had to know the chances he would escape Foncé's lair were minuscule. But he was unwilling to desert his wife.

Sophia sighed. That was love. That was romance.

She snuggled into Adrian's warm embrace and closed her eyes again. "Love!" she gasped and sat up.

"Wha—?" Adrian tried to pull her back, but she resisted.

"That's it." She climbed out of bed, lit a taper, and stumbled to her desk. She rifled through the papers, turning them over and trying to read them in the dim light.

"Do I want to know what you are doing?" Adrian mumbled from the bed.

"It has to do with Foncé."

"It cannot wait until morning?"

"This is it!" She held a piece of parchment aloft.

"Dear God."

She carried the paper to the bed, where Adrian had buried his head in his pillow.

"Look at this. It's a report from several years ago by one of our operatives who was tracking Foncé."

Adrian lifted his head. "This is about the Maîtriser group? Who was the operative?"

"Ah…" She scanned the parchment. "Poseidon."

"He's dead. Foncé must have spotted him."

"Yes, but not before Poseidon filed this report."

Adrian took the paper, squinted, and scanned it. "We've been to all of these locations. Foncé is not headquartered there. Baron and Melbourne checked them all again when Lady Keating was taken. Nothing."

"That's because Melbourne and Baron had only the locations listed investigated."

Adrian gave her a look, the look that said if this was one of her intuitive deductions, he was going to hit her with a pillow. "How are we to investigate locations not listed? That would include the whole of London."

"No, it would not. We need only determine where Foncé's mistress resides."

Adrian shook his head. "He has no mistress. There have been no reports of one." He held up a hand. "No recent reports. Yes, I've read Poseidon's entry. I know at that time Foncé was seen with a woman presumed to be his mistress. But that was several years ago."

"And several years have passed in which Foncé was headquartered outside London."

"Exactly."

"Yes, exactly!"

He gave her that look again, and she almost laughed. Almost, because Adrian was exceedingly grouchy when he was tired and had little to no sense of humor at those times. "Where would Foncé go when he returns, a hunted man, in need of a place to hide and formulate a plan?"

"I suppose you are going to enlighten me at some point this evening."

"To his former mistress's home."

"And you know this because...?"

"Because it makes sense! He would go somewhere familiar, somewhere comfortable. He cannot return to the house where we found him, so where is the next most logical—?" She pointed to him. "Logic, see? I'm using logic."

Adrian looked unimpressed.

"—so where is the next most logical location? Voilà!" She spread her arms for emphasis.

"This is a hunch," Adrian said, voice dark.

"It's based on logic, though."

"But you have no proof."

"I cannot sleep, because I keep thinking about it. That's proof."

He frowned. "I thought your nose itched when you had a hunch."

She shrugged. "Perhaps now that my body is changing with the pregnancy, I have sleeplessness rather than an itchy nose. Adrian, you must admit this is, at minimum, an avenue to explore."

"Fine." He pushed the covers back and stood. She took a moment to admire his nakedness—the long, lean torso, the muscled back and legs. "Where is this house?"

Sophia studied the parchment, willing that small detail to suddenly appear.

"Sophia?"

"I don't know. Poseidon does not say, but he gives the name of the mistress. We can determine where she lived during that period, surely."

Adrian ran a hand through his hair. "You know what that will require?"

"Yes, and if I'm correct, it is quite worth the inconvenience. Baron needs us. It may already be too late."

"No. Foncé will wait until morning. He'll want to be well rested before he goes to work."

Sophia shuddered. She did not like to think of

Foncé and his tools. "If it's any help to you," she said, watching Adrian dress. He moved with what she thought might be termed resignation. "I plan to go to Melbourne's residence with you."

"No." Adrian's answer was quick and definitive. "You're staying here. You are to rest."

"I feel fine. I'm not going to faint again, and I want to be a part of this."

"No. I can handle Melbourne's annoyance and this search."

"I know you can." She went to him, put her arms around him, placing her cheek against his bare chest. "But I can handle it too. And, Adrian," she said when he began to protest again. "One way or another, I will have a part."

He sighed. "I *knew* you were going to say that."

❧

Elinor grasped the first thing within reach, which happened to be a large book. It would probably not deter Foncé or his men for very long, but it might give Winn and her the chance they needed to escape. She scanned the parlor. Not that escape from this room was possible. There was a small window, but the glass was thick and would be difficult to break. And even if they managed it, she did not think either of them could fit through it.

"Stand back," Winn said, pushing her behind him. She was still angry at him, still exceedingly annoyed that he had never planned to rescue her, but at least he was making some effort now. At the end. When their cause was lost. "Stay behind me and be ready to run."

She let out an exasperated puff of air. "I'm not going to run. I'm going to stay and fight."

He gave her an incredulous look. "With what? A novel? Darling, I regret to inform you that the poets have it wrong. The pen is not truly mightier than the sword."

"And what do you have?" she countered. "Not even a novel!"

"I have my fists and years of training."

The footsteps stopped before the door, and the voices quieted. Winn pushed her back, keeping his hand on her arm. Elinor said a silent prayer, grateful for Winn's touch. The door burst open, and two men stormed inside. Winn didn't move—so much for his training—but Elinor hefted her book at the younger of the two men, hitting him squarely in the forehead.

"Ow! Bloody hell!" He put a palm to his forehead and winced in pain.

"You might have done better to introduce yourself," a petite woman with dark brown hair said from the doorway. "She doesn't know you are on her side." The woman wore a pink day gown, gloves, and a pretty straw hat. Instead of a reticule, she carried a sharp-looking dagger. She curtsied prettily. "I thought this just the thing for a morning call."

Elinor shook her head. Where was Foncé? Who were these people?

"How'd you find us?" Winn asked.

The man she'd hit in the head waved his thumb at the woman. "Saint had a hunch. Bloody hell but that hurt."

"I'm sorry?" Elinor said tentatively. She was beginning to realize these were not Foncé's men at all.

"And you got Foncé?" Winn asked.

The older man shook his head. "I have a couple of agents searching the house, but I think it safe to say he fled. Probably had a lookout and a back exit."

Winn gestured to the guard on the floor. "This one didn't heed the warning."

"Oh, good!" the woman said, bending to take a closer look at the man. "He might come in useful. That's quite a bump." She looked at Elinor and nodded toward the lump on the guard's head. "Your work, I presume?"

"Yes."

"I recognize your signature style." The woman gave a sympathetic look toward the man Elinor had hit with the book. Elinor thought the woman must be having some fun at her expense, but she could not be certain. "You must think us all terribly rude." The woman stood and held out a hand. "I am Sophia Galloway, Lady Smythe. The man you hit with that rather large novel is my husband, Viscount Smythe. And this distinguished gentleman glaring at me because I am breeching etiquette by introducing myself is Lord Melbourne."

"They are members of the Barbican group," Winn added, "and better known as Wolf"—he pointed to the man with a rather large welt forming on his forehead—"Saint"—he pointed to the woman—"and my superior."

"I see. I must say I am pleased to find at least someone within your ranks had a plan to rescue us."

Melbourne laughed. "You should direct all your thanks to Lady Smythe. Baron, I am certain you would like nothing better than to escort your wife home, but I cannot let you do so until we two have had a lengthy discussion. I want to know everything."

Something crashed on one of the floors above them, and Elinor jumped.

"Do not concern yourself," Melbourne told her. "Those are my men. We are searching for anything Foncé might have left behind, especially regarding the plot against the regent."

Elinor inhaled sharply. "That's true? I don't understand why anyone would want to murder the Prince of Wales."

The older man gave her a long, direct look. "The Maîtriser group is one we've been trying to quash for quite some time now. They deal in blackmail and extortion, but I've long believed they had more sinister practices as well. I believe they are in league with Napoleon Bonaparte."

"But he's in prison now."

"And who put him there?" Winn asked. "He's escaped once before. All he needs is another opportunity."

"And what better opportunity than if England is in turmoil because our future King and regent has been assassinated," Elinor said slowly.

Melbourne and Winn exchanged a look, but Elinor could hardly wonder over the meaning behind their shared glance.

It was true. There *was* a plot to kill Prinny. It had not been some elaborate ruse planned by Winn to impress or frighten her. She glanced at him. She'd believed he was a spy, but seeing him now, in that capacity, drove the meaning home. Did he do this sort of thing all the time? Break into buildings, fight with armed men, work side by side with beautiful women?

Elinor glanced at Lady Smythe again, not certain

why she was suddenly feeling jealous. Elinor supposed it was because she had not known women could serve any function above organizing a household, bearing children, or warming her husband's bed. Lady Smythe was married, but that meant nothing these days. How could a man like Winn resist a woman like this Saint? She was beautiful and had an air of intrigue about her.

"Would you like to send your wife home and report to my offices?" Melbourne was asking Winn.

"No," Elinor said suddenly. Her voice was a bit louder than she intended, and everyone's attention focused on her. "What I mean to say is, I want to help. I don't want to go home. I'm part of this now."

"Oh, no. That is out of the question," Winn said.

But Elinor was not going to back down now. Yes, she could admit she'd been terrified for part of this ordeal, that there had been a moment when she wanted to give up, but she was also willing to admit, if only to herself, that she'd also been elated. For the first time in years—perhaps in forever—she had been part of something exciting, something dangerous, something important. She had planned hundreds of balls and fetes and soirees, but she derived no true pleasure from such undertakings. The tasks were her duty as the wife of a baron of the *ton*.

But right now, her heart was pounding against her ribs, her vision was clear, and her entire body felt alive. She had never felt so alive before. She would not give it up so easily.

"Actually," Melbourne said, "I would not mind hearing your wife's account. She may be able to add something useful. After all, she did spend several hours with Foncé before we located her."

"Well, that's settled then," Elinor said.

"No, it's not." Winn took her elbow and steered her toward a corner of the room. It was a small room, and his action did little more than give the illusion of privacy. "I do not want you involved in this. In fact, I want you to go home, pack your valise, and go to my mother's."

"No."

He blinked at her, and she realized this might very well be the first time she had blatantly defied him. "Excuse me?"

"No. I want to help you find Foncé. I want to help protect the prince."

"Elinor, you are not trained in this sort of work. You would only endanger yourself—"

"Actually," Lady Smythe said from across the room where she was making no pretense of not listening, unlike her husband and Melbourne, "we use civilians all the time. Think of our informants and those we pay to ferret out information."

"This is hardly the same thing," Winn said, and Elinor thought his jaw might have been clenched rather tightly.

"Sophia, stay out of it," Lord Smythe said.

"The situation is not exactly the same," Lady Smythe added, obviously ignoring her husband's injunction, "but I think Lady Keating might be of use to us."

"She is my wife. I am not going to use her in that manner."

Elinor opened her mouth to point out that he had used her abduction to locate Foncé just the night before, but Winn raised a finger. "Do not say it. Now, you are to go home, pack your things, and leave Town."

"Is this because she is a woman, or is this because

you truly do not see how she would be beneficial?" Lady Smythe asked. Elinor could not help but stare at her. She did not seem to care one whit that both her husband and Winn were glaring at her. She stood, twirling her dagger in some fancy dance across her fingers and looking as pretty as a debutante at her first garden party. "Because any day you want to test your skills against mine, Baron, I'm open to the challenge."

Elinor barely had time to flinch, much less scream, before the dagger flew across the room. She whirled about and saw it had wedged itself directly in the center of the nose of the man in the portrait opposite.

Winn did not even turn and look. He might have fooled the others into thinking he was unimpressed, but she could see his fingers flexing. That was a sign he had taken note of Lady Smythe's agility with the dagger. "This is not about you, Lady Smythe. This is a domestic issue."

"Really? Well, tell that to Foncé, because he seemed to think he had every right to abduct your wife."

"Sophia, perhaps we might assist with the search," Lord Smythe said, taking her arm and leading her from the room.

Elinor prepared for another argument with Winn, but Melbourne spoke first. "Saint has a point, Baron. Sending her away will not protect her. The only thing that will do that is capturing Foncé."

"Are you suggesting I involve my wife further in this mission?" Winn asked.

"I'm not suggesting it, old boy. I'm ordering it."

Fourteen

WINN DID NOT UNDERSTAND WHAT HAD HAPPENED. When had women become spies? And when had they taken over the Barbican group? He'd never even seen a woman step through its doors before, and now there were two women in Melbourne's office, and they were wreaking havoc. Wolf did not look as though he shared Winn's opinion. He was watching Saint and smiling. "What are you smiling about?" Winn asked.

Wolf laughed. "It was a shock to me at first, but you'll become used to the idea."

"What idea?" Winn was appalled. "My wife is not going to become a spy."

Wolf shrugged. "Too bad. She'd make a damn fine one."

Winn could not argue with that. He'd always admired her efficiency and eye for detail. He'd watched her organize a lavish ball in three days flat. She could coordinate food, invitations, decoration, and musicians all at once and make it look easy.

But this was not a ball. This was serious. The Maîtriser group was a threat to the sovereignty of the nation, not a social event. "The problem," Winn said, interrupting whatever the women were prattling on about, "is now that Foncé has relocated, we are back to where we started. Not to mention, I was not able to gather any intelligence regarding the plot to assassinate the prince regent. I'm afraid His Highness is still in grave danger."

"Well, fortunately, as I was saying before you interrupted, I was able to gather intelligence on the plot," Saint said.

"The *assassination* plot?" Winn asked incredulously. "I don't think so."

Wolf leaned closer. "Would you like me to hand you a shovel? That hole you are digging grows rather large."

"I think Lord Melbourne can be the judge of that." Saint opened the beaded scrap of fabric dangling from her wrist and pulled out two sheets of parchment. She unfolded them, smoothed them, and handed them to Melbourne.

Melbourne, who was leaning back in his chair and sipping brandy, took the papers and perused them. Winn had to resist the urge to snatch them out of Melbourne's hand. Melbourne looked up at him, almost as though he'd read Winn's mind. "Interesting reading. Where did you find this?"

Sophia smiled. "Adrian and I rifled one of the bedrooms. Those were in the desk."

Winn scowled. He'd never even had a chance to search the house.

"The plans are not specific as to time and place," Melbourne said, "but they do contain coded references. I'll have one of our ciphers take a look."

"I've already deciphered it," Saint said, handing

Melbourne a sheet of foolscap. "It lists names of agents working for the Maîtriser group."

"If those agents are mentioned in the plans," Elinor said, "they must be in London. Finding one of them might be the key to finding Foncé."

Of course it was, Winn thought, still scowling. But it was annoying to have his wife think of the idea. She was *not* going to become a spy.

"Good point," Melbourne said. Winn wanted to roll his eyes. Damn the secretary for encouraging her. "I'll have some of our agents start canvassing the area. Unfortunately, most of our men are abroad."

Winn was relieved to hear the secretary say *men*. He did not think he could have tolerated more women in the group.

"You four—"

"Three," Winn interjected. Elinor gave him an annoyed glance.

But Melbourne continued unperturbed. "—will have to investigate as well. And that's not all."

"Bodyguards," Wolf said, even as Winn thought it. Were they now going to be reduced to acting as the prince's bodyguards?

"I'll speak to His Royal Highness," Melbourne said, "but you know how he is. He will be initially terrified and amenable to staying out of the public eye."

"And then he'll grow bored," Saint added, "and want to venture out. I think this is an area where Lady Keating and I could prove even more useful."

"How is that?" Elinor asked.

"No one will suspect two women as part of the prince's entourage. I can protect him while Lady

Keating watches for anyone or anything suspicious. If the Maîtriser group thinks the prince is unprotected, it might make Foncé's men bolder. And if they act, I can intercept them."

"Capital idea," Melbourne said.

Winn clenched his hands around the arms of the chair. It was not capital, not at all. What Saint had not said explicitly was that everyone would think Lady Smythe and Lady Keating were the prince's mistresses. Winn glanced at Wolf, who seemed to find the whole situation... if not amusing, not distressing. But Winn did not want his wife associated with the prince and the man's lascivious tastes.

"All of you should go home and rest," Melbourne directed. "I'll send for you later and let you know my plan."

Wolf and Saint rose to depart, but Winn hesitated. Elinor did as well, clearly waiting to hear what Winn had to say. Fine, let her hear it.

"My lord," Winn said, "I respect your experience and authority."

Melbourne's brow rose. "Good. Let's keep it that way."

"But I prefer my wife not become involved in this. She is not an agent of the Barbican group. She's my wife and the mother of my children."

"And you think that means I would not make a good agent?" Elinor challenged him, hands on her hips. He glared at her, willing her to silence. He planned to deal with her when they arrived home.

"I'm aware of Lady Keating's identity," Melbourne said, "but I believe she has skills that might serve us well. She managed to incapacitate one of Foncé's men, remained calm and collected in the face of danger, not to mention she escaped Foncé himself. Many of our own cannot make that claim. However, I respect your authority as her husband. If you do not want her involved—"

"How dare you!" Elinor stepped in front of Winn and poked her finger in his chest. "How dare you treat me as though I were a child. I am perfectly capable of making my own decisions. I have done so without you for the last fourteen years. And my decision is that I wish to be a part of this case. I am already involved, and became so the moment Foncé abducted me."

"She has a point there," Melbourne muttered.

Winn gave him a dark look. "We'll discuss this at home," he told Elinor.

"Oh, no we will not." Elinor turned to Melbourne. "I am going to assist, one way or another. If you leave me out, you will be sorry."

Winn grabbed her elbow and pulled her out of the room and into the corridor. The Smythes were not to be seen, and Winn thanked God for small mercies. "What the devil are you about?" he demanded. "You do not threaten the head of the Barbican group."

"What the devil are *you* about?" she countered. "Who are you to tell me what to do? It's your fault I am involved in this to begin with." She pulled away from him and marched ahead.

"And I'm ending your involvement right now!" he called after her.

"Go ahead and try!" She hailed a hackney cab at the corner, and when Winn went after her, she told the jarvey to drive on. Winn had to flag his own hackney down, and he did so fuming. She wasn't going to escape him long. He would show her he was not so easy to dismiss.

When Winn arrived home, Bramson took his coat and informed him Lady Keating had also just arrived. "I know," Winn snapped. He knew he should take the time to reassure the servant that the baroness was well and unharmed, but he was in no mood to deal with anyone. "Where is she?"

"I believe she retired to her bedchamber, my lord."

"Good." He took the steps two at a time, marched down the corridor to his room. He entered, tossed his cravat on the bed, and went to the adjoining door. It was locked.

Fury engulfed him, and he gritted his teeth. He was not going to knock on his own door in his own house. She had never locked him out before, and she was not going to start today. Winn raised one booted foot and smashed it into the door. The door splintered but held.

"I see you do not require my assistance at the moment, my lord," his valet said from the doorway.

"No, I do not," Winn said, stepping back and preparing to kick the door again.

"I might have a key for that door," the valet offered.

Winn considered. "Thank you, but I prefer this approach." He took a final step back, raised his leg, and kicked the door in. He stormed in and stared at an empty room. And then he heard a woman's voice and started for Elinor's dressing room. The door was closed, but he did not let that stop him. He kicked it open and burst inside. And was greeted with two shrieks.

Elinor sat in a hip tub, her back to him, but her head turned so he could see her wide, startled eyes.

Her maid was kneeling on the floor, holding a wash-cloth and soap.

"What in God's name are you doing?" Elinor demanded.

Winn looked at the maid. "Get out."

The woman rose hastily. "Yes, my lord."

"No! Bridget! Stay!"

It annoyed Winn that the maid hesitated, but he was also pleased to see his wife inspired that much loyalty in the servants. It explained why they rarely had to hire new help and why Society never buzzed with rumors about them. The maid glanced up at him, and Winn raised a brow. "I imagine you have something to press or sew, Bridget."

"Yes, my lord." The maid bobbed.

"Her ladyship will send for you when we have finished our conversation."

"Yes, my lord. I am sorry, my lady." And the maid rushed from the room. Winn waited until he heard the outer door close, and then he folded his arms. He had her exactly where he wanted her. Her knees were pulled up to her chest, the wet chemise revealing the pale skin of her legs. She had her arms crossed over her chest, but Winn could imagine the way the wet material would cling and mold to her skin there too.

Suddenly, he was not so angry.

"Not so easy to escape me now, is it?"

"I was not trying to evade you. I simply did not wish to continue our conversation." She shifted, leaning down and wrapping her arms about her knees. "If your intent is to come in here and dictate what I can and cannot do, then you might as well leave."

Oh, he was not leaving. Not now. Not until he had her stripped bare.

"Why is it so unpleasant to obey my orders? You might find it pleasurable. If you were willing to try it."

Her eyes narrowed. "Are we speaking of the Barbican group?"

He approached the tub and held a hand out. "Stand up, and we shall see."

"No." She shook her head. "I don't want this."

"You're my wife. You do not have a choice."

Her brows lowered in annoyance. Winn was annoyed himself. What was wrong with him today? Even if the law dictated she was his property, reminding her of her subordinate status was not the best approach.

"Do you intend to rape me then? Is that why you came in here?"

"No." Didn't she know him any better than that? Or did she know him just well enough to realize how much that barb would sting? "Although I must admit I am on unfamiliar ground. You have never refused me before."

"Accustom yourself to it." Her voice shook slightly, and he realized she was probably getting chilled in the cooling water. And still, she'd rather sit in cold water and shiver than step into his arms. The idea would have deflated the ego of another man. Her reaction didn't exactly speak to his prowess as a lover. So perhaps he would have to show her he was preferable to chattering teeth and shivering flesh.

"Or perhaps I might persuade you to try things my way."

She shook her head. For the first time, Winn began to feel that perhaps he was not going to be able to earn her love again. Perhaps his efforts were futile. But he wasn't ready to give up yet. He had to try. "Just this once. If you don't like what I'm doing, you may stop me at any time."

"Really? You will stop?"

"Test me." But she wasn't going to want him to stop.

"Fine. Hand me that robe." She stood, and though she crossed her arms over her chest, she could not hide everything at once, and the material clung to her rounded hips and thighs. Winn felt his throat go dry. The last thing he wanted to do was hand her a robe, but she was shivering, and he didn't want her to catch cold either.

He handed her the robe and watched her shrug it on, then step out of the tub and disappear behind a screen. A moment later, the wet chemise appeared over the edge of the screen, and Elinor emerged, brushing her hair over one shoulder.

"Come here," he said, holding a hand out. It was extremely hard to be patient, knowing she was naked beneath that flimsy robe. Knowing one tug of the knot at her waist would bare all of her to him.

"Has the test begun then?"

"Come here."

"What if I do not like the way you order me about?"

He smiled, masking his annoyance. He had been trained in the art of patience and endurance. He could wait her out. "Why don't you come here? You might like what I order you to do."

Her face flushed, and if he was not mistaken, her chest rose and fell just a little quicker. She still wanted him. Now he had to show her that her desire would be rewarded. In the back of his mind, he was aware this had begun as a way to force her to give up the

Barbican group. But at some point he had forgotten that goal. Perhaps it was when he'd seen she was in the bath. Perhaps it was when she'd stood.

All Winn knew was at that moment he didn't care one farthing whether she became a spy or not. He wanted her naked beneath him. Or on top of him. And she thought he wasn't adaptable.

She took one step and then another, and Winn took one himself to meet her in the middle. The bed, and his goal, were in the next room, but he would find his way there. In the meantime, he saw a sturdy dressing table he might make use of.

Winn put an arm around her waist and drew her close. She smelled of the soap she'd been using, something clean and sweet and not too heavy. That was Elinor. She never overpowered.

For once, Winn thought he might like to be overpowered.

But that was not for today.

"Do you know why I was so angry at the Ramsgates' ball?" he murmured, stroking a finger over one warm cheek and down the curve of her jaw.

"Because you are unreasonable?"

He laughed. Had she always been this amusing? "Try again."

"Because I was dancing with that boy?"

She'd called the puppy a *boy*, and he liked her all the more. "No, though I wasn't pleased to see his hands on you." He slid one hand down her neck to her collarbone.

"His hands were not on me." She began to pull away, but he held her.

"I was angry at myself."

He could tell from the arch of her brows she did not believe him.

"It's true. I was late, and I disappointed you again." It couldn't have been helped, but he did not add that now. Instead, he walked his fingers down to the V of her robe.

"I didn't think you cared."

"I do. I may not show it, but I hate disappointing you."

"Then don't," she whispered as his fingers parted the material of her robe slowly.

"Oh, I won't. But that was not the only reason I was angry."

"No?" Her breath was fast now as he slid the silk slowly over the pink skin of her breasts, baring them.

"No, it was because I had forgotten, until that moment, how utterly ravishing you are."

"No, I'm—"

He lowered his mouth to her nipple, and her voice ended in a choked moan. He sucked gently, pulling back to tease the hard nub with his tongue. "Yes, you are. I cannot keep my hands off you. I can hardly stop myself from taking you right now."

"Then don't."

This was the Elinor he knew. This was the Elinor who always wanted him. Always complied with all of his wishes. But he did not want compliance now. He wanted heat and passion and a glimpse of the woman he saw when she defied him.

"Drop your robe."

"I…"

"I want to see you. Touch you. Everywhere."

She hesitated, lifting her hands but not moving to comply. He'd never made this request before. He'd never wanted to make her uncomfortable. Of course, he'd seen her without clothing, but never like this, never watched her disrobe for him.

Her hands hovered near the slit in the material, and he waited. He was very good at waiting. He'd had years to perfect his skills, but waiting for her to take off the robe rather than ripping it off her himself was the hardest thing he'd ever done.

Finally, after what felt like months of torture, she allowed the material to slide off her shoulders, down her hips, along her legs, and puddle in a heap on the floor. Winn swallowed. He had been a fool. All of this sensuousness had been his, and he had virtually ignored it. Ignored her.

That would end now. "I do not deserve you," he whispered.

"Should we go to the bed?"

He could see her hands starting to come up, and knew she was feeling self-conscious. "Not yet. As I said, I want to touch you." He put his hands on her ribs, just below the swell of her breasts. "Everywhere." He slid his hands down, over the curve of her hips, then cupped her bottom. His fingers itched to delve inside her, to see if she was as hot and wet as he suspected, but he resisted. Instead, he lowered his mouth to hers and kissed her softly, nibbling at the corner of her lips. She smiled, and he could feel her body relax. He kissed a light path across her cheeks to her ear. He breathed into it and felt her shiver. "I'm going to make you tremble with pleasure," he whispered. "I want to hear you call my name."

She opened her mouth, but he put a finger over it to

silence her. If she invited him to take her now, he did not
know if he could resist. Her tongue darted out to tease
the pad of his finger, and he felt himself go rock hard.
Patience would be more difficult than he anticipated.

Gritting his teeth for control, Winn withdrew his
finger and dragged it over her lip, down the slight
point of her chin to the silky skin of her neck. With
so much of her bare skin to explore, he really needed
to make use of both hands.

And his mouth.

He followed the path of his finger with his mouth,
kissing the hollow of her neck and flicking his tongue out
to tease her flesh, which was already pebbling with antici-
pation. He tasted her shoulder and the inside of her elbow
before settling where he really wanted—her ample breasts.

He could still remember when they had first married.
She'd had small, pert breasts that fit in the palm of his
hand. After the birth of two children, they were not so
pert, but they more than filled his hand, and they had a
satisfying heaviness he found irresistible. He found one
erect nipple and teased it with his tongue. Ellie writhed
against him, her breath coming short. "Winn, please."

He smiled, intent on continuing the torture.

She tasted clean, of bathwater and silk, but underneath that, he could taste her—Elinor. It was a taste he
would never forget. It was a taste he had not sampled
in far too long.

Winn fitted his hands around her waist and lifted her.
She immediately wrapped her legs about him, and he
kissed her lips to keep her from exploring with them.
She had never been what one might call an adventurous
lover, but over the years she had certainly learned

where to touch him and what sensations pleased him. He had to hold her at bay for just a little longer.

He kissed her deeply, drugging her with his mouth upon hers and slowly moving her backward. When he reached the dressing table, he set her on it and continued exploring her mouth with his tongue. He filled her, teased her, nipped, and sucked, and she gasped in response. He'd always been careful not to shock her before—not to offend his wife's delicate sensibilities. But now he had no such qualms. Something about seeing her in Melbourne's office, seeing her take charge in Foncé's cellar, made him throw away propriety. There was no room for it between them now. He wanted her, and on his own terms.

Reluctantly, he abandoned her mouth and kissed a path down her torso. She arched back for him, and he paused to tease her breasts again, but he did not linger. When he kissed her abdomen, she tried to sit forward.

"What are you—?"

"Shh. Let me kiss you."

She continued to struggle. "You said you would cease if I did not like something. I do not want you to kiss me there."

Winn rested his hands on her thighs, stroking small circles with his thumbs. He felt her muscles tense. "What is it?"

She put her hands over her belly. "I don't want you to touch me there."

He frowned. "I want to touch you everywhere."

"Not there. My skin sags, and I have the scars from pregnancy."

He looked down at her rounded stomach, ripe and

sensual in his opinion. Yes, he could see the faint marks where her skin had stretched with her two pregnancies, but he did not find them distasteful at all. "These?" He traced a hand over one of the faded marks.

"Don't." She caught his hand. "They are ugly."

"Nothing about you is ugly. In particular, the badges you wear from carrying my children are not ugly. I find you beautiful."

She looked at him as though she did not know him, and perhaps she did not. "Winn." She shook her head in disbelief.

"Women should be round and soft. I liked your body when we first married, but I love your body now. I cannot resist you." Gently, he lifted her hands from her belly and kissed the soft flesh there.

"Winn…" But her protests were dying away. He flicked his tongue out, teasing her skin and kissing every one of her scars. He remembered wanting to kiss her distended abdomen when she was with child, but she had kept it hidden from him, and he, not wanting to hurt the child within her, had abstained from his marriage rights. Now he wished he had not been so careful and considerate. Now he wished he had seen her swollen with child and kissed every angry red mark until she was shivering as she was now.

Her breathing had grown rapid again, and he dipped his head lower, kissing the fine light brown hair at the juncture of her thighs. His hands still rested on those thighs, and he moved them inward, teasing her and skittering upward until she was shaking with need. He opened her thighs and knelt before her.

"Winn!" She tried to close her legs, but he was

between them now, and he was determined to taste her here. He knew she must feel exposed. She was seated on the dressing table, and he was kneeling before her. But that was how he wanted her. This was how he wanted to see her. The lamps cast a soft glow, and the light from the open windows of her bedroom added to the illumination. He could see the soft pink of her flesh. How long had it been since he'd gazed on her like this?

Years. He had done this only once before, and that had been shortly after they were married. He had cared about her pleasure then. When had he ceased worrying about it? When had he begun to content himself with assuming she reached fulfillment? He would never assume again. He wanted to feel her climax. He wanted to hear her moaning his name.

Winn bent, kissed the velvet skin of her inner thigh, and then tasted her.

&c&o

Elinor bucked in shock. She knew what Winn was doing. She remembered being mortified when he'd done this years ago, but also climaxing harder and faster than she ever had before or since. He'd brought her intermittent pleasure in the years between. Still, she never forgot the touch of his mouth and the lick of his tongue *there*. She had never ceased to crave the sensation again, though she had been too mortified to ask him to do it again. If he but noticed her, she counted herself fortunate.

No longer. She had not asked for this. She was no longer his simpering wife, impossibly in love with him with no hope of requite. She would never be that woman again. If he wanted her now, then she would give herself to him because she was enjoying herself. She would not fall in love with him again.

She looked down at his bent head, his bronze hands on her pale skin, and just then he gazed up at her. His emerald-green eyes were full of mischief and dark with pleasure. He was enjoying this almost as much as she.

Very well, then. She would not fall *very much* in love with him.

And then his tongue flicked out and touched her core, and she really could not think at all. It had been so long since her body had spiraled with pleasure like this, so long since she'd felt the first stirrings of ecstasy. She knew it was wanton, but she could not help but spread her legs farther, and Winn took it as invitation and slid a finger inside her. His tongue continued its assault, battering her with tiny licks and taps until she was moving her hips against Winn's mouth and crying for release. "Yes! Please!"

Elinor did not care about the servants. She did not care that Winn was seeing her lose all control. She only knew she had never felt so utterly close to breaking apart before. She only knew that the greatest pleasure she had known was coming. She was already drunk on pleasure, and she could feel more and more and more mounting.

And then Winn scraped his tongue against her, and she exploded. She cried out, gripping the edges of her dressing table for balance. Her hips bucked, and she rose up, and still Winn did not cease his assault. The world was bright white with pleasure, her body was hot with sensation, and when she peaked, she called his name.

The aftermath left her body warm and sluggish and still thrumming with ecstasy. She was vaguely aware that Winn had scooped her up and carried her into her bedchamber. She was vaguely aware that the drapes were open, and she would have preferred they were closed so her body was not quite so exposed. And, in the midst of the last eddies of pleasure, she was vaguely aware that Winn was undressing. She glanced up, from where she was sprawled on the bed, and saw him pull his shirt over his head.

His body was bruised and battered. Blue, yellow, and green splotches mottled his torso and ribs. She was no stranger to his scars and abrasions. She had seen him bandaged and bloody, but she had always believed him when he claimed to have fallen off a horse. Now, she knew differently. His muscles bunched as he pulled the shirt off, and she thought what a perfect specimen he was, despite the injuries. He was no soft-bellied gentleman of leisure. He was slim and fit and powerfully built.

A shot of arousal pierced her. She did not know where it had come from. How could she want him again? How could her body be warming with desire? She did not think even Winn's skilled touch could make her feel anything more today. But the sight of his hard, bare chest made her mouth go dry. She wanted to touch that skin, drag her teeth over it, rub her sensitive nipples against him.

He reached for the fall of his trousers, and she moaned. She could still feel the last waves of her climax pulsing through her. But when she saw his erection—how hard he was, and all for her—she could not stop herself from reaching for him. But he was faster. He bent and grasped her wrists, pinning them over her head. Elinor knew if she protested he would release her.

She looked into his eyes, into the hot desire she saw there, and had a moment's pause. Would he release her? Did she want him to?

His mouth was on hers again. His bare chest grazed the tips of her breasts, and she gasped with pleasure. His hips settled between her thighs, nudging her open, though he did not enter her. She could feel the tip of him—hard and velvet—poised against her most delicate core, but he seemed in no rush. Once again, he was kissing her senseless. Once again, he was drugging her, making her forget who she was and all the years between them.

Seemingly of their own accord, her legs wrapped around him, urging him closer. She wanted to feel him inside her, filling her, completing her.

"Tell me you want me."

"I want you." She pressed him closer with her legs, raising her hips to meet him.

"Say my name," he murmured in her ear. Elinor gritted her teeth. Would the man not hurry?

"Winn, I want you. *Now.*"

He drove into her, and she gasped at the sudden rush of sensation. His thrust pushed her down into the bed and sent a shock of pleasure swirling through her.

"Are you hurt?" He'd never been so rough with her. Never taken her with so much force before. He was pulling back, but she reached up and grabbed his back, holding him in place. "I hurt you."

"No." She couldn't imagine him hurting her physically. "I like it."

He looked down at her, surprise in those vivid

green eyes. He moved inside her, thrusting deeply. "Do you like this?"

She could hardly speak. "Yes," she breathed.

He moved again, this time slow and languorous, stroking her until her toes were curling and she thought she would die from the mounting pleasure. "*Yes*. Yes. Please." She did not even know what she was asking. She only knew she needed him and only him. "*Winn*."

His hands lifted her hips, bringing her into closer contact and making her moan. He slid in and out, driving harder and faster until she was clenching him so tightly her legs began to ache. But she could not let go. She was so close, so close…

And then he groaned and thrust fast and hard, and she shattered. She bit down on a scream, and though it seemed impossible, she clenched Winn more tightly. The pleasure seemed to go on and on until she was floating, weightless and tingling and sated.

"That's going to leave a mark," Winn said, rolling off of her.

She was vaguely aware he had spoken and did not even open her eyes when he pulled her close, cradling her in his arms. Drowsily, she realized he had never done this before, never shown her tenderness *after* their lovemaking. "Hmm?" she said on a sigh. She was so tired. She knew there was something she wanted to discuss with him, something important, but right now she needed to sleep.

"My shoulder," he was saying. "You bit it when… never mind."

She felt his lips brush against her cheek.

"Sleep now. I'll stay right here beside you."

And she drifted away, safe and warm in his arms.

Fifteen

ELINOR ROLLED OVER TO A COLD, EMPTY BED. SHE opened her eyes and shivered, pulling the counterpane over the bare skin of her shoulders. It was draped around her legs, which meant at some point someone, presumably Winn, had attempted to cover her. But she must have thrown the covers off. And now the room was dark and cold.

And she was alone.

She thought about ringing for Bridget. The girl would not usually have allowed the fire to burn down, but after her dismissal by Winn earlier, poor Bridget was unlikely ever to enter again without an invitation.

Elinor dragged herself up and peered out the window, whose drapes were still open. Winn would not have thought to close them. It was dark now, probably past the dinner hour, judging by the rumbling in her stomach. She heard footsteps patter on the runner outside her room, but knew by the light tread they were not Winn's. Where was he? Had she only dreamed he had said he would stay with her?

But why should she start believing him now? He'd

lied to her for years. And now that she finally knew the truth, he wanted her to forget she'd ever learned it. He wanted her to go back to her mundane life of balls and soirees and music lessons for Caro and Georgiana, and pretend he wasn't living a parallel existence full of mystery and intrigue.

Absolutely not. If he would not give up his position in the Barbican group, why should she not agree to assist if asked? Lord Melbourne had said she might be useful. Lord Melbourne had said she had skills.

No one had ever remarked upon her skills before. Well, that was not strictly true. Mary and Lady Hollingshead both praised her entertaining and organizing skills, but Elinor wanted more than days spent choosing the perfect engraving for an invitation or the best arrangement for a dinner party.

She loved her daughters, but they did not need her as much anymore. Oh, there was much to look forward to—their come-outs, presentation at court, their first Seasons. But what happened after the girls were married? What would she do then?

She rose and moved to close the draperies. Her room was dark, but she did not intend to give a passing footman or gardener even an inadvertent view of her nakedness. But as she loosed one side of the drapes, a movement in the garden below caught her eye. She paused and peered from behind the material.

A man was standing in the garden with a lone figure. The man was facing away from her, but she knew immediately it must be Winn. Winn was so tall and broad shouldered, one could not mistake him. He was dressed in coat, trousers, and boots, so he must

have been up and about for some time. He seemed
to be listening intently to what his companion was
saying. The companion wore a cape with a hood, and
Elinor could not see the man. Why did Winn not
invite him inside and converse in the library?

Or was the other man a spy? But Winn had
said he did not involve his home and family in his
activities for the Barbican group, so the other man
must be—

Elinor's jaw dropped as the hood of the cape fell
back, and she caught a glimpse of the woman's face. It
was not a man at all, but a woman with golden-blond
hair and smooth, porcelain cheeks. The woman was
young, hardly more than a girl, and she looked up at
Winn with undisguised adoration.

Elinor felt her face flush with shame. This could
not be what she thought. But if this woman—this
girl—was not Winn's mistress, who was she? And why
would she come in the dark, in secret?

How could he? How could he leave her bed to
meet with his mistress?

And how could he take a mistress only a few years
older than Georgiana? It made Elinor feel sick and
angry at herself. She was such a fool to ever believe
what had passed between them this afternoon made
any difference. To ever believe that Winn cared for
her as more than the mother of his children and the
woman bearing the title of Lady Keating.

When would she ever learn?

She moved to close the other drapery, and the
movement must have caught the girl's eye. She looked
up, and Winn followed. Elinor allowed the drape to

close, but she could not be certain Winn had not seen her standing there.

And so what if he had? She had not done anything wrong. He was the one conversing with his mistress under his wife's window.

Elinor stalked to her dressing room, performed her usual ablutions, and pulled on a dressing gown. She could not dress without Bridget's help, but before she called her maid, she had best determine her plans.

She would go to Melbourne. That was what she would do. She would offer her services and tell him Winn could go to hell. He might not listen. Technically, she was under Winn's authority, but perhaps Melbourne was more freethinking. After all, Lady Smythe was a spy. Would a man who stood on outdated customs and practices employ a woman as a spy? Elinor did not think so. She walked back into her room, heading for the servant's bell to summon Bridget, when the door opened, and Winn stepped inside.

He had come from the corridor, not his room, which meant he had probably come to her room directly from the garden. Elinor paused with her hand on the bellpull. "What do you want?"

He sighed. "I was afraid of this. It is not what you think."

"Oh, really? So you were not conversing with a beautiful woman under my window just now?"

"Tell me you did not conclude she was my mistress."

Elinor put her hands on her hips. "Why would I assume that? Because it is dark outside and you were meeting her in secret? Because I've never seen her before, which means she must be someone with whom I am not acquainted? Because she was looking up at you adoringly?"

"Ellie—"

"Don't call me that." She pointed a finger at him, mostly because she could tell he was thinking about moving closer to her, and she did not want him to touch her.

"She is not my mistress."

"Then who is she?"

He paused. "I cannot say."

"Of course not." She rolled her eyes. "How silly of me to demand an explanation. I forget you are an all-important spy, and the rules that apply to the rest of us do not apply to you. Very well, then, I shall behave as a good wife and pretend I know nothing. In the meantime, I have a call to make myself."

He frowned. "You're going out?"

"That's right." She reached for the bellpull, but he moved quickly and caught her hand. She snatched her fingers away, loathe to touch him. How quickly her desire for him had evaporated. "Get out of my way. I need Bridget to help me dress."

"I know where you're going, and I forbid it."

Elinor raised her brows in the same manner she did when Caroline attempted to defy her. But Winn was not a twelve-year-old girl, and he did not back down. "You are not to call on Melbourne."

"I see. So working for the Barbican group is acceptable for you but not for me."

"I have training."

"Your own Melbourne said I have skills. I am certain I can be trained, just as you were."

Winn's look grew dark, and he took several steps toward her, until Elinor was forced to back up against the wall. Winn put his hands on either side of her shoulders and bent close. "I'm trying to protect you," he growled in a most unprotective manner.

"I don't want your protection."

"You have it regardless."

Elinor decided to try a new tack. "If the work is so dangerous, then why do you not retire?"

"I have training."

"Yes, I saw the results of your training earlier today." She poked his bruised ribs, and he inhaled quickly. "Your daughters need you as much as they need me. Retire, and I will forget I ever heard of Melbourne or the Barbican group."

Winn shook his head. "I can't do that, Ellie. Not with the Maîtriser group at large and the prince in danger. Perhaps when they have been decimated—"

"Then you will find another mission. No. If you refuse to retire, then I refuse to stay uninvolved. After all, I am involved with the apprehension of Foncé and the Maîtriser group now as well."

Winn's hands fisted beside her head, but Elinor held his stare. She was not afraid of him. Whatever else Winn was—liar, cheat, spy—he was not a man prone to violence. "I'm trying to keep you safe."

"Perhaps I am tired of being kept safe. Perhaps I find it tedious and want some adventure."

"Risking your life is not adventure!"

"Then leave the group."

"I don't want you to be hurt or killed."

"Likewise."

"Damn it!" He slammed his fist against the wall. "I cannot lose you too, Ellie!" The words echoed in the room, and Winn swore again and pushed away from her. But she was finally breaking through, and she was not going to allow him to retreat now.

"What does that mean? Whom did you lose?" She followed him across the room to where he paused in front of the window overlooking the garden. He pulled the draperies aside and stood, much as she had a little while before, and looked down.

"I cannot discuss it."

Elinor was tempted to force the issue by summoning Bridget and dressing to go out, but Winn looked so defeated, so broken. She had never seen him like this. She put a hand on his back. "You can trust me. I will keep your confidence."

"I should not tell you this."

"It will never leave this room, I swear it."

He stared down at the garden for what seemed hours. Elinor held her breath, waiting to see if he would trust her, if he would let her in.

"Crow was my partner. That was his code name— Crow. His real name is—was—Edward, and the woman you saw me speaking to in the garden was his sister."

Elinor did not speak. With her children she had learned that sometimes when one thought a person had said all there was to say, a moment of silence would reveal more.

"We worked together for years. Not all agents work together. Most work alone, but we had complementary skills. We first worked together on a mission in Switzerland in '06. After that, we rarely worked alone."

"You must have become good friends."

"More than that. We were like brothers. We knew all about each other's lives." Winn looked at her. "Though he never met you, he knew all about you and the girls. He used to call you his surrogate family."

"Was he not married?"

"No. His only family was his sister, and she was in a convent school for much of the time I knew him."

"You speak of him as though he is gone. What happened?"

"I killed him."

Elinor started at the vehemence in his voice. But there was something else there too. Hatred? Blame? Self-loathing? "I don't believe you."

He looked at her, his expression unreadable. "I made a mistake that cost Crow his life. It was my error that killed him."

"What happened?"

Winn shook his head. "I can't."

Gently, Elinor pulled him away from the window and took his face in her hands. "Tell me, Winn. You have to tell someone. I can see it's devouring you from the inside out."

"We were in Europe on a termination assignment. It's better if you don't know the particulars."

Elinor nodded, but she had to inquire. "Termination assignment?"

Winn gave her a wry smile. "Believe it or not, I am quite capable of murder when called upon to act in my country's name and best interests. *Termination* is the code for assassination. Our orders were to assassinate..." He cleared his throat. "Someone important.

Very important. Crow and I planned everything meticulously. He would complete the actual termination, and I would smuggle us in and out. But something went wrong that night. The guards' schedule had changed, or perhaps they sensed something was amiss. Nothing went as planned, and we never even managed to come within arm's reach of—this important person. Instead, we ended up fleeing for our lives. I went one way, and Crow went another. I heard the shots, but I had no reason to think he would have been hit. We'd been shot at so many times…"

Elinor took a breath and bit her tongue. How many times had she almost lost Winn? How many times had she been a breath away from becoming a widow?

"He didn't come to the rendezvous. I waited for hours, all night. I went back, though it was dangerous, and looked for him. Finally, I found him."

Elinor did not want to hear this. She did not know what Winn would say next, but she could see in his eyes it was killing him. Part of her hoped she was mistaken and the story would not have a tragic ending. Part of her wished Edward—this Crow—would turn out to be just fine. But she knew that hope was false. It was *Romeo and Juliet* all over again. No matter how many times she watched the play and held her breath for a fairy-tale ending, it always ended in sorrow.

"Where?" she finally asked, her voice little more than a croak. "Where did you find him?"

Winn's jaw tightened, the only visible indication of how difficult remembering the experience was for him. "In pieces. He'd been cut into pieces, stuck on pikes, and was on display outside the palace. A warning to any other who might attempt to strike at—who might attempt what we had."

"Winn." Elinor pulled him into her arms, feeling him crumple against her. Suddenly, she'd become the strong one. Suddenly, the man who had always seemed so solid, so stalwart needed her. "Winn, I'm so sorry."

"It was my fault."

"No!" She pulled back and looked into his stricken face. "No! Edward could have so easily been you."

He shook his head, not hearing her. "I missed something. I should have known the guards' pattern would change."

"How could you? Crow didn't know any more than you did."

"I should have gone back for him. When I heard the pistols. I should have gone back."

"Then you would be dead as well."

"Some days and nights, I think that would be preferable."

"No." She pulled him close, and when his legs gave way, they sank to the floor together, locked in each other's arms. "No," she said, clinging to him. "How could I have gone on without you?"

She heard him give a short, bitter laugh. "Easily. I have not been the husband you deserve."

"I…" She wanted to reassure him, but this was one point on which she agreed. He had not been much of a husband to her. "It's not too late to change." As soon as the words were past her lips, everything began to make sense. Winn's new interest in her, his change of attitude toward the girls. Crow's death had shown Winn the value in his own life.

"For a long time I was numb," Winn was saying. They still embraced, and Elinor made no move to see his face. These words were hard enough to say without looking each other in the eye. "But I had a duty. I promised Edward I would take care of his sister, and I have. Her needs have been taken care of. She has a lady's companion, lodgings, safety. But she hardly knew her brother. She does not mourn him. No one mourns him. Life goes on, and no one cares that he is dead." Winn pulled back, and Elinor saw the anger in his expression.

"You remember him."

"And who cares for me? If I had been the one to die, rather than Crow, would anyone have mourned me?"

Elinor wanted to say yes, but he would know she was lying.

"That's what I thought."

"Then leave the Barbican group. Spend more time with the girls and with me. They cannot mourn a father they never knew, and I cannot mourn a husband who is little more than a stranger to me."

Winn dropped his head into his hands. "I have tried to retire. I think of it every day, but I cannot leave. Not yet. Not with Foncé on the loose and you and the girls at risk."

Elinor raised his head and looked into his eyes. "Then let me in. If you cannot let your work go, then share it with me."

"It's not that simple."

"Yes, it is. Your own director has said he wants my assistance. For once, let's work together on something."

"And if something happens to you, how will I ever forgive myself?"

"By realizing it was my own choice to become

involved. I'm not a fool. I understand the risks and accept them."

"I don't like it…"

Elinor could see she was swaying him, though, and she was not going to back down now. "Then let me prove myself to you."

Winn raised a brow. "How?"

That was a very good question. "I… don't know. Not yet. But I'll make an agreement with you. Before I agree to any assignment, I have to pass your test."

"I still don't like it. A test is nothing like the actual experience—"

"Winn." Her voice held more than a note of warning. "This is the best offer you are likely to receive, and more than generous, in my opinion. You would do well to accept."

The man had obviously negotiated before, because he gave a heavy sigh, indicating he knew he was matched. "Very well. I accept."

She put her hand out, but he looked at it as though it were a foreign object. "We should shake on it, like men do."

"That was not the method I had in mind for solidifying our agreement." He had that wicked glint in his eye, the one she saw so rarely. The one that made her heart feel as though it might pound itself right out of her chest. But she was not going to give in. Not this time. They had work to do.

She rose and pulled the bell cord before he could protest. "That will have to wait. I have a meeting with Lord Melbourne, and I need time to dress."

Sixteen

ELINOR COULD HARDLY KEEP STILL, SITTING IN Melbourne's office. This was like some sort of dream. She was a spy. She was a *real* spy! In the armchair beside her, Winn was looking sullen and glum, but she was not going to allow his sour mood to infect hers. She was right where she wanted to be.

As an added bonus, before they had departed—together for once—they had received a message from Georgiana, telling them all was well with their grandmother. She wrote extensively on the topic of each and every hunter, racing horse, and town hack in the stables and those she had been privileged to ride and those she had been told she would be able to ride when her skills improved. She was obviously having a wonderful time, and though Elinor was not pleased that Foncé and the Maîtriser group necessitated the girls' leaving, she was happy the result was so pleasant.

Caroline had inserted a short note with Georgiana's treatise. It read:

Grandmother says we must not neglect our studies and

has employed two (this underlined several times) *tutors. Must I really study whilst on holiday?*

Elinor had laughed and tucked the note in her reticule to keep that little portion of Caro close to her. Her youngest daughter would never be much of a scholar, she feared. Winn and she had better make the girl a good match.

And then Elinor smiled again, because it had been so long since she had thought of Winn and herself in the same sentence. It had been a long time since he had been a part of her life or of their family.

"Why are you smiling?" he asked, keeping his voice low, even though Lord Melbourne had been called away momentarily.

"No reason."

"Do not look so happy to be here."

"Oh, good point. I should practice the art of deception."

He scowled at her, and she tried to look serious. And then the door opened, and they both turned to see Lord Smythe, Agent Wolf, enter. Elinor waited for his wife to follow, but Melbourne came in after Wolf and closed the door.

Wolf seemed to read the question on her face—she really must practice disguising her expressions—and said, "Lady Smythe is not feeling well. She is resting, and I will give her a report when I return."

Elinor's eyes widened, and Wolf met her gaze. His expression told her nothing, but that did not mean she did not suspect. Agent Saint had seemed nothing if not hale and hearty this afternoon. She was a capable woman, and not the sort to accept being told to stay home and rest. Unless there was a reason.

Elinor could think of only one very good reason—she was with child. Now this was truly amazing, because as much as Winn protested her involvement now, she knew his objections would increase a hundredfold if she were pregnant. But that time in her life was over. After Caro's birth, they had attempted to have another child, an heir, but she had not conceived again. Winn seemed content with the situation and happy to pass the title on to his younger brother or nephew.

"I am glad to see all of you back," Melbourne was saying. He gave Elinor a brisk nod, and she heard Winn curse under his breath. "I have important information to relay, and I have new assignments for each of you." He turned to Agent Wolf. "You will inform me if Lady Smythe is not feeling up to the task I assign her?"

"Of course, but she has never turned down an assignment yet."

Melbourne smiled. "There's a first time for everything." He looked at Winn and Elinor, seated across from him. "I do not need to remind you that what I say here must remain strictly confidential. You should not speak of it outside this room unless you may be assured no one will overhear."

"Of course," Elinor said.

Melbourne nodded. "Good. Here is what I now know."

❧

Winn had to admire the skill of the agent who'd uncovered the whereabouts of Foncé's second-in-command.

Finding Foncé would be a great deal more difficult, but his lieutenant could very well lead them straight to the leader of the Maîtriser group. He had a suspicion Blue was responsible for the intelligence, but he would never have violated protocol to inquire. "Is it possible," Winn asked, "that Foncé is also hiding at this brothel?"

"There is that possibility," Melbourne said with a nod. "However, it is highly unlikely." The hour was late now, and he had offered everyone brandy. Elinor had shaken her head at the offer, taking tea instead. It was a small concession to propriety, and most likely for his benefit, Winn decided.

"If Foncé isn't at the brothel," Smythe said, turning his snifter in his hands, "I'd say there's still a high likelihood he could be spotted there. His lieutenant and he must meet somewhere to discuss plans."

"Exactly." Melbourne nodded. "I have men watching the brothel, but we dare not get too close."

"Which means we need someone on the inside." Winn drained the last of his brandy, not liking the direction the conversation was taking. Not to mention that Elinor was suspiciously silent. He wondered what she was thinking.

"I need an agent to get close to Lefèbvre, find out if he is who we think he is, determine whether or not he is in contact with Foncé, and what plans have been made for the assassination of the prince."

"You need a woman," Smythe said. "No man he doesn't know is going to get close to Foncé's lieutenant in a house of pleasure."

"I did have Saint in mind," Melbourne said, his

gaze on Smythe, and yet, Winn felt his fingers curl around the arm of the chair.

"No." Smythe shook his head. "If you ask her, she will agree. She would do anything to stop the Maîtriser group and protect the prince. But I am requesting you find another agent for this mission. Sophia is under a doctor's care. She needs to rest, or we may very well lose this baby."

Winn blinked in surprise. Saint was with child? This was unexpected. He glanced at Elinor, but she was nodding as though she had suspected as much. "How far along is she?" Elinor asked.

"A couple of months." Quite suddenly, Smythe looked exhausted. Elinor rose and went to him. Winn exchanged a glance with Melbourne, and Winn deduced the secretary was as relieved as he that a woman was here to offer Wolf comfort. Winn sure as hell didn't know what to say.

"She has made it this far before," Smythe told Elinor, "and lost everything, so we don't really dare hope. And yet..."

"You do hope. Of course you do." She smiled at Smythe, and then her gaze drifted to Winn. For a moment, he remembered the secret pleasure he had when he'd found out Elinor was breeding. They had kept it to themselves for a little while, and it had formed a special bond he hadn't even realized was still there. Until now. In her eyes, he saw that softness again, and he knew she could love him again. If he managed not to do everything wrong.

"And you are right to protect her," Elinor said, which was a surprise, because only hours before she had argued women did not need men to protect them. "And that is why I am going to take this assignment."

"What?" Winn jumped to his feet. "No, you are not."

Smythe's expression turned sheepish, as though he had known this would be the outcome of his revelation.

Elinor was looking at Melbourne, who sat with his fingers steepled. "Do you have another female agent?" she asked Melbourne.

The secretary looked at Winn. "No."

"There's no one else?" Winn sputtered.

"The Barbican group is not rife with female operatives. Lady Keating is our only option at the moment."

"Then we will have to formulate a new plan."

Elinor held up a hand. "Wait a moment. My lord, may I speak to you in private?"

Winn gaped at her. Surely she did not think a brief chat was going to change his mind. He had just freed her from the claws of the Maîtriser group. He wasn't going to send her back in.

"Winn?" She arched a brow.

"Fine." He moved toward the door, but Melbourne waved him away. "Wolf and I will step outside. Take as long as you like."

With a last apologetic look, Wolf closed the door, leaving Winn and Elinor alone. She looked at him, the picture of composure.

Winn didn't like it.

He would have much preferred her anger and indignity. That he was used to.

"Have you already forgotten our conversation earlier?"

Winn opened his mouth to say that of course he

hadn't, before he realized he had no idea which conversation she referred to. "We discussed quite a few topics."

"We made an agreement."

Winn frowned. "Remind me."

"I will accept your decision if you believe a mission is beyond me, but you must agree to test me first."

"It's coming back to me now," he muttered.

"Good. Then before you forbid me to accept Melbourne's offer—"

"Melbourne's offer? *You* are the one who made the suggestion!"

"—you must devise a test."

Winn was in no mood to devise a test for her, especially considering whatever test he devised would have to be one she failed. "We don't have time for this," he argued. "Foncé may decide to kill the prince at any moment. Time is of the essence."

"Then sending me in would be the fastest way to get close to this Lefèbvre."

"You're not going into a brothel. You'd have to masquerade as a…" He tried to think of a word for *prostitute* he could use in the presence of his wife. "A fallen woman. Once you went inside, anything could happen to you. A place like that is no place for my wife."

She narrowed her eyes. "You seem familiar with these establishments."

Bloody hell. *Now* she chose to play the jealous wife? "At times my work has taken me into less than savory locations. I do not frequent them for personal pleasure."

"Then where do you go for personal pleasure? It has not been my bed, not for a long time."

Winn did not need to be reminded of that fact, but the lack of intimacy between them did not mean he had turned his affections elsewhere. He had made a vow to Elinor, and he had kept it. Still, he did not think he would have stayed away from her bed if she had invited him. It was true that, until recently, she never refused him, but she never seduced him either.

Winn blinked. That was the answer.

"Now what?" Elinor asked.

"You requested a test," Winn said slowly.

"I did."

"Good. I have a test for you."

Seventeen

Elinor did not know why she should be nervous. Perhaps the feeling stemmed from Winn's refusal to tell her the nature of his test. Perhaps the feeling stemmed from the triumphant glint in his eye when they had been alone in Lord Melbourne's office. Or perhaps the feeling grew out of her own fears of inadequacy. What if she did not have the skills to become a spy? What if being a wife and mother were all she could do?

She had always been proud of these roles, but now she wanted more—adventure, excitement. And she wanted to be part of something bigger than herself. She wanted to know she'd had a hand in preserving the British monarchy and protecting her future sovereign.

She peered through the windows of the carriage she and Winn occupied, watching the other conveyances rattle by. Their lights jounced brightly, and she could hear the happy, excited voices of the occupants they passed. The *ton* was flitting here and there, to this event or that, without a care in the world other than who would hop into whose bed. Once she had been so bored and desperate for entertainment, she'd thought that existence exciting—or at least desirable. She had coveted the most sought-after invitations and spent fortunes on the newest French styles.

Now she wore a gown she had barely glanced at when Bridget dressed her, and she was going home rather than to the theater.

Winn was seated across from her, and she couldn't have been happier.

Except she still had to pass his test.

"You look nervous," he said. His eyes had been closed, and she would have sworn he was dozing.

"Not nervous, merely curious. What did you tell Melbourne when you spoke to him?" When she and Winn had exited Melbourne's office, Smythe and the secretary were waiting outside. Winn had nodded to his superior, and she'd strained to overhear the conversation. Coincidentally—or had it been?—Lord Smythe had spoken to her that same moment, and she hadn't been able to hear.

"I told him you would give him your answer tomorrow." He peered at his pocket watch. "Which I suppose means later today."

"*I* will give him an answer?"

"If you pass the test, you may give him whatever answer you choose. If you fail, you must tell him you will not be a part of this mission."

She would not fail. "How will I know I have passed?"

"You will know."

Those words did little to reassure her, and her stomach was tied in knots by the time they arrived at their town house. Winn escorted her inside, and they silently handed wraps, hats, and gloves to the butler and footman.

Relieved of her outer garments, Elinor stood immobile and uncertain. Should she retire to the drawing room? Winn's library? Where would this test commence?

Winn leaned down and whispered in her ear. "Prepare for bed then dismiss your maid. When you are alone, I'll tell you the nature of your test."

"Am I to take it tonight?" she asked.

"I see no point in putting it off."

Elinor nodded and climbed the stairs. What would Winn have her do? Prove she could disguise herself? Escape a locked room? Decipher a coded message? She was not certain she could successfully accomplish any of those feats.

"Are you feeling unwell, my lady?" Bridget asked as she helped Elinor don a robe over her serviceable linen night shift. Elinor had not known what one wore when taking a spy test, and she had chosen the most practical thing she could think of. Winn had told her to prepare for bed. Why did he not want her to prepare to sneak out of the town house undetected?

"I'm fine, Bridget. Merely tired. Thank you. I will do the rest. You are dismissed."

Bridget bobbed. "Yes, my lady."

As soon as the door closed, Elinor ran to bolt it. Then she checked to be certain the door between her chambers and Winn's was unlocked. She'd already checked it, and it was still unlocked. She pressed her ear to the wood and heard the low rumble of masculine voices and then Winn's chuckle. He certainly did not seem nervous.

She took a seat on her bed, rose, paced, sat down again, and folded her hands in her lap. Then she decided perhaps sitting on the bed was all wrong, jumped off and raced to a small chair in the corner. She crossed her legs, uncrossed them, tried to look bored, and even lifted a book and pretended to read.

Where was Winn? What was taking him so long?

Unable to stay seated, she jumped up again and paced the room, pausing to glance at her reflection in the looking glass. Her cheeks were flushed and her eyes bright. Her hair hung down her back in loose waves, and she wondered if she should have told Bridget to leave it pinned up. Elinor grabbed a pin and hastily secured her hair in a severe bun. Was that the look she wanted?

"Are you ready?" a voice said from behind her. She spun around and stared at Winn, who was resting one shoulder on the door frame. His arms were crossed over his chest.

His bare chest.

Elinor swallowed.

He still wore his boots and his black trousers, and in his hand he held a glass of what appeared to be wine.

Elinor smoothed her robe. "Of course. I'd prefer to get this over with."

Winn gave her a fleeting smile. "Wine?" He held the glass out to her, pushing off the wall and walking toward her.

She frowned. "That is for me?"

"I thought you might need it."

Was this a trick? Had he drugged the wine? Poisoned it? Was this part of the test? As though he read her mind—or more likely the expression on her face—Winn said, "This is not part of the test." He set the wine on a small table next to the bed. "I was merely being courteous. A rare thing, I know."

Elinor really believed she would scream if he did not tell her the nature of the test soon. Her nerves were frayed, and she was exerting an immense amount of willpower not to begin wringing her hands.

Winn walked toward her, and she had to check the urge to take a step back. There was something feral and almost lionlike about him when he was without his shirt. His chest gleamed bronze in the firelight, and the muscles tensed as he moved, like those of a predatory animal. "It occurred to me in Lord Melbourne's office," Winn was saying, "that you have probably never encountered a fallen woman."

Elinor blinked. She had not expected him to return to this conversation. "I have seen members of the demimonde at the theater and at various balls and such."

"And how did these courtesans strike you?" He took another step closer, and she caught the faint scent of the polish used to shine his leather boots. It was a dark, masculine scent, and underneath it she detected the barest hint of the spicy scent of his shaving soap. Had he shaved for her?

"I don't understand."

"What was your impression of these women?" Winn was before her now, and he raised one hand and tucked a finger in a lock of hair beside her ear. Slowly, he pulled the curl free of its confines so it slid over her shoulder, tickling her neck.

"I..." It was difficult to think with Winn touching her, but perhaps this was part of the test. She thought back to the courtesans she'd seen. She'd been curious about the women. She was not supposed to take an interest in them, which made them all the more intriguing. "They were fashionable," she said slowly, trying not to think about the way Winn wrapped her hair around his finger. "And laughing. Flirtatious, I suppose. Surrounded by men."

"Is that all?"

She sensed there was something more he was waiting for her to say. She closed her eyes in an attempt to recall the courtesans as much as to avoid looking into Winn's alluring gaze. "Sensual," she said, the word crossing her lips before she even had time to think it. She remembered full red lips, plunging bodices, round, white shoulders, dark, knowing eyes. "I suppose they struck me as sensual creatures." She opened her eyes.

Winn was looking at her, his expression unreadable. "And do you see yourself in this light?"

Elinor's heart began to pound again. Her brain screamed a warning, but she had come too far now. She thought of her prim necklines, her matronly figure, her always-proper behavior. "No. But—" Elinor recalled the scarlet gown she had worn to Mary's ball, the one that had made Winn's eyes go dark with desire.

"But?" Winn prodded.

"But I do not think I am completely devoid of sensuality."

"Good."

"Good?"

"You will need that quality to pass this test." Winn's hand slid down her robe, gliding over her breast and pausing at her waist. He flicked open the knot of her robe and pushed the garment off her shoulders. "Your test, Ellie, is to seduce me."

❧

Winn returned to his room and slumped in the chair beside his bed. Elinor had looked so shocked, so... completely at a loss when he'd told her of the test, that he'd taken pity on her and allowed her a few moments to prepare. He had no hope she would pass this test. And that was exactly the result he wanted. He did not want her to pass the test. She'd be safer at home. The Barbican group would find a way to apprehend Foncé and dismantle the Maîtriser group without involving his wife and family.

As the hand on the bracket clock beside his bed inched slowly around the clock's face, Winn became more and more certain Elinor was not even going to attempt the test. He was not surprised. She had never been one to take the initiative when it came to their lovemaking. And yet, Winn couldn't help but feel somewhat disappointed. Would it have been so bad if Elinor had at least attempted his test? Wouldn't it have been rather enjoyable if she had passed? Not that he would have allowed her actually to seduce him. He would have stopped her.

Probably.

She had never tried to seduce him, at least not overtly. And this was why she could not be allowed to risk her life playing the role of a prostitute at a brothel.

This was no game. If Foncé's lieutenant suspected she was a spy or in the service of the Barbican group, he would not hesitate to kill her. And Elinor would never be believed in the role of a wanton.

Suddenly, the door between their rooms creaked open. The doorway was empty. Frowning, Winn craned his neck, supposing he had simply not latched the door properly when he'd shut it.

And then Elinor appeared, and Winn's jaw dropped. The fire burned in the hearth, and the lamp beside his bed illuminated the room, but they did little to chase away the shadows. And yet, even in the dim light, Winn could see enough that a jab of arousal cut through him. Elinor stood in the doorway in a pretty white chemise with a wide neck, held together by silk ribbons tied in an innocent bow. But what she had done to the chemise was anything but innocent. The linen material was damp. It had to be to cling to her body so. And cling it did, molding to her every curve and slope. She moved forward, and the linen dragged against her legs, revealing the rounded shape of them—and yet revealing nothing, as she was still covered from neck to knee. Winn felt his mouth go dry.

"No greeting?" she said, still moving forward. She moved slowly, a feat he had not thought her capable of. She was always moving quickly and efficiently. There was nothing efficient in her movements now. They were languorous, smooth, and—God help him—sensual. What had possessed her to dampen the material? And why had he never thought to douse her with water before? He would have, had he realized the effect.

"Is your tongue tied in knots?" Her brows arched. "I sincerely hope not. You might need it."

Winn blinked. Had his wife just made an innuendo? She had never done so before in his memory. What, exactly, had happened in the half hour they had been apart?

"I did not think you would come," he finally replied.

She nodded, stopping directly in front of him. Her dark nipples were hard and pushed through the wet fabric clinging to the swell of her breasts. The fabric then fell to her waist, where it slid into a V at the juncture of her thighs. "It took me a few moments to dress."

"I see that. Are you cold?"

"Freezing."

He reached for her, but she stepped to the side. "And I will need you to warm me with your hands, your body, and your mouth."

Winn's hands gripped the arms of the chair, sensing if he rose now, she would only find another way to avoid him.

"But not yet," she said, reaching out and putting a finger on his chest. "First, we must rectify a most distressing situation." She pouted, and Winn gaped at her. He had never seen his wife pout. Not once in all of the fourteen years he had known her. And yet, her full red lips had turned down in a moue he found irresistible. He could think of so many things he'd like her to do with those lips. Winn shook his head. This was his wife. He had to remember that, but she was making it quite difficult. She was acting far more the role of the—

Bloody hell. She was doing it. She was playing the courtesan, and she was succeeding. She was going to pass this bloody test if things went on as they had been. He needed to make it more difficult on her. Mentally, he was aware he needed to ensure she failed.

But physically—physically, he was desperate for her to succeed.

"What situation?" he asked warily.

"You, my lord, are wearing too many clothes." She moved toward him, and Winn tried to scoot back—a feat all but impossible in the chair. But he could see where this would lead. If she managed to undress him, he would never be able to keep his wits about him. But instead of reaching for him, she turned her back on him. For a moment, Winn was confused. For a moment, he was completely and utterly distracted by the way the thin, wet fabric clung to her bottom.

And then she bent over, took one boot between her knees, and pulled. She had never removed his boots before. It was a task relegated to his valet, and not one Winn ever paid much attention to. But he was paying attention now. He could not help but stare at the way her hips wiggled and the way the fabric of the chemise only hinted at what he wanted to see. Horrified, he pulled back his hand just before it could clamp on the flesh of her bottom.

"There!" She dropped the first boot on the floor and looked over her shoulder at him. "That's one."

Oh, how he wanted to put his hands on her hips and bury himself inside her. It would take nothing to lift the chemise and plunge into her warm depths. She was not wearing anything underneath. He could see that quite clearly.

She lifted the other boot, positioned it, and wriggled it off. He could have told her that was not the best way to go about the task, but he could not seem to form words with her bottom wriggling like that. He was doomed. If this continued, he was never going to be able to resist her.

No man would.

She turned to face him again, smiling mysteriously. "And now, my lord, we may begin."

Winn swallowed and hoped she had not noticed he was waving the white flag.

Elinor saw Winn's throat working and did not know what it meant. Was he having a difficult time keeping the bile from rising in his throat? Was she completely disgusting him? She dared not risk a glance at his nether regions, and so she did not know if she was succeeding in her seduction or, as she feared, a complete and utter failure. Oh, she was going to make a fool of herself, that much was patently obvious. But at least she had tried. Winn said he did not think she was coming. Well, she had never been one to give up easily, and she was not done with him yet.

She only wished he would show some indication of what he felt. Did she arouse him at all?

And why had she said, "we may begin"? What did that mean, and what was she supposed to do now? He was looking at her expectantly, and she supposed she had better do something soon or she would fail this test before she had even begun. Seduction... seduction... She had no idea what to do next. Perhaps she would do something to keep him from staring at her so intently. She bent and pressed her lips lightly to his. She had to rest her hands on something to keep from toppling over, and the closest available surface was Winn himself. She slid her hands over his thighs and forgot she was supposed to be the seducer. How could his thighs be so muscular? How could they be so hard and solid and sculpted beneath her hands?

Her belly tightened, and she tried to focus on something else. She'd been kissing him lightly, but now she nipped playfully at his lips as she ran her hands up and down the length of his thighs. She could feel his muscles tightening beneath her hands. Did that mean she was affecting him? If she were truly a courtesan, she would not falter. She would not question her power. If she were truly a woman of pleasure, she would take her pleasure. Her way.

And what gave her pleasure? Kissing Winn. The feel of his mouth against hers. She deepened the kiss, slanting her mouth over his. How strange to be the one controlling everything. She was so used to Winn kissing her, Winn touching her. But now she could do as she liked. And she wanted to continue kissing him, to explore his mouth, revel in the taste of him, savor the feeling of being joined together—mouth to mouth—and soon body to body.

She teased his lips until he opened for her, then dipped her tongue inside his mouth. He tasted of mint, the same mint with which she cleaned her teeth. Hesitantly, she touched her tongue to his and felt a shock of arousal flash through her. Kissing him like this was familiar and novel all at once. In some sense they were still Elinor and Winn, but in another she was a wanton Cyprian and he the man who wanted her, the man who would pay any price to possess her.

She kissed him more deeply, sliding her hands up his thighs until she felt the bare skin of his abdomen. His muscles were tight there too, his body hard, his stomach flat. It rippled beneath her fingertips, and for the first time she thought she might be affecting him. She thought she might be seducing him. She stroked his tongue with hers and stroked his chest with her hands, noting how his muscles bunched when she caressed his skin, how his nipples had hardened, the way he sucked in a breath when she tweaked them.

Elinor could not have said what possessed her, but she could not resist closing what little distance remained between them. She straddled him, one leg on either side of his, and slid up his body, resting her bottom on his thighs and taking him by the shoulders. Even his shoulders were sculpted, the muscles beneath giving her a sense of the power he held leashed. He could take over at any moment. He could throw her to the floor, lift her into his arms, take her swiftly and hard. But he was allowing her to take control. Her hands scraped over the planes of his back and then dove into his hair to tangle with the short dark curls. She fisted a hand and moved his head so she could better access his mouth. Amazingly, he did not protest, but allowed her to have her way.

Feeling bold, she slid her body closer to his until they were joined but for the scraps of clothing between them. But even through the material, she could feel the heat of him. She could feel the heavy, hard maleness of him, straining against the fall of his trousers.

He wanted her, and she wanted to feel his need.

She reached between them and released the material covering him. He sprang into her hands, hard and hot and velvet. She took him by the root and ran her hand up and down, teasing the tip of him until she felt a bead of wetness well up. He groaned now, and she almost smiled. Instead, she pressed kisses along his jaw and his neck, feeling him shiver and jump in her hand as she continued her ministrations.

Without her mouth on his, she could hear his quick

intakes of breath, his muffled groans, and the growl in the back of his throat as she touched him with long, slow strokes. She dipped her head, kissing his hard chest, sliding her body down until she knelt between his legs and could run her tongue over his muscled abdomen.

She remembered what he had done to her—had it been only hours before?—and bent to touch her tongue to the tip of him. For the first time, his hands gripped her shoulders and he pushed her back. "Stop." The word was more of a growl than human speech.

But she had felt his body's reaction. "You like it," she countered. "You don't really want me to stop."

His hands on her shoulders tightened. "I do like it, but if you're going to do that, if you're going to touch me that way, kiss me like that, I don't want this to be a game between us."

She frowned. "You devised the test."

"I'm ending it. I want to know this is something you do because you want it, not because you want to pass some test."

How could she help but fall in love with him again? Even if she'd still been fighting it, she would have fallen helplessly at that moment. "I want this," she murmured, stroking him again. "I want you. I always have."

She touched her tongue to him again, swirling it around his tip then taking him slowly inside her mouth. In her peripheral vision, she could see his hands tighten on the chair, the skin white where he exerted pressure and attempted to maintain control.

"Ellie, you are killing me."

And she would have liked to see what it took for his control to break, but her own arousal was building, and she needed him inside her, buried deep, the two of them frantically reaching for their joint release. Reluctantly, she released him and stood. The sheer expression of regret on his face all but made her laugh. He actually thought she was going to stop.

Instead, she bent and grasped the hem of her damp chemise. The material had grown cold and heavy, and she was glad to remove it. She wanted to feel his hot skin against her own cool flesh. Before, when she'd been in any state of undress in his presence, she'd always felt exposed and slightly embarrassed. But now she looked into the dark emerald of his eyes and saw how much he wanted her. She saw how beautiful she was to him. It made her want him all the more. It made her ache with love for this man who wanted her despite all her flaws.

"Now you," she said, reaching for his trousers. He helped her yank them off, and she could not help but pause to admire his long, lean form. He was so perfect, so strong, so wonderfully male. She pressed herself against him, feeling the light dusting of hair on his chest rasp against the sensitive skin of her breasts. He was hot, she cool, and the contrast between them made her sigh with pleasure. She settled her bottom on his thighs, wrapped her arms around his neck, and kissed him. He rocked against her, and just the press of his heavy flesh against her sensitive core made her ache with need. She rose, positioning him, then whispered in his ear, "I want you."

"Now," he said between teeth clenched for control.

She was going to test that control further, because although she could tell he wanted to thrust into her hard and fast, she wanted slow and tantalizing. She was wet and hot and took him inch by inch, feeling every sensation to the fullest before he finally filled her completely. She was having difficulty holding back now as well, but she held on, knowing she would be rewarded. This was a new position for her. Years ago, before she'd conceived Georgiana, she could remember one night when they'd both drank too much champagne, and he'd set her on top of him. She'd been embarrassed then and unsure. She did not feel that way now.

Now she only knew she was controlling her own pleasure. Now she only knew that with each stroke she brought herself, and him, closer to climax. Now, she only knew if she resisted the frenzy her body called for, the mind-numbing pleasure building would explode into an ecstasy the likes of which she had never experienced.

She rode him slowly, steadily, until he was calling her name and clutching her, begging her for release. But she did not give in. She could not. Her entire body was straining for the peak of the swirl of pleasure rising within her. As soon as she thought she'd reached the summit, another peak crested, until finally she went over the edge. She trembled, bucked, exploded. Her body was alive with sensation so acute, so sharply pleasurable, she could not comprehend it. All she could do was give in to the sensation.

All she could do was let go.

With a cry, she bowed back and allowed herself to fall, knowing Winn would catch her. Knowing he would be there when she came back to herself.

Eighteen

WINN OPENED HIS EYES, HEARING A RINGING IN HIS ears. What the hell had just happened? He had never felt anything like that before, never felt pleasure so strong he all but went blind. And still bright stars shot in front of his eyes. He shook his head and felt Elinor, warm and relaxed against his chest.

If the servants had wondered at their activities before, there was no need to wonder now. Half of Mayfair knew she had climaxed. He would have smiled with pleasure at her fulfillment, but he could hardly take much credit for it. He put his arms around her, holding her until her breathing slowed. Her silky hair brushed against his arm, and her soft skin was all but impossible to resist. He had to touch her, to stroke her, to feel her warm and soft against him.

When it became apparent she was not going to rise anytime soon, he stood awkwardly and lifted her into his arms. She was still so hot he would have thought her fevered if he had not known her better, so it was not the warmth of his bed but the comfort he sought. He yanked the covers back and tumbled onto the soft mattress, pulling her against him. Her head nestled against his shoulder, and her body curled into him. She fit against him perfectly, as she always had.

Her breathing slowed, and he knew she slept. He should sleep too. He doubted he would be able to rest in the following days, knowing the danger she would face. He would have denied her the position in the Barbican group if he could have, but she had more than proven herself capable of seduction.

Winn had not intended to allow the seduction to reach its completion, but he had found himself unable to resist her. His hands curled into fists as he thought of her seducing another man, even though he knew she would not allow it to go very far. But the idea of another man looking at her, lusting after her, attempting to touch her, kiss her...

Winn gritted his teeth and tried to control his fury. She was his wife. *His*. He was supposed to protect her, keep her safe, and he was going to allow her to walk into the lair of one of the most dangerous organizations known to the Barbican group. He'd risked his own life countless times and rarely thought much of it. Now he had a sense of what Elinor would feel if and when he continued with the Barbican group. Winn supposed fair was fair. He would never forgive himself if he lost her, but he knew she would never forgive him if he tried to wrap her in a cocoon.

Winn and Crow used to joke during long, cold, cramped nights on dangerous missions, that the good citizens of His Majesty's Britain had no idea what the agents for the Crown endured to keep the people safe in their cozy houses. Winn used to think about Elinor,

Georgiana, and Caroline sleeping peacefully in their warm beds. He would picture them snuggled under piles of covers, their heads resting on fluffed pillows. Somehow that made the cold and the boredom and the fear—because only a man who didn't want to live anymore didn't fear death—bearable.

But now Crow was dead, and Winn would never be able to think of Elinor sleeping peacefully away from him. He hadn't understood before what it was to want, to long, to yearn. She'd longed for him, and he had not understood the emotion. But now he would have his own taste of it, and he did not relish the reversal of their positions.

Crow would have said it was Fate's way of keeping the scales even. Winn would have probably wanted to punch him, because that would have been easier than admitting his partner was right.

Elinor sighed against him, and Winn pulled her close. How he missed Crow. How he would have liked to tell him about this remarkable turn of events. How he would have liked to speak with his friend one last time.

The old sense of guilt welled up inside him, but this time, instead of succumbing, he tamped it down. He could not absolve himself of guilt, but neither was he willing to take all of the blame for Crow's death anymore.

The Barbican's investigation had cleared him of any misconduct. Melbourne had told Winn he had done all that was to be expected. Perhaps it was time he believed them. Perhaps it was time he stopped regretting his life and began to live it.

He looked down at Elinor, her red lips parted slightly in sleep. Now he had something to live for.

≈

Elinor woke slowly, puzzling over the unfamiliar surroundings. She stared at the dark shape above her as it gradually formed into a canopy. She blinked and turned her head. She was in Winn's bed, his large, dark mahogany tester bed. She studied the ornate carvings over her head, wondering how many hours Winn himself had spent gazing at them.

He was asleep beside her, his body solid and comforting, one of his arms slung over her middle. Neither of them were wearing any clothing, and she supposed that should have embarrassed her, but she was still too sated from their earlier lovemaking to feel even remotely embarrassed. She would have done it all again. She smiled.

Perhaps she would.

But had what they shared meant anything? Had she passed his test? At some point she had stopped caring about the test and just enjoyed being with Winn. She'd never felt so close to him. She'd never before felt as though they'd shared a moment of true intimacy.

She looked up at the bed again. She'd never before slept in his bed. Did this new circumstance mean something? Was Winn inviting her into his life?

"I don't suppose I can convince you to go back to sleep," a deep, groggy voice said.

She smiled. "I thought you were asleep."

"Someone has to lie here and worry while you

sleep. Now that you're awake and worrying so loudly I can hear you, perhaps I can get some rest."

Footsteps sounded in the corridor, and she squinted at the heavy draperies, which would have blocked out even the brightest sunlight. "I hear the staff moving about. It must be morning." And she was ready to find out what the day held. Would she be working for the Barbican group? Had she passed Winn's test?

"It is barely seven, which in many quarters is still considered the middle of the night."

"You have never been the sort to loll in bed."

"Neither have you." He propped himself up on one elbow and looked down at her. "I like waking up with you."

Elinor blinked, taken off guard.

"Does that surprise you?"

"I suppose. We have always slept apart. I thought you enjoyed your solitude."

"I did, but I stayed away from you more because I did not want to arouse suspicion when I had to leave in the middle of the night. Now there are no secrets between us."

Elinor was not ready to agree that no secrets existed between them, but there were certainly fewer. Although there was one matter she would like resolved as soon as possible. "This is the first time I have slept in your bed," she said.

"Is it?" He frowned. "Do you find it comfortable?"

She laughed. "Yes… Winn, please tell me already. Did I pass your test?"

He stroked her face with one finger, and she braced herself for disappointment.

"Of course. You more than passed."

She rose on her elbows. "I did?"

He shook his head. "Do not look so pleased. There is nothing about putting yourself in a position to die a slow, painful death that should please you."

"I passed," she said, hearing the wonder in her own voice. "I am going to work as an operative for the Barbican group."

"For the record, I had not intended to allow the seduction to go that far. You were perhaps too good at playing the courtesan."

"Really?"

"Mmm." He brushed a lock of hair back from her temple. "I beg you not to play your role quite so well with Foncé's lieutenant."

"Of course not! I will not be required to... What I mean to say is, I will not have to."

She saw the muscle in Winn's jaw tense. "As your husband, I would like absolutely to forbid you from even looking at another man, but as an operative, I will say that no one can predict what will happen during a mission. You are not expected to seduce Foncé's man, but he may have other ideas, and he may not appreciate being refused."

"I see." Elinor slid back down.

"You do not have to do this," Winn said. "God knows I'd prefer it if you stayed home."

"And if we all stayed home, where would we be? Someone must stand and fight for King and country. You have done so for years."

"And I have never been in a position where my powers of seduction were called upon."

She laughed. "I am happy to hear it. And I am ready to do my duty."

Winn nodded resolutely, as though he'd been expecting this.

"But I do have one small request first."

He raised a brow.

"Before we go to Melbourne, there is someone I must see."

❧

Lord and Lady Smythe's house on Charles Street was quiet and unassuming. Elinor would never have guessed two of England's foremost spies lived under such seemingly normal auspices. Of course, she'd lived with a spy for years and had no idea. So perhaps it was not so difficult to believe after all. "Are you certain this is the correct house?" she asked after the footman handed her down from the coach. Winn took her elbow.

"Yes. I'm certain." He seemed mildly amused as he led her up the walk and to the door. He rapped three times, and the door was promptly opened by a distinguished-looking butler.

"Good afternoon, Wallace." Winn handed the servant his card. "Are their lordships at home?"

"One moment." He ushered Elinor and Winn inside a very normal-looking vestibule and clicked along the marble before opening a wood-paneled door and disappearing inside.

Winn nodded. "Wolf's library."

"That is his code name?" At his nod, she added, "And hers is Saint?"

"Yes."

"I understand why his name is Wolf."

Winn raised a brow.

"He has a predatory look about him," she explained.

"I see." His smile widened, indicating she was still amusing him.

"Why is her code name Saint?"

"Because she's perfect. She's known for her flawless missions and rarely makes a mistake."

"But Foncé escaped her."

"And do not think she has forgotten," a man's voice said. Elinor glanced up and saw Lord Smythe making his way toward them. "She will have him in the end, I promise you."

Elinor smiled. "Lord Smythe." She curtsied.

He took her hand and kissed it. "Lady Keating. My lord. Shall we convene in the drawing room?"

"Actually," Elinor said before Smythe could direct them toward the stairs, "I was hoping to speak to Lady Smythe alone. Would that be possible?"

"Of course. She is in her room. I will have her maid take you to her."

"I don't wish to disturb her."

Smythe waved a hand. "She will be glad for the distraction. She is going mad with all the enforced relaxation." A maid appeared and beckoned Elinor to follow her up the stairs. Elinor complied, watching Winn and Smythe make their way back toward Smythe's library. She was willing to wager there would be talk of strategy, and though it was early yet, once they began discussing strategy, she had a feeling Winn would also want brandy.

She had plenty of time.

Lady Smythe was lounging on a chaise when Elinor

was shown into her boudoir. The viscountess could not have known Elinor was coming, and yet Lady Smythe did not seem surprised at her arrival. "Lady Keating." The dark-haired beauty smiled widely, emphasizing her full lips. "How good to see you. Would you care for tea?" Without waiting for a response, she gestured to her maid. "She will return in a moment, and we can talk freely then. How lovely you look today. Green is your color."

"Thank you." Though she realized this was probably the sort of thing any lady would say when called upon, Elinor felt her cheeks heat with pleasure. "How are you feeling?"

"Very well." Lady Smythe gestured to a stack of papers. "Trying to keep busy. Ah, here is the tea."

It took two servants to wheel the heavy tray into the room, and Elinor rather thought it was more of a meal than tea. Besides the steaming teapot and its accoutrements, there were sandwiches, scones, clotted cream, crumpets, jam, cakes, tarts, and candied violets. Elinor blinked at it, but Lady Smythe merely reached for a cup and saucer. "Cream and sugar?"

"Cream, please." Elinor took the delicate china cup and a small sandwich. Her belly was in knots, and she did not think she could even stomach that much. She did sip the tea, knowing it would calm her nerves, and watched Lady Smythe pile two scones, a crumpet, three cakes, and a sandwich on her own plate.

"They are trying to make certain I eat," Lady Smythe said, nodding at the servants leaving the room. She poured her own cup of tea and added both sugar and cream. "I have not been hungry, of late."

Elinor wondered what the woman ate when she *was* hungry.

"But then this morning I woke up feeling famished. I cannot seem to eat enough."

Elinor smiled. "I remember feeling the same way when I was carrying my girls. For weeks, the very thought of food made me ill, and then all of a sudden I was so hungry I could have eaten my dinner and Lord Keating's as well."

"Then you think this a good sign?" She looked so hopeful, so desperate for good news, that even if Elinor had thought it a horrible sign, she would never have said so.

"I do. It means the baby is growing and needs sustenance."

Lady Smythe was nodding and popping bites of scone in her mouth. "If this continues, I shall be as big as the prince in a month. I've never eaten so much."

"Eventually, the baby will take up more and more room, and there will be less and less for your stomach. You won't be quite so hungry then." She did not mention that Lady Smythe would instead be tired and uncomfortable. Elinor did not remember the last weeks of either pregnancy fondly. It seemed she could not stand or sit or lie comfortably, she was always too warm, and her back screamed in constant pain.

And how quickly she forgot all of that once she held her daughters in her arms.

"Adrian tells me you have been chosen to infiltrate the Maîtriser group's lair."

"Yes. I am going to Melbourne's offices after this to formally accept the assignment."

Lady Smythe nibbled a cake. "How does Baron feel about this?"

"He is not pleased."

Lady Smythe laughed. "I should think not, but he has faith in you."

Elinor wrinkled her forehead. "How do you know that?"

"Because if he did not, you would not be going."

Elinor wanted to bristle at the words, but she had a feeling it was more of a compliment for Winn than a slight directed toward her.

"What do you want to ask me?" Lady Smythe lifted her sandwich and ate it in two bites.

Elinor took a deep breath. What did she want to ask? "I suppose I'm nervous."

Lady Smythe nodded as she spread jam on a crumpet. "Of course you are, and that is good. Nerves keep you alert, and that is what we want." She bit into the crumpet.

"What sort of things should I look for?"

"Anything to do with the prince, or any evidence Foncé has been there. If Lefèbvre and Foncé are not meeting at this brothel, where are they meeting?" She gestured to the stack of papers surrounding her chaise longue. "I have looked at all of these reports on the Maîtriser group again and again, and I cannot help but think there is something I am missing. Why the prince regent? What could Foncé possibly hope to gain?" She lifted a scone and peered at her plate. "I thought I had chosen a sandwich."

"You…" Elinor decided against informing the viscountess she had already eaten it. Instead, she took a bite of her own. "You should try them. They are delicious."

"Thank you." She reached for another. "I will. Now, the other thing," she said when she had swallowed, "is that you will be infiltrating a brothel. I imagine you'll be presented to the abbess in some manner or other. You want to appear believable, but not so believable that you are cornered in a bedroom and forced to knee a man in order to escape."

Elinor nodded, making note of kneeing as a possible exit strategy.

"Look pretty but uninteresting. You do not want to catch Lefèbvre's eye. I imagine at this point, he has seen his fill and barely looks twice at the girls. That should work to your advantage."

Elinor nodded. "What if I am presented with a customer?"

"Tease him," Lady Smythe said around a candied violet, "and promise him all manner of things, and then hide until he's gone. You want to get in and out as quickly as possible. Stay only as long as it takes to gain entrance to Lefèbvre's personal quarters. When he is occupied or absent, sneak in, rifle his belongings, and steal anything you think might have merit." Lady Smythe sat back. "I am really quite envious of you. This mission sounds excessively diverting."

Elinor did not think she would have described it as diverting. Terrifying would have been her description of choice, but then she had chosen this path, and it was infinitely more diverting than supervising preparations for yet another soiree.

"Honestly," Lady Smythe said, leaning forward

to refresh Elinor's untouched tea. "You will do very well. You are a natural. Trust me. I am a good judge of these things."

"Thank you." Elinor could not say why, but Lady Smythe's words calmed her enough that her hands stopped shaking and she was able to sip her tea without the cup trembling. She could do this. She had proven last night that she was strong and powerful. She could do anything.

Lady Smythe yawned, and Elinor realized she should take her leave.

"I'm terribly sorry," the viscountess apologized. "I am so tired today."

"Then perhaps I might give you some advice," Elinor said, rising. "Rest now. You shall have none when the babe arrives."

Lady Smythe actually looked wistful at the thought of little or no sleep. "If there is a babe."

Elinor glanced at the ravaged tea cart. "There will be a babe. Mark my words."

❧

Winn tapped his foot irritably and resisted grabbing Elinor's mantle and throwing it over her scantily clad form. He did not know where Melbourne had acquired such a disguise, and he didn't want to know. What he wanted was for this whole thing to be over. Winn wanted his wife back in her demure gowns, seated in her comfortable chair in the front parlor, his daughters bickering over some hair ribbon or other, and Foncé a distant memory.

"It is too dangerous for you to carry any sort of weapon on your person," Melbourne was telling

Elinor. For her part, she was nodding sagely. "In the past, when Agent Saint encountered this problem, we devised an alternate solution."

Winn wanted to ask how often Agent Saint was called upon to dress as a prostitute and hide a weapon, but he refrained. Now he knew why Agent Wolf's advice to him while the women were ensconced in Lady Smythe's chambers had been, "Have a strong drink and find someone to punch. You'll feel better."

"What solution is that?" Elinor asked.

Melbourne gestured to Elinor's head. "If you would not mind, could you style your hair so it is a bit more… puffy."

"Puffy?" Winn repeated.

Elinor merely smiled. "I think I know what Lord Melbourne has in mind. One moment." There was a small oval mirror with an ornate frame encasing it hanging on the wall near the door. Elinor went to it, took down her simple, austere bun, and repinned it so the style was looser and, Winn had to admit, puffier. "How is this?" she asked.

"Splendid." Melbourne opened a drawer in his desk and pulled out a small silver dagger. It was the length of Winn's longest finger and perhaps double that in width. His hand would have swallowed the weapon, but when Melbourne handed it to Elinor, it seemed to fit her slender palm perfectly.

"This is not a weapon that will inflict much damage, but it might afford you enough time to run, if the need arises."

Elinor took a shaky breath and nodded. "I am to hide it in my hair?"

"Precisely. Foncé's men will not be looking at your—er, hair." Melbourne reddened, and Winn raised a brow. He had never seen the secretary look abashed before.

With a nod, Elinor expertly slid the small dagger into her hair and arranged the style so the weapon was completely covered. She shook her head slightly, adjusted the weapon so the point was lodged firmly in the thick coil at the crown of her head, and nodded. "I have it. What else?"

"Because you are new and relatively untried," Melbourne said, "you will be allowed only four hours inside."

Winn sat straight, but Elinor shook her head. "What if I am not able to complete my mission in that time?"

"Then you get out and save your life," Winn answered.

She scowled at him and looked pointedly at Melbourne. "My lord?"

"We might be able to send you in again, but Agent Baron is correct. Any observation you make will prove valuable, and God knows we have already lost enough agents to Foncé and his Maîtriser group. I won't lose another."

"And if she does not emerge after four hours?" Winn asked.

Melbourne nodded. "Then we assume the worst and go in after her."

"I volunteer for that operation."

"Winn." Elinor shook her head.

"I thought you might," Melbourne conceded. "Normally, I would not consent. You are too close to this case, but I have no one else available at the moment. It will have to be you, and if I can pull Blue from his watch over the prince, I will send him to assist you."

Winn nodded then looked at Elinor. "Are you certain you want to do this? It is not too late to change your mind."

"I am certain," Elinor said, her face set in what Winn recognized as determination. "I am ready." At Winn's frown, she amended, "Or as ready as I am likely to be."

Melbourne checked his pocket watch. "Night is falling. Both of you be in position by full dark."

"Yes, sir," Winn answered. He escorted Elinor to the door, throwing her mantle over her before he did so. He opened the door, and with his hand at the small of her back, was ushering her through when he heard Melbourne's last words.

"And God go with you."

Nineteen

ELINOR HUDDLED BESIDE WINN IN THE DARKENED doorway of a seamstress's shop. Most of the shops on the street were closed and locked tight for the evening. Across the way, light and raucous laughter spilled from a tavern, along with men in various military uniforms and others in the garb of the working man. The building beside the tavern glowed with soft light, and a steady stream of men went into its doors. If she had been passing by in a carriage, Elinor would not have looked twice at what appeared to be an ordinary street in London. She never would have wondered what went on behind the drawn curtains of the old but neatly kept building across from her.

Not for the first time since arriving, she questioned whether this was the correct location. The large detached house did not look at all how she pictured a pleasure house to look. From the outside she would have guessed the structure had been built sometime in the mid-eighteenth century. It had two floors and what was probably a cramped attic space. Steps at the front of the house indicated a basement entrance for servants.

Apparently, not all brothels had half-dressed women hanging out of windows, and gaudy red decoration.

"Once you go in," Winn said, "I'll move to the rear of the building. There's less chance I'll be spotted there, and more shadows. If Blue is able to join me, I'll station him in this position. Do not worry about me. Just get out, if need be. I will find you."

Elinor nodded. She was shaking with nerves and tension, but Winn's words calmed her. He would find her. She was not alone in this. There was something comforting in knowing he would be only steps away.

"If you do not emerge in four hours," Winn said, "four exactly, I am coming for you." As if to emphasize his words, low-pitched church bells clanged ominously in the distance.

Elinor swallowed, dismayed to find her throat seemed to be blocked by a large lump.

Winn took her by the shoulders, and even through the thick wool of her mantle, she could feel the warmth of his hands. "You do not have to do this. You can still change your mind."

"I want to do this," she told him, pushing down that lump in her throat until it thudded into her belly and rested there, heavy as a boulder.

He sighed, seeming resigned, and she reached out and stroked his cheek. She had always been the one seeking comfort, and now she felt a little dizzy at the change in their stations. "I will be fine, Winn. I know what I am doing." Perhaps if she said that enough, she would begin to believe it.

"No, you don't, but I love that you rush in anyway."

Elinor blinked. This was the closest he had ever

come to telling her he loved her. Loving something about her was not the same as loving her, but it was better than nothing.

"And I love that you will stand and protect me," she answered after a pause. "Just think of the stories we will have to tell our grandchildren."

"Just remember, you need to live so we might have the chance to meet those grandchildren."

She nodded. "Point taken." The clock clanged its last, the bell reverberating through the night. "I suppose that is my cue," she said.

"Yes."

She took a breath and stepped away from him. "I will see you in four hours." She turned away and started for the appointed house, but before she could take more than a step, she was spun back around and enveloped in Winn's warm embrace.

"Winn!"

His mouth, warm and possessive, closed over hers, cutting off her protest. She tried to free herself, but as he deepened the kiss with expert skill, she found her legs weakening instead and her arms reaching up to grasp him by the shoulders. She suddenly needed the support. His hands slid up her arms and cupped her face, and the kiss changed from possessive to tender. It was so tender she almost wanted to weep, so tender she never wanted it to end. She had longed to be kissed like this. She had longed to feel cherished and beautiful and utterly irresistible. Winn made her feel that now. Winn made her feel as though he could not exist without her.

And then slowly, reluctantly, he broke the kiss. "Be

careful," he said, his voice husky with a need she felt as well. She nodded, still slightly dazzled but startled into awareness when she felt the cold bite of the cool night air. Winn pulled her mantle off her shoulders and threw it over his arm. "Now you are a fallen woman. Act like one."

With a deep breath, she turned away from him.

As she stepped into the street, she heard his last whispered command. "Come back to me."

She turned to tell him she would, but when she looked back, he was gone.

The interior of the house of pleasure was much more what Elinor had expected. It was decorated in red with provocative art hung on the walls. Men were shepherded into a drawing room, where the ladies of the house congregated to entertain them. It sounded like any soiree in any London drawing room, until Elinor noted most of the women were in some state of undress, and couples frequently departed together, climbing the stairs with what appeared to be frantic need.

As she'd expected, she'd been shown to a small parlor and introduced to the proprietor of the establishment, otherwise known as the abbess, and referred to here as Madam Limoge. Elinor was about as French as the woman who stood before her, speaking in a very bad French accent.

"You are pretty enough, *oui*? But why do you want to work for Madame Limoge?"

Elinor had been schooled in the proper responses. "I hear you're fair. You give a girl what she's owed." She lowered her eyes. "And I have need of blunt."

The abbess nodded. "Lost your protector, did ya?" Her accent seemed to falter. "Think you can find a new one here?"

"I think a partnership between us might be mutually beneficial."

The abbess narrowed her eyes. "Yer a smart one, no doubt." She gave Elinor a lengthy perusal from head to toe. "Pretty too. You've got curves, *oui*? So many of the girls I get here are all skin and bones. Gentlemen like curves."

Elinor bit her lip, thinking she should probably make some response, but completely at a loss as to what the appropriate response might be.

"What did you say your name was again?"

Elinor had been schooled here as well. "Mrs. Smith, but my friends call me Chastity."

The abbess laughed, and Elinor felt all the color rush from her face. Melbourne had said *Chastity*, had he not?

"Amusing too," the abbess remarked. "All right, I'll give you a chance. I'll show you to the room you can use."

This was what Elinor had been waiting for. She needed to get inside the house to be able to look around and find Foncé's lieutenant. Melbourne suspected the man was ensconced in one of the rooms on the upper floors. Elinor needed access to those rooms and those floors in order to search for the man.

She followed the abbess through the house of pleasure as the woman pointed out various points of interest—kitchens in the basement below, dining room adjacent to the drawing room on the ground floor, and on the first floor, what she called pleasure rooms. These were bedrooms, whose doors were closed when occupied. As it was a large house, there were half a dozen bedchambers and one or two were presently open, and Elinor could see they were plain in nature, boasting a bed, dresser, and worn rug. But she supposed little else was needed for the activities that went on there. Finally, the abbess came to the end of the hallway and opened the last door. "Here you are, Mrs. Smith. Best room in the house."

Elinor peeked inside. It looked similar to the other bedrooms. The bed was made, though she was suspicious of the cleanliness of the sheets, and a pitcher of water with two glasses had been placed on the bedside table. "Thank you," she said, moving inside. "I need but a few moments to ready myself." She would not be here long. There was a door a few paces away she suspected led to the attic, and she intended to investigate that level.

"Just a moment," the abbess said, catching the door before Elinor could close it. "There are a few rules."

Elinor raised a brow.

"First of all, no filching."

"Filching?"

"First girl to call a man has rights. You don't try and filch him from her."

"I see."

"And another rule. Don't act so carried away you scream the house down."

Elinor's eyes widened. "I don't take your meaning."

"A man likes you to act satisfied, but the rest of the men—those waiting for yer attentions, so to speak—also like to imagine they are the only ones. So keep your screams and hollers down."

"Of course." Elinor prayed this was the end of the lecture and began to close the door again in hopes of encouraging the abbess to depart.

"One last thing," Madam Limoge said, wedging her foot in the door. "See that there door?"

Elinor looked around blankly and pretended to notice the door. "That one?"

"Right. Don't go near it. The attic is private."

Elinor nodded. "Is that where your rooms are?"

"It's private. In fact, it's best if you don't take too much notice about who comes and goes through that door, if you take my meaning."

"I do."

"Good. I'll see you downstairs. *Oui?* You're the new girl, which means all the gentlemen will want a quarter hour of your time. I expect to turn a nice profit."

Elinor forced a smile and finally shoved the door closed. She leaned against the wood, feeling it rattle. It certainly would be no protection against any who wished to gain entrance. She wondered how long she had before her absence in the drawing room below was noted. Assuming she had very little time, she creaked the door opened, peeked out, and started for the door to the forbidden attic.

❧

Winn had sat in every imaginable pigsty in the whole of Europe. He'd endured snowstorms and rainstorms, sweltering heat and bitter cold, mud, grime, and everything in between. But no hellhole had ever been worse than the one in which he currently found himself.

It was not that the yard behind the brothel was particularly uncomfortable. He'd found a broken stool on which to sit. Admittedly, it was somewhat lopsided, but Winn did not find that a cause for complaint. The weather was tolerable—neither too cold nor too hot, and for once it was not raining in London. Considering the current weather conditions, the fog would not creep in until the early morning hours, which meant he had an excellent view of the building he was surveying.

Which meant Winn noted precisely when Foncé's man entered through the rear door. Elinor had been inside a little over an hour, and all appeared to be well. Business seemed to progress as usual, and Winn could only hope she'd managed to avoid that business and had been able to take a peek into Lefèbvre's chambers.

Until he saw Lefèbvre.

And then it was all Winn could do not to rush into the bawdy house and warn her.

"You'll only put her in more danger," a soft voice said near his ear. A hand came down on his shoulder, and Winn, who already had his hand on his dagger, released it and looked into the eyes Blue had been named for.

"I thought you were guarding the prince," Winn grumbled.

"He's in bed with his latest mistress and unlikely to leave her side tonight. Perhaps I should be guarding your back. You did not even hear me approach."

"A lapse I suppose I will never be able to live down."

Blue smiled. "You know me too well."

"I don't know you at all."

"But I know you, and you were on the verge of going in there." Blue nodded at the brothel. A dim rectangle of light had spilled from the doorway a few moments before, but when Lefèbvre closed it behind him, the yard went dark again.

"Foncé's lieutenant is inside."

"I followed him here."

Winn stiffened. "He was at Carlton House?"

"The Maîtriser group has been watching it and the regent. They will strike soon."

"Do you think they have a plan in place?"

Blue shrugged. "If not, I would be very surprised. I hope she can uncover it for us. Even a small clue would be helpful. Right now, I am at a loss."

Those were not sentiments Winn wanted to hear from one of the Barbican group's best. If Blue was puzzled by Foncé's intentions, then they were all in trouble.

"If Lefèbvre discovers Elinor…" Winn began, unable to finish the sentiment.

"She appears clever and resourceful. She will find a way." Blue extracted a pocket watch from inside his black cape. Winn might have sworn he saw the shine of silk and brocade underneath, but why would Blue be wearing such fripperies? "What time is the rendezvous?"

"Two and three-quarter hours." Winn did not even have to look at his own pocket watch. He felt every moment's slow passage in the beating of his heart.

"Good." Blue snapped the watch closed. "You want me in front?"

Winn nodded, and Blue started for the path that

would skirt the building and keep him out of sight. "Blue?" Winn hissed.

Blue looked back.

"Thank you."

"Do not thank me yet."

❧

Elinor eased the forbidden door near her room open, wincing at the loud whine the hinges made. Heavens! Did no one oil the hinges in this establishment? The sound was enough to wake the dead. She half expected the closed bedroom doors along the corridor to snap open, revealing accusatory looks from Madam Limoge's girls and their clients, but no door opened, and the sounds of merriment from below did not falter.

Elinor swallowed the bile rising in her throat and willed her heart to slow its thundering against her chest. Instead, she eased the door closed behind her and looked up at a steep flight of stairs leading to the attic floor of the brothel. A weak candle sputtered in the sconce to her right, and Elinor squinted in the gloom. She supposed gloom was what she wanted. After all, if Foncé's lieutenant was in residence, he would want more light. Now was the perfect time to have a look around. Elinor used the candle to light the lamp she held, then tiptoed up the steep steps. The attic was cramped and narrow and consisted of a corridor with several doors on either side. No rug lined the wood floor, and it had not been polished in some time. She could see tracks in the dust leading to one of the rooms.

Similar tracks led to the other rooms, but they were not as numerous or as recent.

That first room was the one she wanted. She was sure of it.

She padded along the dusty floor until she stood before the closed door. Her heart pounded in her ears, the sound like that of the mail coach thundering down on her.

Dear God, please let the door be unlocked.

Her hand shook as she reached for the handle, rattling the tarnished metal when she touched it. Gingerly, she pushed it down. It would not move.

She let out a shaky breath and closed her eyes. Now she would see if Winn's work had paid off. She reached into her skirts, found the pocket hidden within, and extracted a key. The metal clattered against the door as she fit the key into the lock. Wonder of wonders, it fit! She turned it, hearing the scrape of metal on metal and a click. She felt the lock give, but the door did not swing open.

With another look at the stairs behind her, Elinor set down her lamp and wedged a shoulder against the door and shoved, feeling her face grow hot from the exertion. With a scrape of metal on wood, the door eased inward. A bead of perspiration ran down her temple, but she ignored it, and turning her back on the door, dug in her heels and heaved.

She flew backward, falling into the dark room. She grimaced at the noise she had made and prayed her room really was the one directly below this one. Crawling back toward the hallway, she lifted her lamp, pocketed the key again, and turned in a half-circle to study her surroundings.

Besides the low sloped ceiling, the room where

she stood was little different from those she had seen below, though this one had a desk and a man's coat thrown over the bed. The desk's surface was obscured by stacks of papers, and Elinor felt her heart leap with excitement. There had to be something here!

She dashed to the desk, setting her lamp on top of a stack of papers she hoped would not tumble over from the additional weight. Her back prickled as she thumbed through the papers in the middle of the desk. What if she were discovered? What if Madam Limoge, or worse, Foncé, walked in and found her?

That wasn't going to happen, she chided herself, frowning at a list of numbers that meant nothing to her. She was going to be in and out in just a few moments. As soon as she found something relating to the prince...

More papers with numbers, more papers with numbers... Elinor shuffled them aside until she spotted something with words. French words. She closed her eyes in frustration. Now was no time to have to rely on the accuracy of her French translation. Perhaps she should simply scoop the lot of the documents into her arms and hope she managed to grab something useful.

Elinor looked down at her gown and shook her head. The bodice was cut so low she would not have been able to hide a ticket to the theater, much less two or three of the papers littering this desk. Her pocket was large enough only to fit the key. She had no choice but to go through the pile. She puzzled over the first document in French, eventually deciphering it to be a list of members of the Maîtriser group and their current salaries. That information might have been useful to the Barbican group, but it was not what she needed at the moment.

Her first priority had to be the prince.

She shuffled another paper to the top and scanned it for words she could quickly translate. It was something about a shipping venture, and she set it aside. Her foot tapped impatiently as she realized this was taking far longer than it should have. Yes, she still had hours before Winn would come after her, but Madame Limoge would expect her to make an appearance in the drawing room shortly. How long did Elinor have before Chastity was missed?

She lifted another paper and tried to concentrate on the words. She had to focus and put the rest of her worries aside. This was no different than helping Lady Hollingshead with her garden party. Then the servants and the tasks had been scattered and disorganized. All Elinor had done was lend some order and focus to the preparations.

That was the key here as well. She would go through these documents in an orderly fashion, concentrating on each one briefly. Very briefly.

She studied the one she held again, scanning the French for familiar words. Instead, a word in English caught her attention.

Regent.

Elinor caught her breath. She'd done it! She'd really found what the Barbican group needed!

And then she heard footsteps on the stairs.

Winn paced back and forth in the shadows behind the brothel. He stared so hard at the building he thought perhaps he would burn through it with his eyes. What the devil was going on inside? Had Elinor been found out? Was she, even now, being forced to seduce some man who had his hands all over her? Was she hiding in a corner and praying he would come and save her? He hated this defenseless feeling. It reminded him too much of what he'd felt when he'd heard those shots and could not go back for Crow.

Winn stopped pacing. He would not make the same mistake again.

He stared at the house again, noted the numerous garments strung along a clothesline in the back, and started forward.

❧

Elinor dropped the paper and turned just in time to see a short, fat man climb the last step and move into the corridor outside the room. His already dark eyes went even darker when his brow came down menacingly. "Who the bloody hell are you?" he asked. His accent was French, heavily French, and Elinor knew she had found her man.

Not that she'd wanted to find Foncé's lieutenant. In fact, she would have been quite happy never to lay eyes on the man. He was coming toward her, his expression menacing, and even though her reflexes were telling her to run, she tossed her hair back, stuck out her chest, and smiled.

Foncé's man slowed.

"*Je suis* Chastity." She gave a little curtsy that was

more of a bow designed to give him a clear view of her breasts spilling out of the low-cut gown. "And that's all the French I know. You are French?" She giggled. She had not giggled in... possibly ever, but she'd heard her daughters giggle often enough.

"What are you doing here?"

Elinor shrugged. "I'm new. I must have taken a wrong turn." She turned in a full circle, as though she had lost her way and had no notion of the way out. "Unless, that is, you want me to stay." She smiled coyly, but when his brow rose with interest, she wondered if perhaps she would not have been better off making a quick exit. Then her gaze strayed to the paper she'd dropped on the floor—the one mentioning the regent. She had to take it with her. She hadn't even had a chance to read it. If she left without it, all of this would have been for nothing.

Elinor stepped closer to the paper, and consequently, closer to Foncé's lieutenant. He reached out a hand, beckoning her. "Do you want to stay?"

Elinor thought of the paper just inches from her foot and nodded.

"Then convince me you can be entertaining."

Elinor let out a slow breath and took Lefèbvre's hand.

༄

"And there are those who mock my sense of style."

Winn spun around and would have punched Blue if the other agent had not stepped to the side. "Stop sneaking up on me."

"Pay better attention, and I will not be able to sneak up on you. Tell me this is not what I think it is."

Winn looked down at the ill-fitting gown he wore. He had tried several before landing on one that fit. It was sturdy and plain, which told him it probably belonged to one of the servants rather than one of the prostitutes. It didn't look half-bad, in his opinion. "I need shoes," he said to Blue. "The boots ruin the effect."

"The stubble ruins the effect. You are not going inside."

"I am. No one will notice me. No one ever notices servants."

"They'll notice one who looks like you. Baron, you look like an ape stuffed into women's garb. This will not work."

Winn bent and shook out a dark mantle. "I admit disguises are not my forte, but if I pull up the hood to cover my short hair and keep my head down…"

Blue shook his head.

"I'm going."

"And if I attempt to stop you?"

"Are you stronger than you look?"

Blue sighed. "Melbourne will have my head for this."

Winn ignored him and turned around. "I cannot fasten this thing. Do you see how it is accomplished?"

"I will see what I can do."

Winn felt the other man fumble with the fabric, and then he went still.

"Do you realize you have what appears to be a bite mark on your shoulder?"

"What?"

Blue touched it. "Here."

Winn had a flash of Elinor sinking her teeth into his flesh as she'd climaxed. "It's nothing."

"Of course not." Blue's voice sounded choked— almost as though he were laughing.

Winn felt the other agent tug at the dress again, and then the material pulled tightly against his ribs.

"Suck in your stomach," Blue said.

Winn did so.

"More."

"I can't," Winn gasped. "That's as far as it will go."

"You make an awful woman." Blue grunted, and the fabric pulled tighter yet. Winn could not breathe, but finally he felt the gown close in the back.

"Do not move, and you shall be fine."

"Excellent," Winn gasped. He struggled to pull the mantle over his shoulder, and Blue assisted him. "Now I know why my wife despairs when her lady's maid has the evening off."

"Yes, I…" Blue gripped Winn's shoulder and shoved him into the shadow of a small, struggling tree. Winn ducked down, feeling the gown's material rip at the seams, but he made no sound as he watched three men stroll into the yard.

Foncé and two of his men.

Blue and Winn exchanged glances and sank farther out of sight. As Winn watched, Foncé went through the door of the brothel, leaving one man to guard the back door and keep watch.

Winn was trapped.

Even worse, Elinor was trapped, for if Foncé saw her, he would kill her.

Twenty

LEFÈBVRE'S HAND WAS CLAMMY, AND ELINOR TRIED not to show her distaste at the touch of his moist skin. He pulled her hard against him, and they were eye to eye. His breath was tinged with the scent of onions, and she attempted to hold her breath.

"S'il vous plaît. Entertain me."

"Ah." Elinor felt light-headed from lack of air. She was relatively certain incidents like this were what Winn had objected to when she'd begged for this mission. But she was more concerned that, at the moment, she could think of nothing she wanted to do more than cast up her accounts. "Shall I dance?" she finally managed. Perhaps if she danced, she could move away from him and catch her breath.

"*Oui*," he said, voice husky. He released her, and she took a step back.

Only to stand completely frozen.

She had to escape. She had to dance. But how was she supposed to dance? Certainly he did not want to see her dance a quadrille or a reel. But she knew no other dances. No, that was not true. She knew the waltz. And only very recently the waltz had been considered quite scandalous. Humming a song in her head, she began to move in the steps of the waltz. She was used to having a partner, but she thought she was doing rather well on her own.

"What are you doing?" Lefèbvre said.

Elinor frowned. Was that not obvious?

"Seduce me."

Elinor gave him a shaky smile. She had to figure some way out of this. And she had to take the letter with the mention of the prince on it as well. Could she grab it and run? Could she hit him with a blunt object? There was an ink blotter on the desk…

"Dance," he demanded.

Elinor jumped and began to waltz again. Hitting him with the ink blotter might not be such a bad idea.

Lefèbvre removed his coat and threw it on a chair. He sprawled on the bed and propped himself on one elbow, giving her his full attention. Elinor did not like this progression of events. "Put your hands down," he ordered.

She complied. She'd been holding them up as though grasping an imaginary man's shoulders.

"Use them to remove your gown."

Elinor froze in mid-dance step and stumbled.

"You are a shy one."

"Yes." That was it. "I am shy."

"Take off your gown."

"Perhaps we could talk a little first…"

"I would be happier talking to you if you wore fewer garments."

Why had she agreed to this mission? Why had she

not listened to Winn? She had no one to blame but herself. She'd created this muddle, and she would have to find a way out of it.

"Would you mind turning around?" she said.

"I would mind."

Why did she expect him to behave as a gentleman? "Please. I promise to make it worth your while."

He studied her a long moment. "I do not like to turn my back, but I will do so. Just this once. Be quick, and when I turn back, I want you undressed."

"You won't see a stitch of my clothing." Because she was going to run at the first opportunity. She reached for her bodice, and Lefèbvre rolled to face away from her. As soon as his back was to her, she bent, snatched up the paper, and ran for the stairs.

She raced down the steps, flung open the door, and stared into the handsomely cruel face of Foncé.

❦

"This is unfortunate," Blue muttered.

"Unfortunate?" Winn grumbled. He reached back to ascertain the damage to his gown. "It's a bloody disaster."

"Not completely," Blue murmured. "We wanted Foncé, and now we have him."

"And he has my wife."

"We don't know that."

"I'm not taking any chances. I'm going in."

Blue sighed. "I knew you were going to say that. I suppose you want me to deal with our friend there."

From their hiding place in the shadows, just a few yards from the brothel's rear entrance, Winn studied Foncé's man. "I could do it."

"Quietly?"

Winn glared at Blue. "Would you like a demonstration? I can throttle you right here without saying a word."

"Point taken." Blue stepped back. "But I have a better idea. A plan, if you like."

He bent his head, and Winn listened, his scowl growing.

❧

"I beg your pardon!" Elinor hurried to say before she realized whom she had plowed into. And then she saw his face, and she ducked her head and attempted to skirt around him.

He deftly caught her arm and jerked her chin up. "Lady Keating. We meet again."

"Who?" Elinor asked. "I'm Mrs. Smith."

"You, my lady, are a very bad liar."

Lefèbvre picked that moment to come roaring down the stairs, but when he saw Foncé, he stopped short. "I'll send her away."

"Oh, no," Foncé said with a smile Elinor did not much care for. "We are well acquainted. Are we not, Lady Keating?"

Elinor glared at him.

"You know her?"

"Oh, yes," Foncé said, gesturing toward the stairs, an indication she should precede the men. "She is the wife of one of the Barbican's last spies. One of the few we haven't exterminated yet. I have a feeling that oversight will be rectified tonight."

Elinor moved to ascend the stairs again. Once in Lefèbvre's chamber, she would be trapped, but she could see no other alternative.

"I trust she did not fool you," Foncé said, climbing the stairs behind her.

"Of course not."

"Good." Foncé ripped the paper with the information about the prince out of her hand. "We would not want sensitive documents to fall into the enemy's possession."

It was at that moment Elinor realized she might be able to postpone the inevitable. She reached the top of the stairs and tried to remember how Caroline always managed to goad Georgiana into a quarrel. "I really didn't see anything," she told Foncé. "I was here only a few moments before your lieutenant arrived. I merely glanced at these papers."

Lefèbvre's face turned dark. "You read these papers?"

"I only peeked," she said. "They were in plain view."

Foncé rounded on his lieutenant. "I have told you, time and again, to burn our correspondence or lock it in a drawer."

"I do."

Foncé gestured to the stack of papers littering the desk. "Then what is this?"

"I was not concerned. None of the girls here can read."

They were fighting each other now, and Elinor scooted to the right, closer to the stairwell. She would have to slip past Foncé, but if she could wait until he was absorbed enough in the argument and not looking her way…

Foncé pointed to her. "*She* can read." He held aloft the paper she'd stolen. "And she read this. You know what that means, do you not?"

Elinor froze. Perhaps her plan was not working as well as she'd hoped. Perhaps it worked well only with silly young girls.

Lefèbvre cracked his knuckles. "It means she must die."

～

"Oh, my," Winn said in an unnaturally high voice that made his throat tickle. He held back a cough. "You are a handsome man."

Foncé's guard turned quickly, raising a pistol.

Winn wanted to knock it out of the man's hand, but if it went off, it would alert those inside to their presence. So Winn held up his hands and said, "Oh! Don't hurt me."

"Who are you?" the guard demanded. Behind him, Winn could see a shadow creeping closer. It was Blue. Just a few more moments of this idiocy.

Winn fluttered his lashes. "Chambermaid. You frightened me." He attempted to look scared.

"Were you scared? Come here then." The guard opened his arms. "I'll make it all better."

Winn cocked a brow. Was the man sincere?

"Come here now," the man said. "I like a woman with a little substance to her."

Winn grimaced. It must have been darker than he'd thought. But if the guard wanted substance, who was Winn to deny him? With a shrug, he stepped into the guard's embrace. Winn tenderly wrapped his arms around the man, then lifted him and slammed him against the side of the building. "I might have a bit more substance than you were expecting," he said in his own voice and punched the man in the stomach.

Blue caught the guard when he stumbled backward, and Winn saluted. "Told you I could handle it."

"Baron, you scare me sometimes."

He scared himself. "Just watch my back." And he stepped into the brothel.

As he'd expected, the back entrance opened into a small anteroom, which was dark and empty at this time of the night. A door in the corner led down to the kitchens and the servants' stairs, and another door opened into what was probably the dining or drawing room. Winn could hear the voices of men and women rising and falling. He doubted Foncé or Elinor were chatting over wine. In fact, Elinor had been instructed to look for Lefèbvre's private chambers. That meant she was upstairs.

Winn looked at the door to the public rooms again. He was never going to gain entrance to those rooms looking like this. He could remove the gown, solicit a woman for the hour, then tie her up and search for Elinor…

The idea had appeal. Except there was that other man who'd come with Foncé. What if he was in the drawing room? Chances were, he would recognize Winn.

That left Winn only one option. He sighed and started for the door housing the stairs down to the kitchens.

He immediately regretted not having taken a moment to search the dining room for a lamp or a candle. The kitchens were dark, and he stumbled down the creaky stairs, feeling his way. The smell of animal fat, onions, and burnt bread permeated his nostrils, making them burn, and when he stepped into the kitchen, he bumped his head on a low-hanging pot. He jostled it, and it clanged softly against the others hanging nearby. It made for an eerie chorus until one pot tumbled to the floor, making a clanging sound. If anyone was down here, they knew they were not alone.

Winn moved to return the pot to its hook and knocked the tongs from the kitchen fireplace. He cursed quietly, replaced the pot then bent to retrieve the tongs. Unfortunately, the heat of the tongs had caught his skirts on fire. "Bloody hell!" How did women manage to cook anything without going up in flames?

He tore the section of skirt off and tossed it aside, where it landed on the stone floor. Winn examined his dress to ensure the fire was out but jerked his head up when he heard a popping sound. He jumped back at the small explosion, shielding his eyes. Fire raced up the wall and across the floor as the fat which had ignited it poured out of a small pail.

He waited for someone to rush in with water or sand to extinguish the fire, but no one came. This was to his advantage because no one would look too closely at him or ask questions. Of course, the disadvantage was that the house was now on fire. He had better be quick.

❧

"That seems a bit harsh," Elinor said, taking a step back. "You do not have to kill me. Really."

Lefèbvre stepped closer, and she retreated again, only to feel the bulk of the bed's mattress push against her calves. "I have never been a supporter of the regent. He is far too frivolous, and a terrible spend-thrift! And once I met him at a ball." She was babbling now, but she feared if she ceased speaking, Foncé would take the opportunity to issue some horrible directive. "He wears a hideous beauty mark just here.

And he practically leered at every woman who passed within five feet."

"Shut up!" Foncé roared.

"I beg your pardon! I am only trying to explain that I am no friend to the prince. If you want to kill him, go right ahead."

Foncé's dark look was not reassuring.

"I mean, if that is your plan. I didn't see anything that would confirm such a plan. I am merely guessing."

"I am going to kill you so I no longer have to listen to your voice," Foncé said. He grabbed her and twisted her arm behind her back. "Find me something with which to secure her. If the Barbican group knows we are here, we must move."

Elinor's arms were jerked roughly into place, and something that felt suspiciously like a drapery cord was wound around her wrists. Tightly. She had no experience escaping bonds, but she knew she would not easily free her hands from this prison.

"Do you want me to kill her?" Lefèbvre asked. With a jolt, Elinor spun around. Lefèbvre grinned at her. What kind of man discussed murder so easily? But this was what Winn had tried to warn her about. She had thought it all adventure and excitement. Why had she not considered that things might not go as she'd hoped?

"Not yet," Foncé answered. "Collect these papers first. I'd rather not have to work in here with a dead body fouling the air."

Elinor inhaled sharply, and Lefèbvre cracked his knuckles. He leaned close to her, so close she could smell the onion on his breath again. "And I thought you wouldn't entertain me."

Elinor watched as Lefèbvre dragged a trunk from one side of the room to the desk. He began sweeping papers into it, tossing in ledgers and books as well. She closed her eyes. Now Foncé would find a new hiding place, and the Barbican group would have to begin all over again. Somehow, in her zeal to help, she'd made everything worse.

And to add to that failure, she was about to die. That thought was none too comforting either.

She watched as the men hurriedly emptied the room, knowing her time was growing shorter and shorter. And then her gaze fell on a slip of paper on the bed. It was the paper with the reference to the regent. The men had forgotten it. If she could somehow hide it from view, perhaps the Barbican group would find it later... when they found her body.

Trying to look nonchalant, she scooted toward that side of the bed. Foncé shot her a look, and she immediately flung herself down, her bottom hiding the parchment. "Do you mind if I sit?"

"By all means, make yourself comfortable. We won't be much longer."

"Take your time."

He gave her a thin smile and went back to his task. Elinor watched to be certain he would not look back at her, then scooted forward and gripped the edge of the paper with her fingers. She could not manage a good grip on it with her hands tied, and it took her several attempts to finally grasp the edge.

Just as she did so, Lefèbvre looked back at her. She froze and tried to look innocent. She imagined she looked about as innocent as Georgiana after she snatched the last tea cake. Elinor would do better to imitate Caroline. That girl had a natural deviousness.

"I think we are about done here," Foncé said.

"Do you want to do it, or shall I?"

Elinor swallowed. "By *it*, I assume you mean who is going to end my life?"

"This doesn't involve you," Lefèbvre said, pointing his finger at her.

"I beg to differ!" She stood, holding the parchment behind her to keep it from view.

"You kill her," Foncé said. "I don't have my tools, and we are short on time."

Lefèbvre cracked his knuckles again and stepped toward her. At the same time, a cry of "Fire!" echoed. Both men started for the door, and Elinor took the opportunity to drop the parchment on the floor and slide it under the bed with her foot.

"See what that is about," Foncé ordered. "It could very well be one of their tricks." He gestured to Elinor, and she was gratified that at least she was considered part of the Barbican group by someone.

"Yes, sir!" Lefèbvre rushed down the stairs, and when Elinor turned back to Foncé, she found him staring intently at her.

"Did you know you have a knife in your hair?"

Elinor tried to reach for her coiffure, but she'd forgotten her hands were tied. Foncé did the honors for her, gently withdrawing the small dagger she'd secured there. It seemed she'd performed the task a lifetime ago, when it had been merely hours. With all of her flopping and running, her hair must have moved enough to make the dagger visible.

Foncé held the small weapon aloft so it glinted in the lamplight.

"It appears I have the tools to kill you after all."

❦

Upon reflection, Winn thought he might have done better to search for Elinor and forgo additions to his disguise. The fire he'd accidentally set spread quickly, and he found himself in the unenviable position of trying to gain entrance to a row of doors, all of which appeared to be locked.

He glanced behind him. The flames in the kitchen pumped like angry fists then raced like gleeful children up the walls to dance on the ceiling.

He was either extremely dedicated to his work, a complete idiot, or madly in love. Probably all three. A sane man would be heading for the exit, not deeper into the house. Trying to keep low, a rather difficult task considering his size and height, he moved along the corridor to face two more closed doors. He had just enough time left to quickly augment his disguise.

Hoping he'd be lucky—as though that ever happened—he tried one of the door handles. Locked. He tried the other. Locked. Who locked all the doors in a house? Bloody hell. He hated breaking doors down. He was definitely too old for this sort of thing

Winn stared at the doors. *Which one? Which one?* He didn't have the time or energy to break into all of them. He said a little rhyme in his head his daughter had enjoyed when she was younger, and pointed to the door his finger landed on.

He took three large steps back, inhaled slowly,

then ran for the door, leading with his shoulder. He rammed it, bounced back, and shook his head. He examined the frame, saw he'd done some damage, and stepped back again. He eyed the door, noting curls of smoke had tiptoed down the corridor.

With a groan of dread, he rammed the door again. This time he separated it enough to kick it in. He was inside the room and stumbling about in the darkness. His shoulder hurt like the devil, but he ignored the pain and looked for a dresser. A promising shape loomed across the room, and Winn approached it, smiling when he saw it was a highboy. Beside it were two pegs, and on one hung a hat. With ribbons. Perfect.

He found some shoes, yanked his boots off, and stuffed his feet in them, wincing with pain. Hobbling, he made his way to the looking glass. He looked like a man wearing a woman's hat. He needed something more...

Ear bobs! He tied a pair on his ears and checked the looking glass again. Better. But what was Elinor always putting on her cheeks? She didn't want him to notice, so he pretended he didn't. Ah, there. Rouge. He stuck his fingers in it and rubbed it in a circle on his cheeks and then his lips. He shrugged at his reflection. Not bad. He was the ugliest woman he'd ever seen, but he thought he might pass, considering the smoke and confusion.

He rubbed his hand on the mantel to rid his fingers of the remaining rouge, and ran for the door.

He promptly tripped over his shoes and had to climb to his feet again. How the devil did women walk in these things? Small, dainty steps, he decided.

Now to find Elinor. Winn tripped and stumbled up the steps, onto the ground floor, and into the dining room.

Without pause, he flung open the door to the drawing room. "Fire!" he screamed in a womanly voice—or as close as he could manage. "The kitchens are on fire. Run!"

There was a long moment when no one moved and no one spoke. Winn half expected them to go about their conversations as though he hadn't spoken. And then pandemonium erupted. Women screamed, men cursed, and people climbed over one another to reach the exits.

Winn waited until they'd filed past him, and then started for the stairs.

But not everyone had fled.

☙

"I think I shall start with your mouth," Foncé said. "I would like to cut out your tongue, so I do not have to hear another word from you."

Elinor was wise enough not to speak.

"Then again, I do so like the sound of screaming. If I cut out your tongue, I won't hear your pleas for mercy when I cut you here." He drew the blade of the dagger across her chest, causing a string of pain and a bright line of blood to appear. It was a shallow cut, but it hurt nonetheless.

"Or here." He flicked the dagger at the front of the gown, tearing the thin material and exposing a swath of her pale abdomen. The dagger flicked again, and another smiling red mouth appeared. Elinor choked back a scream. She wanted to keep her tongue as long as possible.

"Now that is pretty." Foncé wielded the knife again before boots thumped on the stairs.

"It's true!" his second-in-command wheezed, doubling over to catch his breath. "The kitchens. Fire."

"Damn it! I don't have time for this." Foncé thrust the dagger at his lieutenant. "Kill her."

❧

"Who are you?" asked the guard standing in front of the stairs leading to the upper floors, leading to Elinor. Above, all was still silent. No one had thought to warn the girls working upstairs.

"Chambermaid," Winn said in a ridiculously high voice. "I must warn the girls upstairs." Winn risked a glance at the man and saw he looked skeptical. Bloody hell. What was he to do now? Women always needed help, and men seemed to enjoy helping them, so he added, "Can you help me?"

"I…" The man hesitated, and Winn considered that perhaps it was only *attractive* women men enjoyed assisting. Foncé's man leaned closer, scrutinizing him, and Winn decided he'd better not take a chance.

"Oh, dear! Look at that!" he screeched, pointing behind the man. When the guard turned to look, Winn kicked him. The man fell against the stairs, and Winn fell on him, ramming his head into the wooden slats. As the man's eyes drifted closed, Winn muttered, "That's for thinking I wasn't pretty enough."

He jumped over the unconscious man and continued quickly but cautiously up the stairs to the first floor. A woman appeared at the top, and Winn yelled, "Fire! Run!" The woman rushed past him, not seeming to care he was going in the wrong direction. He took the stairs two at a time, reached the landing, and turned in a circle. Where was Elinor? *Where was Elinor?*

At the end of the corridor, the door leading to the attic flew open, and a short, stout man emerged. He was the image of the description Winn had been given for Lefèbvre. Winn jumped back, into the room the whore had just vacated, and closed the door all but a sliver. He peeked through the sliver as Foncé's lieutenant ran past him and down the main stairwell. Winn darted back out of the bedroom, narrowly avoiding a collision with a couple running for the exit, and headed for the attic.

Thin wisps of smoke made the passage hazy, and Winn heard cries of alarm from below. The fire was spreading. Time was growing short.

He reached the door leading to the attic stairs and paused to listen. He thought he heard voices echoing down through the stairwell leading to the topmost floor. A male voice but no female. Winn would wager anything the male voice belonged to Foncé. But where was Elinor? Winn had been an operative for most of his life. A man like Foncé, a man who was so ostensibly an enemy of the Barbican group, was also *his* sworn enemy. A man like that must be dealt with. And for the first time in more than a decade of service, Winn paused. He did not care about Foncé at the moment. It was Elinor whose face he saw in his mind's eye. It was Elinor he was here for, not Foncé. Foncé could hang. When Elinor was safe, Winn would deal with Foncé.

And if Elinor was not safe… Winn would destroy the entire Maîtriser group single-handedly.

He heard the thump of boots and looked over his shoulder to see the Maîtriser group's second-in-command clomping along the first floor corridor toward him. Winn swore and grasped the first door handle within reach. The bedroom was unlocked, and he dove inside, not caring whether it was occupied or not. A quick survey told him it was not. He eased the door open and watched as Lefèbvre stomped up the attic stairs.

If Elinor had been an experienced operative, Winn would have known with absolute certainty she was in one of those attic rooms. The attic above was obviously the domain of the Maîtriser group.

But Elinor was not an experienced operative, and she might never have made it that far. She could be anywhere in the brothel. She could be bound in a room with flames licking at the door.

Winn wanted to pound his fist into something. He never should have allowed her to accept this mission. Panic rose hot and sharp in his throat. Fear and panic were part of any mission, but this time Winn could not manage to tamp them under control. This time they slammed into him, and his legs all but crumpled.

He could not lose Elinor. He could not.

Still uncertain as to what he would do, he threw open the door to the bedroom, just as he heard footsteps in the attic stairwell again. He ducked back and watched as Foncé emerged through the door leading to the attic.

Now Winn's heart pounded with something much stronger than panic. It was the pounding of the hungry predator who has spotted his prey. It was the pounding of the heart of one who knows he has achieved victory.

Winn's vision narrowed, and his mind focused. The smoke and the heat from the rising fire faded from consciousness. The rushing in his ears blotted out everything but Foncé, moving away, blissfully unaware. He made the perfect target. Winn started for Foncé. He would kill the man and be done with it.

And then he heard a woman's scream.

⁂

Elinor knew the struggle was futile, but she wrenched her bound hands behind her back in a desperate attempt to free them from their bonds. There was no mistaking the glint in Lefèbvre's eyes. He was going to kill her. Her one consolation was that he was not going to play with her first. This was a man who cared for efficiency.

He moved toward her, and she dove around the corner of the bed, falling to her knees and struggling to rise again. Lefèbvre was coming for her. "Stop running, and I will make this quick and painless," he promised.

Elinor would have preferred to run and give herself a few more seconds of life. Unfortunately, she had the wall behind her and Lefèbvre before her. Trapped. But God help her if she would stand here and allow him to slit her throat. She waited until he was within arm's reach, then dove across the bed, wriggling to the edge, using only her body.

A hand clamped about her ankle, and she screamed and kicked. Lefèbvre swore, and Elinor rolled away. The bed sagged with his weight as he climbed after her. Like a caught fish, flopping helplessly on a boat, she struggled to reach the other side of the bed. She could see the door to freedom, but the bed was so large, and her arms were caught in the sheets. She threw her shoulders to one side, freeing herself, but just as she would have rolled off the bed, Lefèbvre caught her and pulled her back again.

"No!" she yelled. He was above her and wielding the knife, and she kicked out with all she had, landing a glancing blow with her foot on the side of his head.

He recoiled, but Elinor knew immediately it was not enough to incapacitate him. Now he was angry. "You will pay for that," he threatened.

The acrid smell of smoke flared in her nostrils, and she gasped for a breath of clean air. "This building is on fire," she told him. "You should leave now, while you still can."

"Good suggestion. Too bad you won't be alive to follow your own advice." He gripped her shoulder and raised the knife. Elinor kicked out, tried to dislodge his grip, but he held fast and managed to evade her thrashing feet. She watched the knife, watched the sharp blade come closer, and the faces of Georgiana and Caroline flashed in her mind.

Sweet girls. They knew how much she loved them.

Then she saw Winn's face. Would he ever know? Would he ever forgive her for this failure?

She shut her eyes, moved her lips in a silent prayer, and heard the blast. Her body jerked as something thumped on top of her. She opened her eyes and stared at Lefèbvre's shoulder. With a yelp, she bucked, throwing him off. He rolled slowly, and she spotted movement above and looked up.

The ugliest woman she had ever seen was peering down at her. She wore far too much rouge, large ear bobs, and sported half a day's growth of beard.

"Are you hurt?" she asked. Elinor blinked. The

woman was speaking in Winn's voice. "Ellie?" The woman came closer, bent, and kissed her.

Elinor started.

"It's me. Winn."

Elinor blinked as Winn hauled her up. When she looked at him this way, his features arranged themselves in the correct order. "Winn? Why are you dressed like a woman?"

"Never mind that now, my love. We have to escape."

"But Foncé…"

"He ran right past me." Winn hauled her to her feet, and with practiced efficiency, freed her hands from their bonds.

Elinor rubbed her arms, trying to restore circulation. "Did you capture him?"

Winn cupped her cheek with uncharacteristic tenderness. "No. I had more important matters to attend to." His gaze slid to the bed, and she made the mistake of glancing in that direction. A pool of blood fanned out from Lefèbvre's head and stained the coverlet. She thanked God the man's face was directed away from hers. Winn grabbed her hand and pulled. "Let's go. I started a fire in the kitchens, and while it makes for a good distraction, it's rather indiscriminate about whom it kills."

Elinor allowed him to pull her toward the door, but at the last moment, she broke away. "No. Wait!"

❧

Winn cursed as Elinor ran back into the room, falling at the end of the bed. Had the smoke addled her brain? "Ellie, we have to go."

"Wait. It's here."

"What is here?" Had she dropped a necklace or a hairpin? "We haven't much time." The smoke was thicker now, and he could hear the roar of the fire. It was climbing, hungry, devouring everything its long fingers touched.

"Got it!" Her hand shot into the air, clutching a piece of parchment.

"What is that?"

She handed it to him, and Winn skimmed the document. He felt a slow smile forming on his lips. He looked up and into the beautiful face of his wife, his partner, and now an agent for the Barbican group. "You bloody well did it," he said.

She smiled. "I know."

"I don't bloody well believe it."

Her smile widened. "I know."

Winn tucked the paper in his coat. "You deserve a knighthood if we make it out of here alive and reach the prince in time."

"Women cannot become knights."

He took her hand and pulled her toward the door. "More's the pity."

"Really?" She sounded astonished.

"Really." He was still grinning. His wife was really an operative. He could bluster and protest all he wanted, but he knew skill and talent and luck when he saw it. "We're going to need some of your luck," he said now, pulling her down the stairs. "If I'm not mistaken, our assassin is with the prince at this very moment."

Elinor halted, her hand pulling out of his. "What?"

"I'll explain later. Blue is waiting for us." He threw open the bedroom door and stared at a wall of flame.

Twenty-one

THIS WAS A BAD SIGN. WINN NEED NOT TELL ELINOR that an angry barricade of hot flames posed a problem. He also need not tell her that going through the flames was their only option. They were on the highest level of the house. They could not exactly escape through the window.

"We'll have to escape through the window," Winn said.

"What?" Elinor rubbed her ears. The roar of the flames was deafening.

Winn pulled her back up the stairs, slamming the door closed behind them. "That door won't hold the flames long. We can't go through the house. The fire has probably already engulfed the lower floors." He strode to the window and looked down.

Elinor followed. "We are on the uppermost floor! We can't jump down."

He struggled to push the window open. "We'll have… to… climb… down…"

Elinor couldn't see much, as Winn's body blocked the view from the window, but she doubted there

were stairs or a sufficiently sturdy ladder outside
that window.

"You're not afraid, are you?" Winn said with a grin.

"No!"

He stuck his head out the window and peered down
then began peeling off his women's garb, leaving it in a
pile on the floor. Slowly, he became Winn again—light
brown hair pulled back into a queue, emerald-green
eyes teasing her, a man's hard, solid body.

Elinor closed her eyes. This was no time for desire.
Winn wanted her to climb out a window. Of course
she was afraid! Why had she just said she was not?
She had no intention of going out that window. She
glanced at the door and saw black smoke gathering.
She looked back at the window, rose on tiptoes to
survey the drop, and felt her stomach plummet.

Elinor dug her fingers into her palm. She had not
thought she would escape Lefèbvre, but she had. She
had not thought she would ever be anything more
than a wife and mother, but here she was. She was not
going to permit a small drop to defeat her.

The fall might kill her, but at least she'd die undefeated.

"Blue!" Winn yelled. "Blue!" Winn pulled his head
back in and yanked the bedclothes off the bed.

"What are you doing?" she asked, though she could
clearly see he was fashioning a rope of some sort, tying
it to the heavy bed, and knotting the sheets together.
Did he really think she was going to trust yellowed
linens and hastily tied knots with her life? A tongue
of fire licked across the ceiling, and Elinor grabbed a
handful of cloth and started to tie.

"Who were you calling?" she asked.

"Blue. Melbourne sent him to assist."

Elinor glanced out the window at the empty yard below. "Where is he?"

"I don't know. Maybe he went after Foncé. I hope he returned to Carlton House."

"Why?" Elinor tested a knot she'd tied. It seemed sturdy. "Why did you say the assassin was with the prince? Are we too late?"

"We might be." He threw the newly fashioned "rope" out of the window. Elinor watched it fall. It did not fall for nearly as long as she would have liked. The distance between the rope and the ground was still alarmingly large, even if she did manage to actually climb down the rope. Perhaps she should begin to encourage more tree-climbing in Caroline and Georgiana's education. She could have used those particular skills at present.

"Did you read the missive?" Winn touched his coat, where he'd tucked the paper she'd saved.

Elinor felt her face color—from the encroaching fire's heat, undoubtedly. "No, I..." Her French was abysmal, but she was certainly not going to jump to her death right after admitting such a failure.

"Foncé bribed the regent's mistress. She'll open a secret door to him at midnight while the prince sleeps. Foncé will have all the time he needs to murder the prince, carve him like poultry."

"We have to warn the palace."

"I agree." Winn gestured to the window. "Do you want to go first, or shall I?"

"I think this is one instance where chivalry is best thrown to the wayside."

Winn grinned. How could the man grin at a time like this? "Very well. If you slip and fall, I will attempt to remain chivalrous enough to catch you. Now, watch how I descend, and follow me."

Elinor watched as Winn deftly threw one leg over the casement and then the other. It appeared he had done this a thousand times. She tried to watch closely, but he moved quickly and the night was dark. The heat from the fire howling behind her tended to distract her as well. Peering over the casement, she watched Winn descend. He gripped the bedclothes between his knees, wrapping an ankle around the edge to further secure himself, and then lowered himself with his hands. The sheets swayed precariously, smashing him into the building at one point, but he looked up, grinned, and continued his descent.

He really loved this.

She was scared out of her mind, her heart was racing, and she knew she was about to die, but she was also having the best night of her life. She did not want to be anywhere else—well, other than safely on the ground. But nothing could have prevented her from experiencing this exhilaration.

A boom resounded through the building, and the floor shook beneath her. The room began to slide, and Elinor grabbed the window frame for support. "Winn!" she called.

"The building is collapsing. Go now before it's too late."

Go now. Go now. Elinor nodded and sat on the edge of the windowsill. She put one foot out the window until she straddled it. She tried very, very hard not to look down. But she had to grope for the bedclothes' rope, and she accidentally caught a glimpse of the drop below her. The world spun for a moment, and she closed her eyes.

She could do this. She would rather take her chances on the rope than sit here and burn to death. Taking a deep breath, Elinor opened her eyes and reached for the rope. Winn's weight kept it straight, but she still had to lean down to grasp it. There was no avoiding the drop that way.

Winn had held the rope and jumped over the side of the window. She was not so confident. She could slide out, with both feet ahead of her, but what if she did not catch hold of the rope when she was through the window?

"Elinor, go!" Winn yelled. "Go, now!"

"All right!" She clamped her jaw tight, closed her eyes, wrapped her hands around the rope, and pushed off. For a moment, all she felt was nothingness under her toes. For a moment, all was silent, and she was floating.

And then she slammed into the building, and she had to remember not to release the rope or else she would fall. She tried to catch the rope between her knees, but her skirts, flimsy as they were, made the task all but impossible. And she was far heavier than she realized. It took all of her strength and then some to support her weight. Already, her hands were slick with perspiration.

"I'm at the end," Winn called up. "I'm letting go. You'll feel some give."

"What does that mean?" She kept her eyes tightly shut. At some point she was going to need to start lowering herself, but she was loathe to release her death grip on the linen.

"Just hold on."

The rope tensed and then relaxed, and she slammed into the building again. She shrieked, but she held on.

"Elinor, open your eyes."

"No." She shook her head. If she opened her eyes, she would freeze.

"Open your eyes and see how I descend the rest of the way. You'll have to follow me."

Oh, God. Oh, she was going to die. She opened her eyes and watched as he climbed, like some sort of spider, down the side of the building. She was doomed. She would never be able to duplicate that.

"Just catch hold of the nooks and outcrops in the building," Winn yelled, jumping nimbly to his feet. "There are enough to see you safely to the ground."

"All right." But she didn't move.

"Climb down now, honey."

"All right." She tried—she really did—to open one of her fists and force herself down the rope, but her hand had a mind of its own.

"Elinor, I don't want to alarm you…"

Never a good way to begin a sentence.

"… but the building is swaying."

Yes, she could feel it. She had thought it was her imagination.

"It's going to collapse. You have to move now." He sounded so logical, so reasonable. As though climbing down the side of a burning building on a flimsy piece of linen were the most natural thing in the world.

And then she heard the sound of a rip, and she jerked down.

"Elinor!" Winn did not sound quite so calm now. "Climb down. Now!"

This was it. This was the moment when it all went horribly wrong and she plummeted to her death on the hard earth below. This was the moment Winn would remember and think, *I should never have allowed her to become an agent.*

This was the moment. *Her* moment.

Elinor opened her eyes, unclenched her fists, and began a slow, clumsy descent. Her hands burned as her palms slid along the coarse linen sheets. She tried to slow her descent, but it seemed the whole building was bowing down on top of her, lowering her much faster than she wanted.

She had to stop imagining the worst.

"That's it, Ellie," Winn called. "You're doing it."

She was doing it. So why did he still sound concerned? Something fiery streaked past her head, bounced off the side of the building, and tumbled to the ground.

Elinor looked up. The building really was coming tumbling down on top of her. "Winn!" she screamed. She was going to die. *"Winn!"*

"You're almost there. Keep climbing," he urged her. She still heard that edge of fear, but he sounded much more controlled than she felt. "You can do this, Ellie."

She could. She *would*.

She lowered herself again, trying to ignore the way her feet flailed in the empty air under them. She had never thought she would appreciate the solid ground beneath her feet so much. She was almost there. She was almost—she looked down, and that was a mistake.

She was *not* almost there. She still had a long, long way to go, and she was never going to make it in time.

Another piece of debris tumbled past her, followed by a broken lamp and several pieces of the roof.

She was too high. She was still too high. "Run!" she yelled to Winn. "It's going to collapse. Run so you won't be caught under it."

"I'm not moving until you're beside me. Climb down."

"Idiot," she muttered and lowered herself again. Slow and steady was the key, but she did not have the time for slowness, and the building was anything but steady.

Still, she kept climbing down, down, down.

A horrible, twisted whine sounded from somewhere deep inside the building. Elinor started, so shocked she almost let loose the rope. "What was that?" she murmured to herself.

"Elinor!" Winn called. "Jump!"

"What?" Surely he had not told her to jump. She looked down. She was much too high to jump...

"Jump!" Winn screamed. But he wasn't looking at her. He was looking above her. She followed his gaze and saw the building was roaring with flames. The top floors had already caved in on themselves, and now the entire structure was bending over like an old man gripping his cane.

"Winn!"

"Let go. I'll catch you."

No! No, no, no. She was too high. She'd kill them both.

"Ellie, let go." This time Winn's voice was strangely peaceful. It was as though he knew everything was going to be fine. She had little choice. She had to trust him.

Elinor closed her eyes and let go.

∾

"You know you're a bloody idiot," someone said. Winn blinked up at the hazy dark above him. "You're lucky nothing is broken."

Was nothing broken? Winn was not quite so certain. Slowly, Blue's features began to take shape. "Where's Ellie?"

"I'm here."

He glanced in the direction of her voice and saw her lying on a patch of grass and weeds. "How did we—?" Winn glanced back at what was left of the brothel. The charred building still smoldered as flames consumed the last of the rubble. It collapsed in on itself and toppled over.

"I pulled both of you out of there before you managed to flatten yourselves. You can thank me later."

Winn had no recollection of Blue pulling either of them to safety. The last he remembered, he moved to catch Elinor, and her weight, multiplied by the length of her fall, sent them reeling. He'd managed to catch her and hold on, but then he'd gone down, unable to muster the strength to carry them out of harm's way. "Why did you call me an idiot?" Winn asked, feeling surly.

"Because you almost broke your necks."

"Do you have a better suggestion for rescuing her?"

"Yes."

Winn waited, but Blue did not elaborate.

"Shouldn't we be attempting to rescue the prince, instead of arguing amongst ourselves?"

Winn scowled at Elinor and noted Blue did the same. "I left him safely ensconced in his bedroom. With his mistress," Blue informed her.

"You may have left His Royal Highness thus, but

he's not safe," Winn said. He pulled the paper from his coat and handed it to Blue. "Lady Keating managed to pilfer this from Lefèbvre's papers."

Elinor stepped closer, watching as Blue read the parchment. "I need a code name," she said.

"No, you don't." Winn wasn't ever going to allow her to do anything this dangerous again. He'd almost lost her. He glanced at her, saw her irritated frown, and pulled her into his arms. Not caring that Blue was standing right beside them, he kissed her with a possessiveness strong enough that it surprised even him. She kissed him back, her hands wrapping around his shoulders as she sighed into him.

"Oh, Winn."

He took her face in his hands. "I thought I'd lost you."

She smiled up at him, an expression on her face he couldn't quite place. She arched up and kissed him tenderly on the lips.

Blue cleared his throat. "There has been a ridiculous amount of kissing within the ranks of the Barbican group lately, and we have more important matters at hand."

"Jealous?" Winn teased.

Blue gave him a mysterious look. All of Blue's looks were mysterious, but this one looked calculated. "Not at all."

"The prince?" Elinor said.

Blue nodded. "We'll never reach him in time. Foncé walked out of the house a half hour ago."

"And you didn't follow?" Winn demanded.

"I thought I was needed here. How silly of me." Blue gave his attention back to Elinor. "He's almost to

Carlton House by now. We'll never reach the prince before he does."

Winn felt frustration slam down on him like a fist. "Bloody hell!"

"But…" Elinor looked from one man to the other. "But we cannot give up. We cannot allow the prince to die."

"The streets are unbearably clogged at this hour, and Carlton House is halfway across London. What would you have us do? The prince has guards who are aware of the danger he is in. There is nothing to do but hope they foil the attempt."

"No."

"No?" Winn echoed Elinor. "What do you mean no?"

"The Season is over, and half of the *ton* is in the country already. The other half are making preparations to leave. The streets will not be nearly as clogged as you think."

Winn nodded. "She makes a good point."

"She does, but it takes only one cart stuck in mud to block a street and keep us stranded for hours."

"We could walk," Elinor suggested.

Blue gave her a cursory perusal. "With you dressed like that and all the pickpockets and cutthroats about? I'd rather not."

"Winn, how did you manage to arrive so quickly at Lady Ramsgate's ball that night? You did not come home first, and surely you were not in Mayfair."

Winn stared at her. She truly was good at this work. Did she even know she'd just given them their solution? "I didn't travel by street."

Blue frowned. "Boat? The Thames—"

"No. We could travel above the street and over the rooftops."

Blue raised a brow. "I had heard you were unconventional." He directed a pointed look at the ear bobs still tied to Winn's ears. "But I thought you were also reasonable."

"I don't need to be reasonable," Winn said, pulling the ear bobs off and wiping his face and the remainder of the rouge on his shirtsleeves. It felt good to be out of the rest of his disguise. If only he hadn't left his boots in the brothel. There was nothing for it.

He'd lost the feminine shoes during his descent, and without any protection, his feet would be bloody by the end of the night.

"I only need to know the rooftops of London." He held his hand out to Blue. "Ten pounds says we make it to Carlton House before Foncé."

Blue took his hand. "Why not make it twenty?"

"Why not stop talking and depart?" Elinor said. "I'm not traveling over the roofs, so I'll just wait here."

Winn's brows rose. "Oh, no you won't." He took her by the shoulders and propelled her toward the nearest building. "I'm not letting you out of my sight. Foncé's men are sure to turn up, as are those who would investigate this fire. I don't want you anywhere near it."

"But I don't like high places, and my balance is horrid."

"Then stick close to me," Blue said with a wink. "I'm nimble as a squirrel."

Winn wrenched open the door of the old, abandoned building, stopping Blue before he could enter. "Is there anything in which you do not excel?"

"Yes."

"What is it?"

Blue grinned. "You don't want to know." He started forward, but Winn stopped him again.

"Yes, I do."

"No, you don't." Blue pushed past him with intention now, urging Elinor up the creaky, dark stairs. Winn followed, frowning when they reached the roof and the breeze slapped at his face. He had not realized how windy it was tonight. That would make their task even more difficult. He stood before Elinor and Blue at the edge of the roof and pointed out toward the dark city. "Carlton House is that way. Toward those lights. Most of the roofs are close enough together that we can hop from one to another."

"And if they're not?" Elinor asked.

Winn shrugged. "We improvise."

Elinor did not like the sound of that. "What do you mean?"

"You'll see." Winn stepped on the roof's ledge and gauged the distance to the next roof. "You want to go first, Blue, or should I?"

Blue bowed. "Oh, ladies first."

Elinor shook her head. "But shouldn't we improvise on this roof? That's too far to jump."

Winn took her cold hand in his. "We're wasting time."

"But—!"

"One, two, three—jump!" And he pulled her into the air.

Twenty-two

ELINOR HAD ALWAYS THOUGHT THAT HER MOTHER'S insistence she act like a perfect lady, which meant Elinor was never allowed to climb trees or jump out of haylofts, meant there were gaps in her education. And while she had never encouraged her own girls to climb trees or jump from haylofts—not that any were nearby—she had not forbidden it either.

But now, as Winn forced her, again and again, to take her life in her hands by jumping from a perfectly stable and solid building and into nothingness, Elinor realized that perhaps it had not been her mother who was primarily responsible for the gap in Elinor's education. She now knew that even had she been allowed to climb trees, she would have preferred to keep her feet planted safely on the ground.

Winn and Blue were another matter entirely. They were more like birds than men. They jumped from building to building as though the feat was nothing. Once Winn had laid a board across the space between two buildings, saying this jump required improvising. But Elinor had thought walking across the far-too-narrow board much more frightening than simply jumping. She preferred no more improvising, thank you very much, and did not protest at all when Winn suggested they travel the remainder of the distance by foot on the ground beneath.

They found a building with a door providing roof access, and made their way through a quiet inn. The public room on the first floor was all but empty, and the innkeeper, who was busy wiping down tables, looked at them curiously as they came down the stairs.

"Lovely accommodations," Blue said breezily. "So sorry we cannot stay."

And they walked out the door and kept on walking. "How do you do that?" Elinor asked. "How do you think of lies so easily?"

"The trick is not to lie," Blue said. "Keep to the truth as much as possible. The accommodations *were* lovely—although not to my taste—and we could *not* stay. All true."

They moved aside as a group of inebriated young men plowed past. Elinor continued, "I would try and explain myself and make a muddle of everything."

"Never explain yourself," Blue told her.

"You've become quite good at that," Winn muttered.

"Why, thank you, old boy. High praise indeed from Baron."

Elinor looked at Winn. "Do you have any rules?"

"Yes," Winn said. "Stay alive." He moved ahead of them, and Elinor glanced at Blue, who was looking studiously at the bare wall of a building they were passing.

"Was it his fault?" she asked quietly.

"To what are you referring?" Blue asked.

"You know," she said. "If *I* know, you know."

Blue sighed, his expression pained. The more she looked at him, the more she realized he really was a very handsome man. He must have been very skilled at disguises to make himself look so plain and nondescript. "I wasn't there. I don't know what went wrong, precisely."

"Then give me your imprecise opinion."

She expected more hedging, but Blue spoke earnestly. "No, it's not his fault. These things happen. That's why this work is dangerous. Plans go wrong. Missions go awry. Our work is unpredictable. But none of that will help him." Blue nodded to Winn, who was striding quickly ahead of them.

"Why not?" Elinor asked.

"Because that's not who he is. He's a protector, and when someone close to him is hurt or killed, he will always blame himself. Did he tell you about the mission?"

"It was an assassination?"

"Yes. Baron is not usually given those assignments. As I said, he's a protector. He does better saving others than he does... disposing of them."

Elinor noted they were nearing Carlton House. She could see the trees of the neighboring park. "What can I say?" she asked. "How can I show him he is not to blame?"

"You'll never show him. He must forgive himself. He must realize he cannot save everyone. Crow knew the risks, as we all do. Baron was no more responsible for him than I am for Baron."

"What about me?"

Blue smiled. "We're all responsible for you, but if we're in time to rescue the prince"—he nodded to the columns lining the portico of Carlton House, just coming into view—"then you might just earn your place among us. With a little training, of course."

Elinor's heart leapt. *She* an actual agent for the Barbican group! She was so caught up in her imaginings, she almost ran right into Winn, who had stopped in front of her. He was looking at Blue. "How do you want to approach this? It's better if we don't alarm the household."

"Agreed. Come with me. I have a secret entrance."

"Let's hope it's not also Foncé's secret entrance."

And just like that, Elinor's excitement faded. The prospect of seeing Foncé again made her knees weak. He'd almost killed her merely hours before. She must be mad to willingly seek him out after her narrow escape. She looked at Blue and Winn. She supposed madness was a trait the Barbican required.

"This way," Blue said, and Elinor followed him into the darkness.

❧

Winn was impressed by Elinor's ability to keep up with him and with how easily she melted into the shadows. Blue led them around the perimeter of the prince's London residence, Carlton House. The house was French in style and furnishings and had been touted by those considered experts as nothing short of *astonishing*. It had cost the country quite a tidy sum to outfit the royal residence with all the opulence the prince required. Winn had never been inside. He didn't remember ever receiving an invitation, though that was more Elinor's arena.

"Have we ever been invited to Carlton House?" he asked in a whisper.

"No," she said. "I suppose we aren't fashionable enough."

"You'll have your chance to see it now," Blue said, "if we aren't shot by the guards." He gestured to the roofs, where Winn spotted the shadow of a man patrolling. "Melbourne asked the prime minister for additional men to protect the prince. His Highness wanted his own men, the 10th Royal Hussars."

Winn almost laughed. A cavalry regiment patrolling Carlton House on foot? Except it was not amusing, because if he and Blue could circumvent the prince's protectors, so could Foncé.

"Shouldn't we alert them to our presence?" Elinor asked, sounding worried.

"Where's the fun in that?" Blue asked.

Elinor looked somewhat nervous at this answer, but that was because she was still sane. A few years of this work, and she'd be as daft as the rest of them.

Blue held up a hand, and Winn stopped, grasping Elinor by the shoulders to halt her as well. Blue tapped quietly on a window. A moment later, the drapes parted, and a woman peered out. As soon as she spotted Blue, her face split into a huge smile. "One of your admirers?" Winn asked.

Blue shrugged then stepped back as the woman pushed the window open. He leaned over to speak to her quietly, and Winn took the opportunity to pull Elinor close.

She was trembling.

"What is it?" he asked.

"Nothing. I'm cold."

Winn could well believe it, considering she was wearing next to nothing and the night was chilly. "Is that all?"

She frowned at him. "Do you ever feel scared?" She shook her head. "Never mind. I'm sure experienced agents don't feel fear."

Winn had the overwhelming urge to pull her into his arms. Since Blue was still talking the woman—probably one of the house staff—into allowing them inside without going through the proper channels, Winn gave in to his urge.

She felt warm and soft in his arms and far too vulnerable. "A good agent always feels fear when it's warranted," he said, his lips brushing her silky hair.

She looked up at him, her brown eyes so dark and lovely. "Is it warranted tonight?"

"Sweetheart, after what you've been through tonight, I'm amazed you're still standing. It's warranted."

"You don't look afraid."

And he realized he wasn't. He wasn't afraid—not for himself. He was afraid for her. And even more than that, he was afraid he would lose her, and it would be too late. "Ellie, I need to tell you something."

She arched her brows in silent question.

Winn cleared his throat. This was his wife; this was the woman he'd fallen in love with. She had told him she loved him more times than he could count. Why should it be so difficult for him to say the words now?

Because she had not told him lately?

Because he feared after so many years of neglect her feelings had changed?

Because he was really a complete and utter coward?

"Ellie—"

"We're in," Blue said. "Ladies first."

Elinor gave Winn a regretful look then turned to climb through the window. Winn watched her go, astounded that he was simply standing there, watching the woman he loved dive—literally, as her leg caught on the sill and she tumbled awkwardly inside—into danger. While the servant helped Ellie to her feet, Winn grabbed Blue's arm.

He nodded to the woman. "Who is she? Can she be trusted?"

"The prince's mistress is with him. She is the current paramour's maid. And no, she cannot be trusted."

"But she's letting us in."

"Only because I told her I knew what her mistress had done, and if she helped me now, I'd look the other way if she happened to run off."

Winn swore.

"You prefer to leave your wife with her?"

"I don't want her near Foncé again."

"We don't always get what we want." Blue gestured to the window. "After you."

Once inside, Blue led them quickly along a dim corridor, decorated with too much red. He supposed it was considered fashionable, as Elinor gasped at almost every new painting or furnishing they passed, but Winn always preferred the simple to the garish.

They turned a corner and faced two armed men standing at attention. "Who goes there?"

"Who goes there?" Winn echoed. "We don't have time for a play set in the Middle Ages."

"It is I," Blue answered with exaggerated formality. "Lower the drawbridge." Apparently, he felt they had all the time in the world.

The men's shoulder's relaxed slightly, and they loosened their grip on their rifles. "Agent Blue," the one on the right said. They were dressed identically in scarlet coats faced with deep yellow, and caps so tall they would have had to duck in any establishment not so spacious as Carlton House. "The prince is not to be disturbed."

"Yes, I know," Blue said. "I was present when he gave the order. I am countermanding it."

"You don't have the authority," the one on the left said.

"We'd obtain the authority," Winn drawled, "but by then the prince will be dead. He might be dead already."

Both men jerked. "What are you saying?"

"Oh, yes, start a panic," Blue muttered.

"I'm saying we have information that points to the collusion between the prince's mistress and the leader of the Maîtriser group. Foncé may be within at this very moment, splitting the prince's fat belly."

"If this is some kind of hoax…" the guard on the left began.

"It's no hoax," Blue said. "Open the door."

The guards exchanged a look. "Open the door!" Blue bellowed. The men jumped to attention and pushed the double doors open just in time for Winn to glimpse the form of a man running through another set of doors.

"I have him," Blue said before racing after the intruder.

Winn started after the woman, who was trying to make an equally quick exit from the antechamber, then realized he needed to give the stunned guards a directive. He looked around helplessly, his gaze landing on Elinor. "Catch her," he ordered his wife, trying not to think too much about the danger he might be sending his wife to face. Elinor looked equally surprised by his order but recovered quickly and raced through the doors.

"Alert the household, and send for more guards to surround the perimeter," Winn told the guards. "Foncé must not be allowed to escape."

"Yes, sir!"

Winn raced after Elinor and saw she'd cut off the other woman's escape route and was backing her against a small desk in a corner. In the prince's bedchamber, there was a shriek and a crash. He jerked his head toward the prince's room. "I have her. Go see to the prince."

"But—"

"Elinor, go!"

With a scowl, she raced through the next set of doors just as another crash, followed by yet another girlish scream, echoed.

Winn glanced back at the prince's mistress just as she raised a pistol and fired. He feinted left, and the ball of a pistol smashed into the wall behind him, shattering a painting of some distinguished woman or other. Baron didn't hesitate. He roared into action and tackled her before she could prime the pistol again.

But she was quick. They hit the floor in a tangle of arms and legs, and she slipped out of his grip, somersaulted away, and was on her feet again. "You bastard!" she spat.

He jumped to his feet. "You're the one who shot at me."

They circled one another. "I'm going to kill you, bastard." She was attractive and moved with agility, despite all the rounded flesh she had on display. He'd thought the prince favored older women married to peers of the *ton*, but he didn't know this woman. And then she pulled a knife from a fastening on her leg and made a slashing motion at him.

Baron's eyes widened. This little vixen was a far cry from the pampered courtesans and spoiled wives of Society. "Who the hell are you?" he asked.

"No one. His Highness's mistress. Let me go."

"I don't think so."

She slashed at him again.

"Is this your idea of foreplay?" he asked, ducking the knife. "Because I rather prefer something with costumes. You could be the saucy chambermaid"—he ducked again—"and I could be the frigid butler who needs warming up."

"I'll show you foreplay," she spat.

He jumped back and narrowly avoided a knife slicing across his gut. He thought about kicking her in the chest—his feet were already bloody and numb from the walk here—but she was a woman, and he still believed in chivalry. "Very well," he conceded, knocking a chair over and tossing it in her path. She had to jump to avoid it, giving him a moment to strategize. "I'll be the saucy chambermaid. But just this once. And I draw the line at frilly aprons."

She gave him a bewildered look, and he lunged, knocking the dagger from her hand. It flew across the room, hitting a candle and toppling it. The room went dark, and he took advantage of the shadows to plow into her. It was a clumsy move, lacking in any semblance of finesse, but brute tactics had their place. He grazed her back, the force of his attack sending her reeling. He was unsettled as well but pivoted and threw himself on her legs, preventing her from regaining them.

"Off me," she hissed.

"You're certainly demanding, but if you prefer to be on top..." He grabbed her by the waist, yanked her over him, then caught her wrists and rolled. She screamed and flailed like a cat caught in a snare as he stared down at her. His hair had come loose from his queue, and it hung over his forehead and slapped at his jaw. "Now," he said, "you are going to stay right here—"

Another crash. "Winn!" That was Elinor's voice. Damn.

"Let me go!" She tried to claw him as he scanned the room for something to use to secure her.

If she'd been a man, he would have simply knocked her unconscious. She might be in league with Foncé, but he wasn't going to hit a woman.

She inhaled sharply, and he frowned. Had she seen something?

"Burn in hell," she spat.

"That's a lovely—" Why did he suddenly smell something burning? He heard a whoosh across the room, and a set of flimsy curtains went up in bright orange flames. He shook his head. "Oh, hell." The bloody knife had knocked the candle over and set the drapes on fire. He was a lodestone for fire tonight, and the prince would not thank him for burning down Carlton House—garish as it was. Now he had to secure the mistress *and* put out a fire.

"Winn!" Elinor again, and she sounded desperate.

"Coming!" He looked down at the woman. "It appears we will have to finish this conversation another time."

"Another time, you'll be dead." Her leg came up, and her knee struck him in the back. She was limber; he would give her that. And the distraction was just enough for her to free a hand. She swiped at him, raking her fingers across his cheek. He was thankful that hand was still gloved, but he knew the act would leave marks.

And how was he going to explain that to his wife? And then he remembered his wife was in the next room. Well, that was one advantage to having Elinor work with him.

He'd flinched back to avoid the worst of her attack, but she'd grabbed whatever she could reach, which unfortunately happened to be a bed warmer. She swung the metal thing at his head, and he raised an arm to ward off the blow. The crack of metal against flesh reverberated through his bones, but he couldn't hear it over what was now a roaring fire. He grabbed her arm and wrestled the bed warmer to the floor, wondering how far the fire had advanced toward the doorway.

There was only one way to check.

He hauled her to her feet, swung her around, and made a quick assessment of the situation. Smoke pooled on the ceiling, and he felt his lungs beginning to burn and his eyes sting. The fire licked across the wall and the carpet, and one thin line jutted across the door. That line would grow as it began to eat up the antique carpet fibers. He needed to act fast. He glanced at the woman, and she shook her head. "Oh, no you don't."

She gave him a hard shove, and he stumbled backward then caught her about the waist as she attempted to flee. He rammed her against the wall, dislodging a sconce and a portrait, but the act served only to make her angry. She swore at him as she crawled to her hands and knees. He fisted his hands and gritted his teeth, prepared to knock her out cold, but as she wobbled to her feet, he just couldn't do it. Why couldn't the impact with the wall have rendered her unconscious?

He glanced at the door again, saw the fire rapidly devouring the carpet and edging toward the hall. Then he heard a shout and saw the guards rushing back. Thank God. "Fire!" he yelled. "Hurry!"

He caught the mistress's hand before she could strike him, and shoved her back against the wall, holding her steady around the throat. He closed his eyes, trying to concentrate.

"Winn?"

He opened his eyes as Elinor rushed in. "I need you. What...?" She looked about the room with dawning horror.

"Slight problem."

"Slight? Winn! You cannot set every building on fire. This is *Carlton House!*"

"I'd have smothered it, but I've been a little busy." He nodded to the woman whose throat he held in his hands. "I need something to secure her hands. If she were a man, I'd hit her, but…"

"Oh, I see." Elinor nodded. "Step aside a moment."

He frowned. "What are you going to do?" But he stepped aside. Truth be told, he was more than relieved to allow a woman to deal with the other woman. Elinor pulled her arm back, and Winn caught it.

He adjusted her fist. "Thumb on the outside, and hit from here." He patted her bicep. Elinor reared back, and the mistress lunged to the side. But Elinor had fast reflexes and anticipated the move. She landed a solid punch, and the prince's mistress crumpled to the floor.

Elinor shook her fist. "Ow."

He blinked at her. "You hit her."

"Well, it was obvious you weren't going to do it." She grabbed his hand. "Quick! Blue needs you."

"Blue?"

Blue never needed anyone. A glance behind him showed Winn the guards were dealing with the fire and had it mostly contained. Ellie pulled at his arm again, and Winn followed her into the prince's bedchamber.

"What the hell?"

It was worse than he'd thought.

Twenty-three

BLUE WAS STILL PATTING THE PRINCE'S SHOULDER when Elinor rushed back into the regent's bedchamber. The prince had graduated from infantile screams to childlike whimpering sounds. He wore a voluminous nightshirt that looked like a tent around his wide girth, and pressed a scented handkerchief to his watering eyes.

"Where's Foncé?" Winn asked as soon as he stepped into the room.

"He went through that door." Blue pointed to a small, square opening in one of the wall panels. "Looks to be a secret tunnel."

"My secret passage," the prince moaned. "How did that awful man know of it?"

"Your Highness, you've had a terrible fright. Please lie back and rest." She turned toward Winn and said, "He's unharmed."

Winn didn't respond. His gaze was fixed on Blue. "Why haven't you gone after him?"

Blue looked chagrined, and Elinor almost felt sorry for him. She'd already guessed the problem.

"Baron, do you remember when you asked me if there was anything at which I did not excel?"

Winn frowned. "What the hell does that have to do with anything?"

"You said we did not want to know," Elinor supplied.

"Because the only reason for you to know," Blue said, still rhythmically patting the prince's arm, "is if my deficiency were to affect us."

"And?" Winn said, tone ominous.

Blue pointed to the tunnel. "I cannot go through there. I have a... dislike of small spaces."

"I have a dislike of being burned to death, but you don't see me cowering at the sight of fire."

"Winn." Elinor put her hand on his arm. "You can argue with Blue, or we can go after Foncé. If we don't go now, we may be too late."

"For heaven's sake," the prince exclaimed. "Go!"

For the first time, Winn looked at the regent. "Yes, Your Highness." He started for the tunnel, and Elinor followed. "You are not coming with me," Winn said.

"Yes—"

"Shh." He put a finger over her lips. "No arguments. I'll not risk your life again. You will not become another Crow around my neck." He pulled her into his arms and kissed her quickly but with heat. "I love you. I don't know if you can ever love me again, but if I don't come back, I want you to know that I love you. I was a fool all those years I didn't love you, Ellie. I'm sorry. God, I am so very sorry for causing you pain." He kissed her again, and before she could speak, he crouched and disappeared into the darkness.

"I love you too," she whispered. "Come back so I

might tell you in the flesh." She wiped a tear from her eye before turning back to the prince and Blue.

The prince was frowning. "I thought that poem was about an albatross, not a crow."

Elinor sighed and closed her eyes, praying Winn was safe.

~∞~

The darkness in the cramped tunnel was complete. Winn could not see his hand in front of his face. He did think of taking a lamp, but then Foncé would see him coming. He needed the element of surprise to kill Foncé.

If he *found* Foncé.

Winn crawled steadily forward, wondering how the prince thought he would ever fit his massive girth into such a tight squeeze. The tunnel must have been built when the regent was somewhat slimmer. The farther Winn moved into the recesses of the tunnel, the more he began to think Foncé was already far, far away. The tunnel had two forks. One led to the kitchens. Winn should not have been surprised the prince wanted unfettered access to the delicacies his chefs prepared. He retraced his steps and took the second fork. From the cool air he began to feel on his face, he knew he was nearing the end of a tunnel leading to the world outside Carlton House.

But when he reached the exit, he found the small gate locked and padlocked. He peeked through the iron bars and saw only trees. The tunnel must lead into what had once been Marylebone Park. And, of course, it was locked in case it should ever be discovered by a dedicated walker.

Winn did not have the key. Presumably Foncé was in possession of a copy, if not the actual key. He lifted the padlock and found it rusted and warped. The damage was such that Winn doubted a key would be of any use. In which case, escape was only possible if the padlock was broken. It was still intact, which meant Foncé had not escaped this way.

How then? Had he escaped through the kitchens?

He might have a chance at escape in all the confusion of the night. But Winn had told the prince's guards to secure the perimeter. And if Foncé was not in the tunnel—a fact Winn knew well from crawling through every small inch of it—and Foncé was not in the park, then Foncé was still in Carlton House.

With Elinor.

With a roar, Winn started back toward the prince's chamber. His mind immediately catapulted back to that night when he lost Crow. He was too late. He'd been too late to save his friend, and now he would be too late to save his wife.

⤥

Elinor stared at the tunnel where Winn had disappeared, and shivered. It had certainly been easier when she hadn't known the danger he was in. She didn't worry about him. How was she going to go back to any semblance of a normal life after this? If Winn was not beside her, she'd be terrified he was off trying to get himself killed.

She heard another loud whimper from the prince and turned to look at Blue. He gave her a pleading look. Poor man. He was not used to dealing with emotional little girls. "Your Highness," she said, walking toward him, "you must be brave."

Blue moved away, and she stealthily took his place, patting the prince's shoulder.

The prince nodded his agreement. "I do believe that man was going to slice me up. I want Lizzie."

Elinor glanced at the doorway to the antechamber. She had a feeling Lizzie was still unconscious, either that or taken to the nearest magistrate. "Someone will be with you any moment now. There was a small fire."

"A fire!"

Elinor grimaced. She should not have mentioned that detail. "Very, very small. I know your staff is anxious to be with you."

Blue, who had been standing before the secret passage, turned now. "Why don't I go and check on the progress?"

"Yes, do," Elinor said. She could see he was still annoyed at himself for not having gone after Foncé. She didn't particularly relish having to stay with the prince, but she would have rather stayed in his chamber in case Winn came back this way.

"I will return momentarily." Blue was away with a whoosh of his cloak.

Elinor and the prince stared after him. A moment later, the regent said, "I wonder who his tailor is. He has excellent taste in fashion, and I find myself envious of that cloak."

Elinor smiled to herself. Somehow she doubted the effete prince would cut the same dashing figure as Blue.

"I believe the spy's tailor is the least of your

worries," a deep voice said. Elinor looked about the room for the speaker, but it was empty, save her and the prince. And then one of the doors to the antechamber swung shut, and Foncé stood smiling at them. He turned and locked the door.

Elinor gaped at him, her gaze drawn to the long, thin knife he held in his hand. The prince gasped and cowered behind her.

"You, madam," Foncé said, moving toward them, "have as many lives as a cat. Do not look so surprised to see me. I have been here the entire time."

She glanced at the tunnel, willing Winn to return. Behind her, the prince buried his face in her skirts and cried, "Save me!"

"I did think to escape through the tunnel," Foncé said, moving still closer. Elinor wished she had some sort of weapon. She had no idea how to fire a pistol, but if she had one, at least she could heft it at him.

"But I quickly saw that would lead me nowhere," Foncé continued, moving inexorably closer.

"But Blue—" Elinor began.

"Was distracted by this nincompoop." Foncé gestured to the regent. "And I slipped back inside." He was directly before Elinor now. "That was a touching display between you and Baron," he said with a sardonic smile. "I am certain he will remember you fondly. Before he, too, dies." Foncé arced the knife toward her, and Elinor lurched violently to the left, dragging the prince with her. She would have been fast enough, if not for her additional burden, and Foncé managed to scrape her arm. She glanced down at the thin line of blood, knowing it was only a surface wound. It barely stung.

"Stand still," Foncé said. "I will make this quick and painless."

"I'll take my chances," Elinor answered. She spotted a heavy vase and scooted toward it. The prince stumbled after her, still clinging to her gown, and Foncé shook his head, looking vastly amused.

"I would like to watch this farce all day," he said, "but I have other matters to attend to."

"Do not let me detain you." Elinor swiped at the vase and grasped it.

Foncé opened his arms as though in challenge.

"No!" Prinny screeched. "Not the Sèvres!"

Foncé made several lunges toward her. She had the feeling he was but playing with her, trying to scare her. It was working wonderfully, but she was not going to use the vase until the last. Finally Foncé smiled and said, "Say good-bye." He lunged, and she sidestepped awkwardly, smashing him over the head with the vase.

"No," the prince cried. "I beg you. My Sèvres!"

Foncé stumbled but went after her. She backed away, reaching for a small plate on a table.

"Absolutely not, madam!" the prince said. "That is from the Ming dynasty."

She ignored him and threw the plate the way one would throw a discus. It hit Foncé on the forehead, and a line of blood appeared. Foncé roared and came for her, his intention clear. He was through playing games. Elinor backed up, pushing the side table over and blocking Foncé's charge.

"My precious pieces," the prince sobbed. "Help! A madwoman is destroying my precious pieces!"

Elinor blew out a frustrated breath and rounded on him. "Your Highness, I am trying to save your life."

"Must my art suffer for it?"

She lifted a porcelain figure of a shepherdess. "I'm afraid so."

Foncé ducked when she hurled it, and kept coming. She saw him slash at her and managed to avoid the point of the knife, but the prince's extra weight on her skirts caused her to lose her balance.

She stumbled, and a strong arm reached out to steady her.

◈

Winn could hear the crashes and shouts as he neared the exit to the tunnel. In the darkness, he'd taken a wrong turn and ended up back in the passage leading to the kitchens. It had taken him several agonizing moments to trace his way back, and now he crawled as quickly as he could toward the flicker of candlelight. He heard Elinor's voice, low and calm, and then he heard the prince's higher, frightened pleas. Foncé had found them. Winn didn't know how he'd done it, but he'd found her.

The tunnel seemed impossibly long, his movements impossibly slow. He would never reach her in time. He would not be able to save her. Without warning, he all but tumbled out of the passage and into the prince's chamber. A slight curve in the passage had obscured the exit.

Winn rolled, came up on his knees, and stared at his wife.

With a knife to her throat.

❦

Elinor saw the desperation on Winn's features, and she knew what he was thinking. He thought he was going to lose her the way he'd lost Crow. He thought he was going to stand there and watch her die.

She was not entirely certain he was incorrect. She was not entirely certain of anything, since the prince was blubbering at full volume, and she could not think what her name was, much less how to escape this predicament.

She refused to think of a knife at her throat as anything more than a predicament. Do that, and she would begin to panic.

"Let her go," Winn said. "Her death is nothing to you."

"You are wrong," Foncé answered. "She's managed to elude me twice. I'm owed her death."

"Take me instead."

"No!" Elinor screamed.

"You'll have the death of another member of the Barbican group to boast about. Either that, or let us both go and gut the prince. Your time grows short, and you can't kill us all."

"Treason!" the prince screamed. "Treason!"

"I am tempted to accept your offer if for no other reason than to shut him up!"

The prince closed his mouth then, looking equally chastised and regally offended.

"But, you see, I kill for sport. And the sport at the moment is to watch your face as she dies. Oh, that will be excessively diverting."

Winn clenched his fists. In his effort to save Ellie, he'd just doomed her. And here he stood, helpless. If he went for Foncé, the man would slit her throat. If he stood here, he would be forced to watch Foncé slice the knife across her pale, graceful neck.

He could do nothing. It was the nightmare of Crow all over again.

The antechamber door rattled unexpectedly, and Blue said, "Hullo! It's me. Open up in there."

Foncé's attention was momentarily diverted, and Winn leapt.

&c&

Elinor felt Foncé turn toward the door, and the knife slipped a fraction from her throat. It was all the diversion she needed. She stomped on Foncé's foot and ducked out of his grasp. He caught her again immediately, but by then Winn had grabbed Foncé's wrist and shook the knife free. Elinor turned and bit the hand holding her, and Foncé squealed and released her. She dove for the door. Winn and Blue together would capture Foncé without problem, but the regent intercepted her.

"Save me!" he screamed, pulling on her shoulder until she toppled over. "Save me!"

"Open the door," Blue yelled. "Or we'll break it down."

Elinor glanced at Foncé and Winn, but she could not tell who was winning. Foncé hit Winn, who winced and rolled away, but when Foncé went for him—with yet another knife he pulled from his boot—Winn kicked him, and Foncé staggered back.

"Break it down!" she screamed and heard the first blows of the axe on the door.

"Don't let him kill me!" the prince cried, clawing at Elinor.

"Your Highness, calm yourself. I will protect you," she said in her best motherly voice.

Winn was on his feet now, and he charged into Foncé, who had fallen against a shelf of books. Foncé hit the shelf hard enough to rattle it, then grabbed Winn's coat and sent him headfirst into the bookshelf.

Elinor gasped as the shelf wobbled and teetered. Foncé saw it too, glanced at the splintered door, and ran for the escape passage just as a tower of books tumbled on top of Winn, all but burying him.

"Winn!" Elinor yelled, but the prince was grasping her arm so tightly she could not go to him.

Foncé turned back. "Au revoir, madam. I will not say adieu, because I know we will see each other soon." He crawled into the passage and vanished.

The door finally came open, and Blue rushed inside. Elinor pointed to the books. "Winn! Help Winn!"

Several guards rushed in after Blue.

"He went through the passage," she told them. "Hurry!"

The prince finally released her, and she ran to Winn. Blue had managed to uncover his head and arms, and he was pulling books off his legs. "Are you hurt?" she asked. He had a cut on his temple, with a slender trickle of blood running down his face.

"Bruised but not broken," Winn answered. "Where's Foncé?"

"The passage." She pointed.

Winn nodded. "He won't go far. It's locked and gated at the end." He glanced at one of the guards. "Send several armed men to the kitchens, in case he tries to escape that way."

The guards rushed to do his bidding, and Winn stood. Elinor all but fell into his arms. "I thought he would kill you," she said.

"You were worried about me?" He laughed. "Madam, I can take care of myself."

Blue moved away, giving them a moment of privacy.

"I know you were thinking of Crow," she said, glancing up at him. "I know you were afraid tonight would end the same way."

"I cannot lose you, Ellie." He cupped her face with his hands.

"You won't," she promised. "I can take care of myself, too. Haven't I proven that to you yet?" She prayed he was not going to demand she give up the Barbican group now, not after all they'd been through. She would hate to defy him, but if she must...

"You need more training before you take on another mission," Winn said.

She smiled. "It is a good thing I know an excellent spy who can help with that."

"Flattery, madam"—he bent and kissed her nose—"is definitely encouraged."

He took her mouth with his, and her knees went weak. When they parted, she said, "I love you, Winn."

He grinned. "It's about time you said it."

Twenty-four

"I TAKE FULL RESPONSIBILITY FOR FONCÉ'S ESCAPE," Blue was saying. "It was my fault entirely."

Winn wouldn't have gone quite that far. He and Elinor bore some of the blame as well. The truth of the matter was that Foncé was very, very good. They'd gone through every inch of Carlton House, as well as its grounds, and Foncé appeared to have disappeared entirely. Winn still couldn't figure out how he'd done it. The gate to the passage had still been secured, but somehow the madman had managed an escape. Foncé had now outwitted four of the Barbican's agents. This slight was added to the indignity of the man having killed a half-dozen Barbican agents over the years.

Blue approached Melbourne, who was seated at his desk, hands folded, brows low and ominous, and held out an envelope sealed with blue wax. "I hereby tender my resignation." Blue gave a bow.

Melbourne looked at the envelope then at Blue. "Are you trying to make the situation worse?"

"No, my lord."

"Then shut up, and sit down."

Winn blinked. He'd never seen Melbourne so angry, and he'd seen Melbourne rather irate on any number of occasions. He glanced at Wolf and Saint, who both looked surprised. Of course, Saint looked more green than anything else. He frowned. Was she ill?

Blue retreated with the envelope, but Melbourne said, "Leave that on my desk. I may yet need it."

Blue nodded, left the envelope, and took a seat next to Saint. The couch moved slightly when he sat, and Saint turned even greener. If Blue wasn't careful, his puce silk coat would be covered in vomit. Winn was prepared to argue the vomit might be an improvement.

Melbourne held up another envelope, and Winn saw the royal seal upon it. "Do you know what this is?"

No one spoke.

"This, my friends, is an irate missive from the Prince of Wales. He has threatened all of us with a holiday in Newgate unless we apprehend Foncé posthaste. To say His Highness is distraught would be an understatement."

"Can the prince do that?" Elinor whispered to Winn.

"Yes," Melbourne said, looking directly at her. "He can accuse us of treason." Melbourne glared at Winn. "I cannot think why."

Winn studied his hands.

"Furthermore, His Highness claims he suffered a loss of many rare and valuable artifacts, and demands restitution."

"Should have let Foncé have him," Winn muttered.

Melbourne looked at Saint and Wolf. "You two were not present, and technically you are retired from the group, but I promise you that if I go down, you go down too."

"My lord," Wolf began.

Melbourne lifted a hand. "Not now, Adrian. Since every last one of you has managed to reveal yourself to Foncé, we have completely lost the element of surprise. Even if we knew where Foncé was hiding, he would see us coming."

"I'm quite good at disguises," Blue said.

"I am aware of that fact, but what I need now is my very best agent."

"At your service, sir," Blue and Winn said at the same time.

Wolf frowned at them. "He was talking to me."

"He was probably talking to me," Saint added, "but I shall have to decline. Excuse me." With her hand over her mouth, she fled the room, closely followed by her husband.

Winn shook his head. "Is she ill?"

Elinor frowned. "For a spy, you are sometimes remarkably obtuse. She is increasing. Remember?"

Ah. He recalled Elinor's bouts with nausea when she'd carried Georgiana. "Then Smythe won't want to leave her side," he said. "Foncé is mine."

"No, he is not," Melbourne said. "You are not my best agent."

Winn looked at Blue, but Melbourne shook his head.

"Then who is he?" Ellie asked.

"The question," Melbourne said, "should be: who is *she*? And you will meet her soon enough."

❧

The girls were home again, and Elinor could not stop smiling. It was so good to hear their incessant chatter. The house had been too quiet without them. She knew she would grow weary of their bickering in a few days, but right now they were babbling on about horses and hay and the spring foaling. She supposed they would all have to visit Winn's mother again soon.

She looked at Winn, and for the first time, when she thought of all of them, she included him. He'd changed. Instead of looking preoccupied by his dinner of mutton and potatoes, he was listening intently, nodding and asking pertinent questions. Both girls loved having his full attention.

Elinor did as well, but that would have to wait.

After dinner, they spent the evening in the drawing room, laughing and reading from books the girls had loved as young children. Finally, Elinor sent them to bed. When she'd kissed both of them, tucked their covers about them, and fluffed their pillows, she went to her room.

Winn was waiting for her. He reclined on her bed, his feet bare, and wearing fitted black trousers and a white shirt open at the throat. Elinor found it very difficult to breathe all of a sudden.

"I dismissed Bridget," he said. "Do you need her?"

She closed the door and locked it. "I cannot undress myself."

A slow smile crept over his face. "I believe I can assist with that."

Elinor went to him, leaning over the bed and taking his mouth with hers. He tasted of the blackberry fool they had eaten for dessert. She wanted to lick the sweetness from his lips. She kissed him more deeply, and he pulled her down on the bed beside him, leaning over her and slanting his lips over hers.

Elinor reached under his shirt to touch his skin, so familiar to her and yet so new. She felt like a new bride with him these past few days. They had discovered a passion neither had known they could possess.

"Hmm. Before we continue," he said against her lips, "I have something for you."

He sat and took something from the bedside table. Elinor frowned and levered up on her elbows. The seal had been broken, so she unfolded the parchment and read the words.

"These are orders to report to Melbourne's office tomorrow morning," she said. She looked up at him and sat. "They are addressed to… Butterfly." She shook her head. "Who is that?"

"You." He grinned. "Your new codename."

Elinor gasped. She had a codename!

"Do you like it?" he asked. "I think it's perfect. You are so many things all in one."

She raised a brow. "Such as?"

"Wife, mother, spy, seductress…"

She laughed.

"My orders were also included." He handed her a small slip of paper. She read it once, twice, three times.

"You will be training me?"

"Someone has to."

She punched him in the arm then read both letters again. "I'm really going to be a spy."

"It appears so."

"But the girls—how can I leave them?"

Winn looked pained. "You are always hinting that your mother should visit more often."

"You'd do that? For me?"

He took her face in his hands. "Ellie, I'd do anything for you. In fact"—he tossed the missives aside—"let me show you."

Acknowledgments

There were so many people who supported and helped me while I wrote this book—my family, my friends, my agents, my web designer, my editor, and the entire Sourcebooks team. In particular, I want to thank the following people.

Amy and Emily, my running/boot camp buddies
Sharie and Tera, my go-to writer friends
My parents and my mother-in-law
Margo, for your invaluable comments and suggestions on this manuscript
Robyn, Emily, Anne—the rest of the Brainstorm Troopers
Joanna MacKenzie
Tina Hergenrader
Gayle and Alora Cochrane
Maddee and Jen at xuni.com
I also want to thank you, my readers, for making this book possible. This book was written because you wanted it. Your support means more to me than you will ever know.

About the Author

Shana Galen is the bestselling author of fast-paced adventurous Regency historicals, including the RT Reviewers' Choice *The Making of a Gentleman*. Her books are published all over the world and have been featured in the Rhapsody and Doubleday Book Clubs. She taught English at the middle and high school level off and on for eleven years. Most of those years were spent working in Houston's inner city. Now she writes full time. She's happily married and has a daughter who is most definitely a romance heroine in the making. Shana loves to hear from readers: visit her website at www.shanagalen.com or see what she's up to daily on Facebook and Twitter.